TAMING HER HIGHLAND LEGEND

Time to Love a Highlander Series
Book Two

by Maeve Greyson

ARE YOU SIGNED UP FOR DRAGONBLADE'S BLOG?

You'll get the latest news and information on exclusive giveaways, exclusive excerpts, coming releases, sales, free books, cover reveals and more.

Check out our complete list of authors, too!

No spam, no junk. That's a promise!

Sign Up Here

www.dragonbladepublishing.com

Dearest Reader;

Thank you for your support of a small press. At Dragonblade Publishing, we strive to bring you the highest quality Historical Romance from some of the best authors in the business. Without your support, there is no 'us', so we sincerely hope you adore these stories and find some new favorite authors along the way.

Happy Reading!

CEO, Dragonblade Publishing

Additional Dragonblade books by Author Maeve Greyson

Time to Love a Highlander Series
Loving Her Highland Thief
Taming Her Highland Legend

Highland Heroes Series
The Guardian
The Warrior
The Judge
The Dreamer
The Bard
The Ghost

CHAPTER ONE

Finchcrest Hospital
London, England
July 28, 2019

E VIE FORCED HERSELF to sit in a calm, composed manner rather than indulge in her trademark fidgeting. Today's massive overstepping of boundaries concerned her. The consequences might reach a level of seriousness she preferred not to think about. Her thoughts raced, searching for a means of atonement that might appease everyone. Nothing came to mind, so she adopted her best fake smile. "I am quite well now, Maggie. I promise."

"This report from your immediate supervisor states otherwise." Dr. Margaret Stroud, respected peer, personal physician, and closest friend, frowned down at the open file on her desk. "Your blood pressure along with statements from several nurses in the unit also confirms that assessment." She looked up, peering over the top of her reading glasses like a professor about to swoop down on a student caught napping. "This is the second time, Evie. And the last according to everyone on the food chain above you."

"So, I'm being dismissed?" The severity of the verdict tightened her fists until her nails dug into her palms. "You drew the short straw then? Won the hatchet to lop off my head for protecting my patient?"

"You recklessly extended the man's surgery by two hours, refused to allow the staff surgeon to close, and when the consultant confronted you about it, you called him a murderous, penny-pinching bastard." Maggie jabbed the air with her pen as her brows rose to judgmental levels. "Not only called him that but yelled it in his face. Several times, in fact. In front of witnesses, no less. Then you escaped the disturbing scene you created by blacking out."

"I did not recklessly extend my patient's surgery. I discovered the possibility of additional bleeds and a blockage that needed immediate attention. If I had followed protocol, the man would've returned to the waiting list and died, considering its current length." She blinked at the telltale flashes of light signaling one hell of a migraine loomed in her near future.

Her friend's intense gaze sharpened. "Your headaches are worse, too. Are they not?"

"Only when I forget to eat."

Cripe's sake, Evie realized she needed to get her rage under control. But a man's life hung in the balance this time. Well, every time if anyone counted all her rants and took notes. And yes, a spiraling rage session ending in a blackout raised some serious flags. But did it warrant letting her go?

"By the way, I'm positive that's why I fainted. In the future, I intend to keep protein bars in my locker to ensure my blood sugar maintains a healthy level." Forcing her hands open, she rubbed her sweaty palms on her scrub pants. Oddly enough, she never perspired during procedures. The operating theatre felt more like home than her tiny flat.

Maggie hissed out a long-suffering sigh as she slipped off her glasses and tossed them to her desk. Evie felt sorry for her friend. Poor Mags. The title of judge and jury fell to her because she had made the fatal mistake of befriending the black sheep surgeon at Finchcrest

Hospital.

Evie decided to make it easier on her friend. "How long do I have to clear out? Today? End of the week perhaps?" She pushed up from the chair and strode over to the window, separating the blinds to stare down into the car park that still needed repaving. She'd miss that weed infested bit of asphalt.

"You are the best surgeon Finchcrest has ever known." Maggie leaned back in her black leather chair and swiveled it back and forth. "Your unmatched talent is all that's saving you, my friend, but you need to understand this is your last lifeline." She opened her top drawer, rummaged through it, then tossed a ring of keys onto the desk. "A month's suspension. With pay, luckily enough." She nodded toward the keys. "Remember my cottage outside Inverness?"

"The place that is far too quiet and remote as hell if I remember correctly?" Evie twitched an indifferent shrug to minimize the situation. "I do not need time off. It's a mere blood sugar thing that I am going to handle." She tapped the folder in front of her friend. "Check the chart. Right there. You have the labs to show it."

"Your blood sugar has nothing to do with your inability to filter your opinions before they come out your mouth, and whether or not you need it, you are taking this leave. Your records show you have taken no time off in over three years, and I know your habit of asking for extra shifts." Maggie leaned forward and rested both hands on top of the folder. "This is not a choice. For both your health and your career, you have one month to get yourself in order and return as a surgeon who plays well with others. Understood?"

"Mags—"

Maggie's warning look cut her off. "Take this chance, Evie. It's the best I could do for you. Either take the time to discover your version of inner peace and lock it in place or clear out by tomorrow."

Evie picked up the keys and slipped them into her pocket. "I'm grateful, Maggie. You didn't have to do this."

With a sad smile, her friend shooed her toward the door. "Yes, I did. Believe it or not, there are people here who care about you, and I'm one of them. Now, go. Enjoy Inverness. Get out and explore. Text me some pictures to make me jealous."

"You bet." Evie nodded, already plotting to spend her thirty days laying low in London.

"Be on the plane, train, or bus to Inverness by this afternoon," Maggie warned. "I am required to follow up and provide proof to personnel that you are cooperating with your recommended therapy."

"Fine." She yanked open the door and shot a frustrated look back. "I'm doing this for you, Maggie."

Maggie shook her head. "Do it for yourself."

ABOUT AN HOUR and a half by plane won out over forever on a train and even longer by bus. Tickets from Heathrow to Inverness weren't all that pricey either. Not that she worried about money. She lived like a monk and saved an embarrassing percentage of her salary. Life alone in her spartan flat cost her very little. So, now she was off to Scotland. What in the world would she do for a month in Inverness? The prospect made her shudder.

After having to stand and step aside three times for the elderly gentleman who probably suffered from prostate issues, she offered him her aisle seat and took his place beside the window. Poor man. What a miserable feeling. A constant urge to pee and little relief no matter how many visits to the loo.

Thankfully, he nodded off soon after, leaving her to sort through her notes in peace. A rental car waited at the airport. Caretaker's name was Gertrude, and she kept the cottage stocked with food, towels, and any necessities needed for an extended stay. If she needed anything else, Gertrude's number was on the board in the kitchen. If not, she would never see the woman. Maggie swore the caretaker was a rare type when it came to respecting everyone's privacy.

Her friend's list of things to see and do waited somewhere in her backpack stowed overhead, and the determined woman continued texting additional possibilities. Once they landed, Evie's forced month of rest, relaxation, and rehabilitation in bonny Scotland began. A dogged sense of tolerating thirty days of boredom taunted her like the throbbing ache of a sore tooth.

A smattering of wispy white clouds skimmed across the shimmering blue lochs and verdant glens below. She didn't see them. All-consuming guilt blinded her as she lamented handing her patients and all their procedures to a different surgeon. Her latest rant had caused her to fail those who trusted her most. She had betrayed them with her mishandling of righteous indignation. Finchcrest should've fired her. Her personnel file provided every justification. The word *difficult* filled its pages in all caps and red lettering.

Her heavy sigh fogged the window. From the change in the engine's whine and her popping ears, their altitude shifted in preparation for landing. Once they touched down, it took less than an hour to claim her bags and pick up her rental. Instead of settling into the cottage, she decided to drive around. Why not start her Scottish adventure right away? After all, her hiking pack stood at the ready, stuffed far fuller than it should be. Airport security had balked some, but let her board when she showed her medical credentials. She wore her jeans and walking boots. What more did she need to start her dubious exploration of the Highlands?

She pulled the car over and searched on her phone for any nearby waterfalls. Maggie had forced an oath from her that she'd find one first thing. Her friend had insisted the sound of tumbling water would help her relax, but Evie had her doubts. Poor Maggie deserved better than a friend like her. Evie managed a grim smile as she checked for oncoming traffic. Exploring as soon as she stepped off the plane definitely counted as first thing. Maggie would be thrilled.

With her virtual list of waterfalls, a general idea of where to hike, and enough water, snacks, and emergency supplies to survive a solid month of any apocalypse the wilderness of the Scottish Highlands threw at her, she honked the horn for luck. Time to keep her word, visit a stream, and send some pictures to Maggie.

"Onward, ho," she grumbled as she pulled out onto the road.

⟫⟫⟩⟨⟨⟪⟪

EVIE SAVORED THE last bite of the bacon and sausage sandwich she had purchased at a cozy little shop in Rosemarkie. She rarely indulged in such delicious greasiness, but this tasted the kind of wicked good that made you shiver. Self-control waning, she barely resisted the urge to lick any remains off the sandwich's wax paper wrapping.

"How scrummy was that?" she announced to the surrounding woods. Also, how ironic? She lectured patients every day about avoiding too much fat.

"I shall walk it off," she informed the birds overhead as they chittered about her hypocrisy. Shouldering her backpack in place, she trudged onward.

Quite pleased with the route she had chosen, she tromped through the area, enjoying the shade offered by the pleasant woods filled with beech, rowan, and oak. Maybe Maggie was right about Scotland being a proper place to relax. She laughed out loud at what her friend might think about her deciding she liked the country. Maggie would admit her for psychiatric evaluation.

A creature of some sort scurried deeper under the bushes alongside the trail. Another amused snort escaped her. Perhaps it was a woodland fairy. She shook her head at the silly thought. All that tasty grease from her lovely sandwich was going to her head.

As a gentle breeze rustled through the leaves, she pulled in a deep breath and blew it out. No, she must never admit to Maggie or Finchcrest's admins that perhaps this wasn't such a dreadful punishment after all. They'd think her over the edge, for sure.

The steady thundering of rushing water up ahead pulled her forward. She checked her phone, but with the spotty signal, it took forever to load the map and reveal the location of the first set of falls. With it powered down to spare the battery, she zipped it into the side pocket of her backpack. A few pics of her woodland stroll had already been sent to Maggie, so her friend should be satisfied for a while.

She chose not to follow the path to the footbridge and endure more nauseating displays of affection from the couple up ahead. Instead, she veered off into the woods to enjoy a unique vantage point of the falls. After all, she wasn't the average touristy hiker. She was here for intense therapy. The steady shushing of the cascading water dared her to risk getting closer. Moisture filled the air from the rising mist as the stream tumbled down to the pool below. She maneuvered closer, balancing on moss-covered boulders and shelves of limestone, finally reaching the point where all she heard was the water's deafening song.

From her seat on the rocks, she drew up her knees and hugged them, watching as the pool swallowed up the tumbling water and spit out the spray. How long since she had sat this still and listened to nothing but her thoughts? Forever, really. She avoided the state of quiet solitude like the plague. Her mind kicked into overdrive, and too many memories reared their ugly heads when she sat still.

An insistent, pitiful mewling managed to break through the water's hypnotic hold. She turned toward it, peering under ferns and bushes and scanning the primrose carpeted embankment. The feline cry grew louder, as if the tiny mite needed rescuing.

"Where are you, kitty?"

It answered, making her edge closer to the falls. She eyed the shelf of water-soaked rocks with apprehension, not relishing the idea of getting her feet or anything else soaked. Then she spotted the crying beastie. A black and gray tiger-striped kitten clung to a swaying branch kept in motion by the stream snagging hold of its tip. The mighty oak stretched across the water, yearning for the sunlight shining down into the pool.

"Bad life choice, cat." Evie climbed higher. If she got close enough and coaxed the mite toward the body of the tree, she just might reach it. "Come this way. Here kitty. Come here, and I'll help you."

The cat flattened its ears, flipped its tail, and hissed.

"Really? Is that nice? I'm trying to help you here." She sidled farther along the rock shelf that disappeared behind the tumbling water. "Come this way." She wiggled her fingers, stretching to steady herself against the branch. "Come on, kitty. I promise to take you to a nice comfy cottage and feed you." Surely, Gertrude stocked a bottle or two of cream at the cottage.

The small cat crept closer, then sat and glared at her.

"Now, see here, I can't help you if you don't work with me." Evie wiggled her fingers along the limb, hoping to tempt the uncertain beast into pouncing close enough to be nabbed. She loved cats. Always had. But couldn't foster one because of her long hours at the hospital. If she rescued this one, she'd care for it during her holiday, then find it a suitable home before heading back to London. "Come on, kitty. Come on," she wheedled in a singsong voice.

The feline charged forward, leapt down to the stone ledge beside her, and shot behind the wall of water. Then it cut loose with a furious yowling.

"You cheeky little…" Evie stared after the cat. If the silly thing liked water that much, Godspeed to it. She crouched to work her way down from the ledge and head back to level ground, but then she heard it again. It carried on with louder pitiful crying as though realizing the error of its daredevil ways.

"Oh, bloody hell." She couldn't leave it. That pathetic sound would haunt her for days. With her pack propped on another ledge, she unzipped one of its multitude of pockets and yanked out the compact square of her folded, clear raincoat. She shrugged it on, pulled up the hood, and settled her pack back in place, snugging the straps tight around her shoulders.

"You better appreciate this," she called out to the feline. "And if you scratch or bite me, we shall have words." Thankfully, her hiking boots possessed extra-rugged tread. She prayed that also meant a better grip on wet rocks. Her face to the cliffside, she hugged the solid backdrop of earth and rock as she sidled behind the curtain of water. Her kind heart would be her undoing. Or so, nanny had told her many times a long time ago.

Halfway across the width of the watery tunnel, she pondered the error of keeping her pack on her back and facing the cliff. It was waterproof and had survived a stint with Doctors Without Borders, so it would be okay. But the full gear pack stretched from just below the top of her head down to her hips. Spray wouldn't soak through it, but if the space narrowed anymore and the force of the water hit it, it might pull her backward off the ledge and send her tumbling. A sideways glance assured her the broad extension of the walkway remained the same. At least, she thought so. The misty half-light behind the falls distorted everything. With the louder drumming of the water, she no longer heard the cat, but it had to be up ahead. Where else could it go?

Her right foot slipped and shot off the ledge. She fumbled to regain her footing, grabbing hold of the cliffside and landing hard on one knee. The falls pounded across her heel, threatening to jerk her downward. Heart rate revving, stomach churning, her choice of that delectably fatty sandwich no longer seemed so wise. And the worst of it was, if she leaned either way to vomit, she'd lose her balance as well as her lunch.

"Ease up, old girl." She pressed her forehead to the cool, wet wall of rock and sucked in deep breaths. "That sandwich cost you five quid. You don't want to chunder it now, do you?" The thrum of the rushing water pounded all around, making her head feel like it swelled to the point of exploding every time she opened her eyes.

She had known it would be some noisier this close to the deluge, but she never expected this strange pressure closing in on all sides. She held her head, pressing the heels of her hands against her temples to keep everything in place. This was worse than any migraine ever.

"Dear God, maybe I'm having a stroke." Bile burned the back of her throat, unleashing more nausea. "Or an aneurysm." She patted her face, flexed both hands, then forced her eyes open. "You are being a hypochondriac, Eves. Just like that time in Afghanistan. Now suck it up, find the damn cat, and get the hell out of here."

Waterfalls. Soon as she got back to London, she'd tell Maggie that the next time she wanted to help—don't. She had rather they fired her than go through this. Jaws clenched, she forced herself to look to the left. Where was that stupid cat? Nowhere in sight. Probably scampered away and took off through the woods. Served her right for being so softhearted. Damn cat.

Inching sideways on her knees, she continued her journey. Her shaky balance took the possibility of standing off the table. "Keep moving," she chanted to herself, focusing on getting to the opposite side. The churning disorientation seemed to ease, and her lunch remained in her stomach. Bloody miracle that was, but she accepted it with gladness.

When she emerged from the watery tunnel, she tumbled off the ledge and hugged the ground. Thank God. She made it. After several deep, calming breaths, she pushed herself up and looked around, praying there wasn't a gaggle of tourists enjoying the show of some fool bumbling out from behind the falls.

Immediate uneasiness shoved away any lingering sheepishness. The surrounding woods seemed different somehow. She couldn't quite put her finger on it. After a hard blink and a rubbing of her eyes, she looked around again. It was so strange. The place was the same, but...not. She massaged her temples, inhaled deeply, then blew the air back out. Probably some silly residual trauma from almost tumbling into the water. How could it not be the same place?

Removing the plastic rain jacket, she shook it out while studying the area. The smattering of tourists annoying her on the main trail were gone. She knew she'd made her own path into the woods, but they should be somewhere close. At least within earshot. This area looked empty of hikers. Not just empty—deserted. She heard nothing other than the crashing water, occasional birdsong, or skittering through the leaves and bushes of some woodland creature. An eerie feeling took hold of her. It was if she was the last soul left on earth. A loud splash that didn't fit the rhythmic sound of the falls drew her attention downward to the pool.

Instinct and years of training took over. Backpack in tow, she charged down the rise, praying the man still lived. He floated in the water, face down and arms outstretched. A dark, bloody cloud swirled around his head. After dropping her pack on the shore, she sloshed into the pond and turned him face up, thankful for the buoyancy of the water. Nothing small about this chap. Muscled like a bodybuilder, he was tall enough to pull thunder from the clouds.

"Bloody hell, they grow them big in Scotland." A determined groan came clear from her toes as she dragged him up the bank. The wound on his head looked vicious, but her immediate concern was his breathing. If he drowned, the gash in the back of his head wouldn't matter.

Wedging her knee behind his shoulders, she propped him on his side and pulled her bag closer. "Lucky for you, my fine fellow, I am mental about always being prepared." She unzipped and laid open the pack. "I've got a complete emergency unit in here." With the stethoscope she never left home without, she listened, pressing it in several spots across his broad back and muscular chest. "Got a bit of water in there, my friend, but at least you're breathing, and your heart is strong. Let's keep you on your side for a while, shall we? With any luck, you'll cough it up in a bit."

Out of habit, she popped the stethoscope out of her ears and looped it around the back of her neck before grabbing a rolled-up t-shirt. She placed it under his head, then positioned her pack behind him to keep him somewhat on his side. "Now, let's check that head of yours." Her peers at Finchcrest always teased her about keeping up a line of chatter with unconscious patients. But who knew? They might hear her and focus on living. She had developed the habit during her charity service abroad. Anything that helped a patient, no matter how odd or silly, always mattered.

As gently as possible, she parted the thickness of his dark mane that looked as though it reached past his shoulders. "Like your hair long, do you?" She went silent and frowned at the gash. It wasn't as bad as she had first feared, but it needed sutures. Head wounds always bled like the dickens, even from the smallest nick.

However, this was not a split from diving and hitting a rock. A clean slice of a blade had split his flesh. From the early swelling at the upper end of the cut, whoever had done it either possessed poor aim or a weak swing. Instead of opening his skull, they'd hit him with a glancing blow and knocked the daylights out of him. "When you wake up, you're in for one hell of a headache, my friend." Even though the injury's severity appeared less than she first assumed, the man needed to be airlifted to the hospital just to be on the safe side.

She found her phone, powered it up, then scowled at the screen. "Of course, there's no service here." All she could do was stabilize him and pray a hiker turned up. They could run for help. It was a fine summer's day, and the place was busy enough. Surely, someone would be along soon.

"Well, let's get that cleaned up, shall we?" She forced herself to use an uplifting tone, even though the delay in getting the man proper aid frustrated her. "Lucky for you, I nicked a bottle of povidone-iodine for my trip." Wearing the gloves also liberated from the hospital's supply room, she washed the wound with the golden-brown liquid. Once satisfied with the emergency disinfection, she sutured the gash. "Just temporary stitches to keep you nice and clean, my friend." After padding it with an antimicrobial dressing, she wrapped gauze around his head and secured it with cloth tape. Proud of her handiwork, she smiled. "Aren't you glad I'm quite the thief when it comes to keeping my emergency supplies stocked?"

A second glance at the serene surroundings compounded her anxiousness to get the man more help. Still no tourists. Several vehicles had sat in the car park when she arrived. Yet no one came upon them? When she returned her stethoscope to the bag, her penlight peeping out of its slot caught her attention. Might as well do a more thorough exam while she waited.

Evie knelt in front of him, eased open one of his eyes, and flashed the light. "What glorious eyes you have, sir." She checked the other one. "So brown they're almost black." Both pupils dilated at the same rate. That consoled her somewhat, but he still needed more care than she or her backpack provided. She sat back on her heels and frowned down at him. "What am I going to do with you 'til help comes?"

For the first time since pulling him out of the water, she noticed his odd clothing. "What's this garb you're wearing? Are you a re-enactor or something?" His linen tunic, almost transparent from its soaking, reached to mid-thigh of the snug black pants he wore tucked into knee-high leather boots. "It's a wonder those boots didn't drag you to the bottom of the pool." That's probably what his attacker intended. This would be a perfect place for hiding a body. Luckily for this brown-eyed hulk, he'd hit the water at a shallow spot and stayed afloat.

She leaned forward and dried his face with the tail of her t-shirt.

"You've been in scrapes before, haven't you?" A thin silvery scar split one of his sleek black brows, and a smaller one ran up the side of his chin. "I wish I had your lashes." She pressed the backs of her fingers against his cheek and smiled. A little warm, but not too bad. And very striking in a handsome, squared-jaw sort of way. An additional scar at the base of his throat caught her eye, making her pull open the loose neck of his tunic and glance at his chest. "Poor man, you've been through it. Are you in the military?" What else would explain all those scars?

He jerked and kicked, rolling toward her with uncontrollable choking.

She sprang into action, supporting his head and shoulders as he lunged forward, coughing and spewing out the water she'd heard sloshing around inside him. "Well done, you!" she praised, thumping her fist between his shoulder blades to keep the fluid moving outward. "That's it. Bring it up. All of it now."

"God's beard!" He yanked away from her and rolled back, baring his straight white teeth as he clutched his head.

"So, you are a Scot." She caught hold of his prying fingers as he discovered the bandage wrapped around his head. "Leave that be, now. You've a nasty wound we need to keep clean until we get you transferred."

"Transferred?" he repeated, flinching as he eased back down onto the rolled shirt. He cracked an eye open and sneered up at her. "I willna go without a fight."

Lovely. He'd lost the plot because of the blow to his head. She hated when patients got combative but wasn't surprised. Especially not with this type of injury. Someone had obviously attacked him. "I would never assume you would go anywhere you did not wish to go." Experience had taught her that agreeing with them sometimes helped.

"Where are they?" he growled, still glaring at her as if she had been the one who axed him.

"Who?"

"Yer men."

This one was turning into quite the challenging puzzle. She shook her head and flipped a hand at the surrounding woods. "Look around. I have no men." Then she smiled. "It's just you and me. I promise."

That knotted his dark brows over his narrowed eyes. "Just yerself then? All alone?"

"Yes." She pointed up the hillside toward the rock shelf protruding out from behind the falls. "In my effort to save an ungrateful cat, I ended up there." Then she jabbed a thumb toward the pool beside them. "I heard an odd splash and spotted you floating face down and bleeding everywhere." With an apologetic shrug, she shook her head. "I tried to phone for help, but there's no signal here." Leaning closer, she peered into his eyes. "Are you able to focus?" She fluttered three fingers in front of his face. "No double vision? Everything clear?"

"In the water," he repeated, eyeing her as though he thought her a liar. "Who pulled me out?"

"I did." If not for the man's injury causing him confusion, she'd be insulted. "Pulled you out, cleaned that head of yours, and closed you up with some temporary sutures. I'm sure they'll remove them to give you a proper cleaning once we get you to the hospital."

"I dinna understand half ye're saying."

"Well, you have had a rough time of it." She pulled out her pen-light and clicked it on.

The man's eyes shot wide open, and he floundered away her. "Witch!"

"No, although I have been called something that rhymes with that. Quite a few times, in fact. Be still now." She leaned closer. "I know the light might hurt, but I need to look in your eyes again now that you're conscious."

"Nay!" He batted her away, his panic and sudden pallor concerning her. "Take it away."

"Fine. Fine. Calm down." She clicked it off and shoved it into the back pocket of her jeans. "I promise I mean you no harm." She gave him her best consoling smile. "Why else would I have saved you?"

"Because I am Chieftain Quinn MacTaggart, ye ken? A valuable prisoner."

Delusions sometimes accompanied head wounds. The man obviously thought himself someone quite important. Better to play along to keep him calm. She gave a polite nod. "It is an honor to meet you, Chieftain MacTaggart. I'm Evie Wortham. A surgeon at Finchcrest Hospital in London." Modesty forbade her from telling him she was Finchcrest's *best* surgeon. She offered him another smile.

Poor, befuddled chap stared at her like she spoke in a language he didn't understand. Disbelief and confusion curled a corner of his mouth higher, revealing a dimple dead center of his cheek. She loved dimples. When he remained silent, she did her best to reassure him. "Mind you, I don't feel you'll need surgery, but that's for further testing to decide. Swelling is our greatest concern at this time."

"Swelling?" He held his head and closed his eyes. "Be a helpful lass and fetch me some whisky, aye?"

She clamped her mouth shut, trapping a curt retort behind her teeth. No. With his cognizance a bit dodgy because of the injury, the man deserved some indulgence. The situation warranted niceness. For a while. "I do not recommend whisky for head injuries." She rose and fetched her water bottle. "Here. Just a few sips, mind you. Especially if you're still feeling queasy."

He glared at her. A fierce glare as if trying to intimidate her. She almost laughed out loud. This man had no idea how many go-to-hell looks she had not only faced in her lifetime but also given right back. "Go on then. Take a sip. It's just water with some electrolytes added. It'll make you feel better."

After a sip, he curled his nose and shoved it back at her. "That doesna taste like water."

"I tried the guava flavor packet. You don't fancy it?"

"It tastes like piss."

"I wouldn't know. Mind you, I don't drink piss." She replaced the cap on the bottle, but not before spotting the hint of a smile from him. Well met. He'd started relaxing around her, and his awareness was improving. Seated cross-legged beside him, she looked around for the umpteenth time, still unable to believe not a single soul had appeared.

After blowing out a heavy sigh, she decided to keep him talking. He mustn't sleep. At least, not for a while. "So, do you remember what happened? How were you hurt?"

He scowled and made to rise, then sagged back on the makeshift pillow, clutching his head. "Do ye see my horse?"

"Sorry, no." She wondered if the horse was real or imagined. Concerned that shock might set in, she pulled a thermal blanket from her pack and covered him. "I promise to look as soon as help comes."

His jaw hardened, and hatred flashed in his eyes. "English?"

"Does it matter?"

"Aye, it does."

"I'll keep that in mind, but right now, I'd settle for any nationality with a stronger cell phone signal than mine."

"Ye are a verra strange woman."

"You have no idea," she said as she powered down her phone again and shoved it back in her pocket. "But I'm all you have for the time being."

CHAPTER TWO

IT GRATED ON his soul that the English had captured him—and one of their female spies at that. Perhaps even one of their witches. He couldn't believe they had resorted to sorcery to seize his lands. Even though the sunlight burned through his skull, he endured the pain and kept her in his sights. This strange woman claimed she had saved him. He wouldn't put it past her to run him through when those she served reappeared.

She paced around the pond's edge, shielding her eyes as she scanned the surrounding wood. Probably searching for soldiers to come and cart him away. She had promised to look for his horse, but he felt sure she lied. All English lied.

Around she went again, circling the water widdershins instead of following the proper direction of the sun. This time faster. Must be casting some sort of dark spell over him. He sent up a prayer for protection as he watched her.

She stopped, tapped on the black band on her wrist, then squinted up at the sky again. Her lovely face tightened into a frustrated scowl that somehow added to her beauty. Aye, for a beauty she was even if she was English. And a witch.

A small bend broke the flawless line of her nose. Up high, almost between her eyes. She must have broken it a long time ago. A faint smile came to him. He liked it. The crooked nose suited her. As did her long hair. Swept up from her face and held high by some strange sort of tie, it was a deep rich brown streaked with gold. A tall lass with hardly any curves at all, but those she possessed filled out those strange blue trews of hers nicely. As the shadows lengthened, she pulled on a coat and covered that scandalously short chemise she wore. It was so small and fitted, when she lifted her arms, a swath of bare flesh as wide as his hand showed above the waistband of her trews. Such nakedness. She must be a whore as well as a sorceress.

"What is it?" he finally asked, unable to bear the wondering about her spell casting any longer.

Her scowl faded into a smile but looked forced. He read her as easily as fresh ink on new parchment. She lifted both hands, then let them drop. "Your horse must have gone home for tea."

"What is tea?"

Both her feathery brows arched to her hairline. A dappling of sunlight across her face shifted what he had thought were green eyes to the tawny coloring of fine whisky. Aye, this one was a witch, all right. Eyes that changed colors? He hardened himself against her. At least, he tried. He'd be lying if he said she didn't captivate him. "Well? Will ye nay do me the courtesy of answering? What is *tea*? Something the English give to their horses for strength?"

"Not the horses." She gave him a teasing wink and tapped her chest. "We drink it for ourselves." Her merriment faded as she blew out a dismal huff. "Sunset soon." With a shake of her head, she flipped a hand at the general area. "I cannot believe all the tourists left so early."

He massaged his brow, trying to recall if she had told him what the word *tourist* meant. God's beard, his head pounded like a fiend. And no matter how hard he tried, he couldn't remember a feckin' thing that happened before he opened his eyes to this strange Englishwoman.

Her cool touch on his arm made him jump.

"I'm sorry." With both hands lifted, she eased back a step, genuine concern flashing in those catlike eyes of hers. "I didn't mean to startle you. Are you warm enough? May I please check you again for fever?"

"Aye." He swayed back when she reached for his face.

"Easy now. I promise I won't hurt you."

"I am nay a horse," he snapped, wishing his head would clear and stop pounding so this infernal situation might make some sense. "Dinna speak to me in such a manner, ye ken?"

"Whatever you say, chieftain." She touched his forehead, his cheeks, and throat. Somehow, her cool fingers against his heated flesh eased him, loosening the furious anxiousness in his chest. A slight frown puckered her brow. "You're entirely too warm for my liking." She scooped up the strange metal bottle that held the noxious liquid and offered it. "Drink this while I fetch some acetaminophen. It will help without increasing the risk of bleeding."

"I willna drink that piss again." He pointed at the falls. "Water. Not any of yer potions, aye?"

She eyed him with a perturbed glare but didn't comment. Just tipped her head to the side and tightened her mouth as though biting back words as she walked away. It might not be wise to anger a witch, but he'd risk it before drinking that swill of hers again. Besides, he found pleasure in making the color rise to her cheeks. She would soon learn; she had overfilled her platter by taking on Quinn MacTaggart.

"Here." She held out a cup and two white pebbles. "Water and acetaminophen."

"What do ye expect me to do with those wee rocks?" He took the cup and downed the water before she answered.

"Well, you were supposed to wash them down with the water. Now, I must get more." With an irritated huff, she snatched the cup away and stomped off. In less than a heartbeat, she returned and held out the pebbles. "Here."

"Since when do men consume rocks?"

"Since they get their heads bashed in by someone. Now, put these in your mouth before I shove them up your nose." She squatted down, held the pebbles closer, and glared at him. "Pills in your mouth. Drink. Swallow. You can do that—right?"

He crossed himself. "Get thee behind me, Satan."

Before he realized what she was doing, she pinched his nose shut. When he opened his mouth for air, she shoved the pebbles inside, followed them with water, then pushed his chin upward with the heel of her hand. It forced him to swallow before knocking her backward. Coughing and spewing, head pounding, he pushed himself to his feet, then grew so dizzy, he fell back to the ground. "Damn ye, witch!"

"Oh, shut up." She picked herself up, rubbing her arse and wincing from where she'd landed on the rocks. "Trust me. I do not like this any better than you do, but I will not abandon an injured man. Not even when I'd like to!" After another wincing rub of her backside, she turned to leave, then paused and looked back at him. "I'm going to get some wood for a fire. If you want to leave, then by all means, scamper off. If not, then stop being an ass. I promise I'll help you any way possible. Your concussion granted you some leeway at first. But your assholery ends now." She marched onward, then stopped again, jerked back around, and stabbed a finger at him. "And do not go to sleep while I'm gone."

With a slight dip of his chin, he dismissed her, making her even angrier. *Assholery.* He liked that word and stored it away for future use. The sway of her buttocks as she stormed away captured his full attention and admiration. When he realized she'd entranced him with her seductiveness, he jerked his head aside to break her hold and immediately regretted it. Another way of shielding himself from her bewitchments needed to be found. Although, the gut-wrenching pain inside his feckin' skull proved quite effective for now.

Intent on sitting upright, he closed his eyes and pushed himself upward. Gut churning, he propped his elbows on his knees and held his throbbing head. This wasn't the only head wound he'd ever experienced, but it was worse than when a mace had caught him with a glancing blow. He gingerly worked his fingers around to the square lump beneath the strange wrappings. The thing was as large as the palm of his hand. Had his skull been split clean open?

The English witch returned, hugging a huge armload of sticks and branches. She dumped them on the ground and began snapping the longer ones in two, breaking them against her knee.

He went to address her, but for the life of him, couldn't remember her name. Damn his clouded mind. "Yer name again?"

"Evie," she said, snapping another branch and tossing it onto the growing pile of shorter sticks. "And by the way, I am sorry for losing my temper earlier. I didn't mean to act so ratty." She blew out a heavy sigh. "That's how I ended up here."

"Mistress Evie," he repeated, determined to remember it this time. He ignored the rest of what she said. The nauseating pound splitting his skull forbade the luxury of word play.

"Your short-term memory may be a bit dodgy for a while, but as stable as you seem to be, I shouldn't worry." She gave him a grudging smile and broke the last branch. Crouching, she selected a few pieces from the pile and stood them on end as if building a wee shelter or trap. After stuffing handfuls of grass and moss inside the thing, she fetched a small square of some sort of metal from her bag. Must be a tinderbox. Instead of striking it with a flint, she pushed it into the grass and moss, then backed away as flames crackled and popped, then licked their way up the sticks. Ever so carefully, she piled larger pieces of wood onto the fire.

"How did you do that so quickly?" Fear for his soul made him cross himself again.

She laughed, then sobered quickly as though fearing she hurt his feelings. Flipping the top off the small square, she rubbed her thumb across the thing and produced a flame. "Sorry—I thought you saw it. My grandfather's old lighter. Still works like a gem. Long as the fluid and flints hold out, it's golden."

"It is nay golden. 'Tis silver. But like an old blade."

Her dubious look shifted to one of concern. "You worry me when you say things like that." She rose and moved to the enormous bag of cloth holding all the tools of her sorcery and unbelted a rolled bundle from one end. With a hard snap, she shook out a heavy, thick blanket and placed it closer to the fire. "If I steady you, do you feel as though you could move over here? You'll find the sleeping bag more comfortable. I promise."

"Sleeping bag," he repeated.

She patted the thing. "Yes. One of the best. I know it's summer, but I don't want you catching a chill with the sun going down and all." She tilted her head the barest bit. "Would you consider stripping down so we might dry your clothes and boots by the fire?" She picked up a pair of sturdy twigs. "Perfect sticks for propping your things to dry. There's quite the supply from a downed tree nearby."

Although he'd *stripped down*, as she called it, in front of women before, this time gave him pause.

"Come now, don't be shy." She came closer with the same sort of smile he'd seen the women of the keep use on the ill or the aged. "I am a doctor, you know. I've seen it all before."

"Maybe so, but ye've nay seen mine." He flinched as the pain in his head shot clear to his churning gut. He needed to remember to speak in a quieter tone. For his aching head's sake.

"I am sure I shall be suitably impressed." Her placating smile infuriated him every time she flashed it. She reached down and supported him with a strong hold on his arm. "Shall we try to stand now?"

"I believe ye already are standing, Mistress Evie." How dare the woman speak to him as if he were a bairn. He glared up at her, willing her to fear him. Soon, he would be healed, and then she would see his might.

"One of those, are we?" Her irritating smile quirked to the side as she pulled on his arm. "Up with you, Chieftain MacCrotchety."

"MacTaggart!" he snapped, immediately regretting it. "In God's name, I command ye to remove this spell of pain that grows worse every time I speak or move."

She rolled her eyes and continued her steady pulling. "I shall do my best. Now, over to the sleeping bag with you. The acetaminophen should kick in soon. It won't get rid of all your pain but should help some."

"I thought you wanted me stripped?" he growled, swaying like a drunkard.

"Good man." She wedged herself against his side and wrapped his arm around her shoulders. "Let's get you over here first, then I'll help you undress. My sleeping bag repels water. Any dampness wipes right off. Once we've gotten your clothes off, I'll zip it open so you won't feel so exposed."

"I dinna understand half what ye said." Pain and nausea battled over which would control him. Once he reached her strange pallet, relief surged through him at being back on the ground.

She helped him to his back, even folded the end of the thick blanket toward him so he might use it as a pillow.

Eyes closed, he blew out the lungful of air he held. He splayed his fingers and smoothed his hands back and forth across the strange slickness of the cloth. Almost slippery like silk, but rougher. A fluffiness to it, too, as if filled with an abundance of goose feathers.

"I'm going to pull your boots off now. It may jerk a bit, but I'll do my best not to."

He braced himself as she hoisted his right foot into the air. It would move him. Always did whenever the wenches pulled them off. One came off, then the other. He exhaled and dared to open his eyes. Not as bad as he had expected. She must've used spell craft to make it easier.

"Thank ye," he breathed.

"Let me turn these up on a stake nearby. Don't want them too close to the fire, do we? Ruin the leather if they dry too fast."

"So, ye're a witch, a healer, and a tanner? What else can ye do, woman?"

With a cocky tip of her head, she winked again. "You can't begin to imagine, mate."

Mate? What did she mean by that? Did she mean what he thought she meant? "Dinna expect any coupling tonight, woman. My head canna bear it."

Her laughter rang out loud and clear, echoing across the pool and startling birds from nearby trees. "While I appreciate your thoughtfulness, Chieftain MacTaggart, I assure you, I do not wish to *couple*. My interest in you is purely in getting you the medical help you need before going along my merry way."

"Insolent wench."

She laughed at him again. "Undo your trousers so I can pull them off. They're next."

"By trousers, I assume ye mean my trews?"

"Yes." She emitted another insulting chortle, then cleared her throat. "Your *trews*."

He undid the flap at the waist, then let his arms drop to his sides. "Done, m'lady."

"M'lady," she repeated, making his insult sound as though she took it as a compliment instead of the slander he intended. "I rather fancy that. Thank you ever so much, m'lord."

"I prefer the address of *Himself* to that of *m'lord*. My chieftainship means more to me than my earldom."

She didn't comment. Nor did she laugh this time. Simply yanked off his trews by the ankles, jolting him so hard, he hissed through clenched teeth. "God's beard, woman!"

"Sorry." But it didn't sound as if she meant it. "Do you need a breather before we get your tunic off?"

"A breather?" He was breathing. Was the woman addled?

"Your consistent difficulty with language concerns me." She crouched by his head, pulled out that infernal stick with the blazing tip, and aimed it at his eyes again. "Let me check the dilation of your pupils."

Before he formed an argument, she leaned over and blinded him with the thing. But damned if she didn't smell nice as she did it. Sweeter than the roses his sister nurtured in their private gardens.

She sat back on her heels, frowning as she caught her bottom lip between her teeth. "Pupils react normally." With a shake of her head, she glanced at the black strap on her wrist. "Blast, I keep forgetting this thing's gone to pot." She tapped on its surface, then shook her head again. "I wish someone would hurry and find us so your MRI could be done sooner rather than later." Still looking perplexed, she slid an arm under his shoulders and nudged. "Help me out, my fine burly Scotsman. Tall and muscular as you are, I bet you weigh over twenty stone."

"Use yer magic as ye did when ye dragged me free of the water." He glared up at her, enjoying the scent of her floating all around him.

"The buoyancy of the water plus slippery grass came to my aid then. I wish there was such a thing as magic. You'll note I didn't pull you far and probably won't be able to move you come morning." She patted his chest. "Now, come on. This is the last of it, then into the bag you go."

A witch who didn't believe in magic? Or was it just words to throw him off? Bracing himself for another surge of pain, he sat up and allowed her to pull his wet *léine* off over his head.

"Don't lay down yet. Hold on." She rubbed her finger and thumb along the edge of the blanket, making it hiss like a snake. Then she separated its layers and folded as much of it aside as possible. "Now, then. Shift your bum over. Down you go. Tuck your feet inside."

Once he'd done as she ordered, she made the bag hiss again, opening it the rest of the way but keeping him covered. "If you get chilly later, you can zip it closed. I didn't want you to feel too constricted." She patted his leg through the thick covering. "Do you feel you might keep down a power bar and more water? The protein and fluids will help you."

"I dinna ken," he mumbled, leery about what a power bar might be. Some form of torture, most likely.

"Well, I'll get one for you and tear the package open. They can be testy little buggers. Try it whenever you wish."

She rummaged through her belongings again, emerging with a shiny object that crackled like brittle parchment. Biting the end of it, she tore the corner, peeled it open, and showed it to him. "Salted caramel. It's a favorite of mine. Quite scrummy, really." She placed it on the corner of his pallet and rose. "I'll get your water."

The English had yet to appear; she had bandaged him, gotten him warm and dry, and now fetched him water and food. Aside from the strange magic of her wee fire box and light stick, she never mumbled any incantations or attempted to do him any harm. Perhaps Mistress Evie was a kind and decent woman, after all. A healer who had saved him from drowning and sinking to the bottom of the fairy pool. But then again, she might be one of the Fae—which was a damn sight worse than any witch.

He risked a taste of the thing she called a bar of power. Perhaps it would gift him with the strength of ten if it came from the Fae. Chewy. Like a tough piece of meat not boiled long enough. But sweet. And salty. A damn sight tastier than any dried meat or oatcake. "'Tis good," he said when she handed him a cup of water.

"I'm glad you like it." But she seemed distracted. Troubled.

"Does someone approach? Do you sense evil?"

"Sense evil?" Brow cocked to an amused angle, she shifted in place with an uneasy glance around. "No. No evil to speak of. Just birds and woodland animals. No motors. No noise at all. That's the problem. There's also no sign of the lights from the car park nor that of a living soul other than you and I. It's not—normal." She pointed eastward. "I know the trees are thick, but with the sun nearly set, the sky should still be lighter in that direction. I distinctly remember security lights at the corners of the park."

"There is nothing to the east but the sea, lass." He resettled himself on the fine pallet and studied the odd wrapping of the confection she had called a *bar*. Such tiny script and long words. He prided himself on being an educated man. To be a proper chieftain demanded it. But the meanings on this bit of strange paper eluded him. "What does all this say?"

She took it from him and shoved it into a pocket of her bundle. "Mumbo jumbo that doesn't really matter. They're all pretty much the same." With a long stick, she poked at the fire. Its glow lit her face, revealing her turmoil.

"Tell me," he ordered, pillowing his head on his arm. It still throbbed like a drumbeat, but the pain had dulled some, becoming a great deal more bearable than before.

"Tell you what?" she asked without looking away from the fire.

"What worries ye?"

She shrugged and gave him another of her careful smiles. "Last time I slept out in the open, bombs kept me awake. I guess I was remembering that night."

"Bombs?" he repeated slowly. "What are bombs?"

With a concerned furrowing of her brow, she stretched toward him and felt his forehead again. "You need an MRI."

"Why type of herb is *MRI*?"

She flinched as she stared at him. "It doesn't matter. I don't think MRIs grow this far north." She looked away, hugged her knees to her chest, and rested her cheek atop them.

"Is this yer pallet?" The thing he laid upon coddled him in a pleasant softness, like the finest spun wool. But he'd nay put her from her bed. He wasn't that ailing. "Lass?"

"Yes," she said without lifting her head and looking his way. "But I don't need a place to sleep. I caught a few hours last night. I'm fine for a while."

She must be one of the Fae to not need rest like a normal mortal.

"Are ye cold?" Worry for her took root and sprouted within him. Even if she was English, she had taken fine care of him. It wasn't proper that she should suffer. "I havena seen ye eat anything. Ye didna give me the last of yer food, did ye?"

With her head still resting on her arms, she huffed out a small laugh. "I am quite fine, thank you. Don't worry about me."

"'Tis a man's duty to worry after women." He smiled. "Especially women such as yerself."

She didn't respond, just lifted her head, propped her chin on her folded arms, and stared into the fire.

"How come ye to be in these woods alone, Mistress Evie?" It was dangerous for a lass to travel the Highlands alone. And unusual, too.

That drew her attention away from the crackling flames but only rewarded him with her pensive scowl.

"Because none of my friends were banished to Scotland along with me."

"Banished?" If she had angered the English enough to get herself banished, that proved she wasn't a dangerous lass. "What caused them to banish ye?"

She returned to staring at the fire and shrugged. "I called the wrong person a murderous, penny-pinching bastard." With a flip of her hand, she tipped her head to one side. "Or something along those lines. Suffice it to say, I insulted the wrong person—for a second time, as a matter of fact." She gifted him with a genuine smile this time. "I say things I shouldn't. A lot. It finally came to a head."

"Ye angered a person of power?"

"You might say that."

The more he learned, the more he decided he liked her, and this woman needed his protection. In fact, since she had saved his life, he was honor-bound to keep her from harm. "I admire ye spoke yer mind. Who were ye protecting?"

Her smile disappeared. "A patient."

"Why does that make ye unhappy?" It amazed him how easily he read her. He had never possessed that talent with any woman before. But then, he hadn't needed the trait. He was a chieftain. And an earl. Fathers seeking a profitable match flocked to him, practically tossed their daughters into his bed. Servants served him. For enough coin, harlots and pub wenches pleasured him. Sometimes even without the coin. Charm and a few kind words got him whatever he wished. But this lass intrigued him. "Tell me, Mistress Evie. What happened to this *patient* of yours?"

"He died," she said, then stood and tossed more wood on the fire. "All my fighting, cursing, and breaking the rules didn't save the poor man after all."

"I am sorry, mistress."

"Evie," she corrected. "Just plain Evie, all right?"

"I daresay there is nothing plain about ye." He eased himself upright to a seated position, pleased to discover that the movement didn't trigger as much misery as before. As he rolled to his knees and pushed himself to his feet, she rushed to him and took hold of his shoulders.

"Let me help you. Where are you trying to go?" She ducked under his arm and hugged his waist as if she thought him unable to walk.

"If ye must know, I need a piss." Surely, she would nay wish to help with that.

"I don't want you to wander too far from the firelight. You're still unsteady, and who's to say what sort of crawly things might be out there in the darkness."

He stared down at her. "I canna make water with ye hugging on me like this."

"I don't want you to fall over."

"I willna fall over." As gently as possible, he unwrapped her arm from around him and set her aside. "Stand here, if ye must, but I'll be moving forward a bit to relieve myself. Alone. Aye?"

Fists propped on her hips, she granted him a stern nod. "Fine then. I'll wait right here. But don't go much farther."

"Ye're nay my mother nor my wife, so, I'll thank ye to mind yer tone, woman." He nearly groaned his relief as he unleashed the stream.

"Well, if I'm ever fortunate enough to meet either of them, I shall offer my commiserations for their tolerating your stubbornness."

"My mother crossed over years ago." His relief complete, he turned back and walked slowly, taking care to avoid any obstacles hidden in the shadows. "As did my wife and child."

"Forgive me for my poor sense of humor." She dropped her gaze, then held out a hand. "Come now. Back to your pallet. I'll get you a fresh cup of water once you're settled."

"So, I'll need another piss?" he teased, striving to lighten the mood and drive the unhappy memories back to the shadows where they belonged.

She smiled. "Yes. So, you'll need another piss."

CHAPTER THREE

E VIE FINALLY RELENTED and stretched out beside him on the sleeping bag. More to silence his archaic sense of chivalry than because she needed the rest. He refused to understand or accept that, as long as she scored a few hours of sleep here and there, she did just fine. Peace finally reigned once she spread the bag open and covered them both with the thermal blanket.

With the mild night, they didn't really need the fire or the blanket, but somehow, both made her feel safer. She also ended up roasting, because the man put out the heat of a furnace and kept snuggling closer. His tendency to throw an arm around her and pull her to him while he slept rattled her at first, but then she decided it wasn't so bad after all. It had been a long time since she shared a closeness with anyone. At least she could pretend for a little while.

At intervals ingrained by years of medical training, she checked his pulse and breathing without waking him. She wished all her patients possessed the recuperative powers of Chieftain MacTaggart. *Quinn,* she silently corrected. Since she had insisted he call her *Evie,* he proclaimed she must call him *Quinn.*

And now she lay on her side, head pillowed on her arm, unable to shake the eeriness that somehow, something seemed very off as in an apocalyptic kind of way. She tried to put her finger on it as the sky grew lighter. With Quinn doing so well, perhaps they could walk back to the car park once he awoke. The sight of that compact blue rental car would make her feel so much better.

She eased out from under his arm, replaced the blanket he'd thrown off yet again, and strolled closer to the pool's edge. An eerie mist floated across the water, perpetually rippling and wavering like a spirit come to warn her about pending evil. She blinked away the silly thought, scolding herself to stop buying into Quinn's delusions.

As the sun rose, the sky turned a lovely shade of pink, then gave way to the clearest blue. The trees came alive with songbirds warbling their morning songs. A gentle breeze rustled the leaves, whispering that it knew what was wrong but refused to tell her.

The mist evaporated so quickly, it made her blink and wonder if she had imagined it. Her gaze followed the rippling waters to where the pond narrowed and turned into a stream flowing to the east. It reminded her of the footbridge she hadn't taken yesterday. Maybe that's why no other hikers had found them. The bridge spanned a smaller set of falls. If a tourist kept to the main trail, they wouldn't discover this waterfall. That realization gave her some comfort, but not much. It was still too bloody quiet.

She returned to the smoldering coals and added enough sticks to get the fire going. Rough camping or not, she insisted on her tea and prided herself on packing her trusty dented pot for boiling water. She always preferred packing supplies instead of extra clothing.

A glance over at Quinn made her smile. He'd kicked away the blanket again and lay sprawled across the pallet as if enjoying the best sleep of his life. A not-so-professional interest in his anatomy begged her to allow her gaze to linger. Genetics had blessed this man with quite the impressive package. His wife had been a lucky woman. Her smile faded. Both his wife and child had died. She wondered how it had happened. A car accident, perhaps?

With the pot filled and nestled in the coals, she added her favorite black tea to a cup and impatiently waited for the water to boil. With the fresh start of a new day and her tea, she could handle anything.

Quinn stirred, groaned out a jaw-cracking yawn, then grabbed his head. "Hell's fire!"

Poor man. He'd feel like proper shit today. "I'm making tea," she said, hoping that would lift his spirits.

"What is *tea*?" he forced out through clenched teeth, sagging to hold his head as though he feared it might scatter into pieces.

She dimly recalled him asking that same thing yesterday and wondered how he still couldn't know. The man definitely needed a full work-up once she got him to the nearest medical facility. Water boiling, she poured some into the cup she had intended for herself. Patients took priority. After it steeped a scant amount of time, she carried it over to him. "Careful now. It's piping hot."

He took a sip and made a face. "*That* is tea?"

"I know. I fancy mine with a bit of cream, but it's better than nothing." She peered into his face. "Drink it all if you can. Caffeine helps. I'll fetch water and acetaminophen for you, too."

"The pebbles," he repeated, squinting up at her as he forced down another sip.

She smiled, even though his ignorance of something as every day as acetaminophen worried her. "Yes. The pebbles."

"Ye are a tender woman, Evie, and I am grateful."

She didn't know what to say. The compliment made her blush. Quite a feat since she thought that trait had left her years ago. When she returned with the pills and water, she found him frowning down into the cup.

"Am I supposed to eat that muck now?" His look said he hoped she would answer *no*.

She laughed and took it away, replacing it with a fresh cup of water. "No. Take your pebbles while I fix a cup for myself. I fear I'm less than human until I've had my morning tea."

"So ye are one of the Fae?" The awe in his voice matched the leeriness flashing in his eyes.

"What?" She tossed out the spent tea leaves, added fresh, and pushed the pot of water deeper into the coals to get it boiling again.

"Ye said ye were nay human." He shrugged and made a swiping motion that included her as well as all of her things. "That would explain much—ye being one of the Fae and all."

Delusions. Unable to grasp reality. The blow to his head appeared to have damaged his reasoning. She had to get him to a medical facility. Soon. "I promise I am not one of the Fae. I'm as normal as you are."

"I have yet to see that, lass."

Time to change the subject. "Once you've dressed, if you feel you can manage it, shall we try to make the walk to my car?" She sipped the hot, black tea, a purr almost escaping her as the wondrous stuff recharged her system.

"Make it to your car? Is that where ye live?" He stood and stretched to his full impressive stature, unashamed in his glorious nakedness like a powerful god descended from the heavens. "I've never heard of a place called *Car*."

"Uhm... sorry?" She blinked, unable to remember what he had just asked. Always one to focus on a patient's health instead of their appearance, her staunch professionalism slipped in appreciation of the impeccable view of Chieftain MacTaggart's sculpted physique. After all, she was a woman. "What did you say?"

"Car," he repeated, flinching as he pulled his tunic down over his head. "Is that yer home?"

"No," she answered slowly, trying to choose the least upsetting explanation as possible. Poor man. What century did he think himself from? It certainly wasn't the current one. "My car is my transport. The way I get around."

"Ah." He relaxed with a smile that fully displayed the handsome dimple in his left cheek. "*Car* is yer horse's name then."

"In a manner of speaking." She didn't want to dive too headlong into his world, or she'd never get him inside the vehicle once he realized a car wasn't a horse.

"I wouldha thought ye'd bring the beast closer to camp. Did ye see to it once I slept?"

"I left it in a safe place. We'll go there once you've dressed, and I've packed everything up."

He yanked on a boot and flinched again but didn't lose his balance. That gave her hope.

By the time she doused the fire and repacked her bag, he'd finished dressing and watched her from his seat on a boulder. The intensity of his stare made the back of her neck tingle, the same way it had while they slept snuggled like spoons in a drawer. She scrubbed away the feeling, then hoisted her pack in place and hooked her thumbs through the padded straps. "Do you have the strength to walk a bit?"

His expression hardened into a scowl. "Aye."

"I didn't mean it as an insult." She turned eastward, determined to follow the stream to the footbridge. The main trail back to the car park would be right there.

In two broad strides, he caught up with her, took hold of her arm, and pulled her to a stop. With a tip of his head toward her pack, he held out his hand. "It isna proper that ye should carry such whilst I walk with nothing. Give it to me. I shall bear it for ye."

"I think not, my good sir." She would entertain his delusions up to a point. Without thinking, she reached up and gently rested her fingertips on the bandage wrapped around his head. "You've done well considering the bashing you took. Concentrate on keeping steady, agreed? I've carried this pack more miles than you can imagine."

When he reached up and covered her hand with his, she jerked away. With the firm tone she always used with her more stubborn patients, she added, "I cannot, however, carry you. Mind your walking now. Right?"

His irritated scowl softened somewhat, but he wasn't pleased. She tugged on his arm. "Come on, then. If you behave, I'll reward you with a bacon and sausage sandwich when we reach Rosemarkie."

He shot her a disbelieving glance as they trudged along. "Rosemarkie, ye say?"

"Yes. There's a shop there that sells the best bacon and sausage sandwiches. Do you know it?" She didn't recall what else their menu offered, but something there would surely tempt him.

"A shop," he repeated. "In Rosemarkie?"

Why did he find that so hard to believe? "Never mind."

She quickened her pace as if walking faster would help her escape the growing sense of uneasiness gnawing at her. The farther they walked, the more the landscape looked noticeably different. As impossible as that seemed—she couldn't ignore it. It was... less civilized, for lack of a better way to describe it. Trees, bushes, and clusters of tall weeds and grasses covered the area. Quite a change from yesterday. Not a single one of the several trails she had seen showed up anywhere. Nor any of the signage that herded the tourists and kept them from getting lost. She slowed to a complete halt and stared up at the monstrosity of a boulder on her right.

"I know there was a blasted sign here," she said under her breath. Pressing both hands on the sun-warmed rock, she kicked aside the overgrown sedge that wasn't there yesterday. She stared at the ground. There was no possible way it grew that quickly. Today, the natural monolith looked in dire need of a thorough trimming.

"This is east, right?" she asked without taking her hands from the stone.

"Aye, we're traveling east." Quinn shielded his eyes, squinted at the horizon, then gave her a quizzical look. "Why?"

She pushed away from the rock. The icy knot tightening in her chest almost cut off her air. A refusal to acknowledge or give in to her growing panic made her square her shoulders and resettle her pack. "I just wanted to make sure I hadn't gotten off track." The distant shush of tumbling waters helped calm her. There it was—the next set of falls. And the too touristy footbridge would be right there. The picnic area. Tables. Trash bins. All just up ahead. The trail back to the car park would be right where she had left it. Everything would be all right, and maybe she'd have her own head examined when she got Quinn's checked.

"Might we get some water and rest in the shade for a wee spell?"

Ashamed that she had ignored her patient while wallowing in her own foolish worries, Evie took hold of his arm. The poor man had gone pale as milk, and a sheen of sweat glistened across his forehead. "Sunshine has your head pounding worse, doesn't it?"

"Aye," he said, as if admitting to it made him less of a man.

She knew he felt a great deal worse when he allowed her to steady him as they made their way down the hillside toward the water's edge. "Mind the stones now," she said, catching hold around his waist as he stumbled. "The last thing you need is a tumble." Her concern grew even more when he didn't even growl or grumble that he could manage it alone.

They made it to a mossy embankment shaded by a large oak. Teeth bared, Quinn lowered himself to one of the gnarled roots that popped up from the earth like the knuckle of a mighty finger. After scrubbing a hand across his face, he leaned forward, propped his elbows on his knees, and held his head. "The wee pebbles are nay working as well today, Evie." His tortured rasping squeezed her heart, making her wish she could erase his suffering completely.

"Today will be bad." She slid off her pack and sorted through it until she found a cup and the t-shirt he'd used as a pillow. "Sit tight. Water and a cool compress are on the way. We'll stay here as long as you need."

She skittered down the bank to the fast-moving water, scooped up a cupful, then soaked the soft cotton shirt and wrung it out. As she straightened, the sight of the falls up ahead gave her the hard jolt of a bared electrical wire. That water feature was the one she had seen on the internet. In fact, her current viewpoint was probably where the travel photographer had taken the shot. One slight problem. Not a bridge in sight. Nor a tourist viewing platform. No smattering of benches offering weary hikers a comfortable place to enjoy the play of the water. Nothing but banks overgrown with ferns and an occasional boulder peeping above them.

"My sanity has left me," she whispered. There was no way on God's green earth that she had lost her way and gotten turned around. Not this time. The bridge. Where was it? Yesterday, she had avoided this place because of the nauseating lovebirds with all their clinginess. She looked off to the left. Yes. Right there. She distinctly remembered turning off into the woods just there. Then she came upon the different waterfall. And the cat. "What in Heaven's name is going on here?"

"Evie?" Quinn's concerned call broke through her paralyzing confusion.

"Coming." She wet the shirt in the cold water again, determined to keep her mind on task to keep from teetering over into hysteria and running screaming through the woods.

"I called ye twice, woman. Dinna make me worry after ye like that again." Some color had returned to his face, but he still looked a bit peaked.

"Sorry." She offered the cup of water, then moved behind him, gently scooped up his hair, and placed the cool, damp cloth against the back of his neck. "Keep leaning forward. I'd prefer your dressing remain dry."

He eased out a sigh and rolled his shoulders. "That helps. Thank ye, lass."

"Of course," she said, speaking the words out of reflex. She sat and massaged her temples. Lost. That was the only plausible excuse. She had somehow gotten turned around.

"Ye dinna look well."

"I *dinna* feel well." She shouldn't do that. This was bloody Scotland. The last thing she needed to do was make fun of his brogue. "How familiar are you with this area?"

His brow furrowed as he resettled himself on the large tree root. "This is the land of my ancestors. MacTaggart is a sept of Ross, but this area has always been under our clan's care."

"So, you would say you're quite familiar with all the waterfalls here?"

"Aye. I've swum in the pools and tickled fish from the streams."

"But you know nothing of a car park over in that direction..." She pointed to be sure he understood. "Say... a couple of kilometers from where we sit now?"

He looked at her as if he thought her mad. "I dinna ken what a car park is, lass."

She must not panic. This man suffered from a concussion. However, the tiny voice in the back of her mind laughed altogether too loudly. That same voice also reminded her how well he appeared to be managing compared to some head injury patients she had treated.

"You are Chieftain Quinn MacTaggart of Clan MacTaggart—right?"

His concerned scrutiny tightened, narrowing his eyes further. "Aye," he agreed, his tone leery.

"When were you born?" She couldn't evade the question any longer.

"Winter of 1266, why?"

"1266," she repeated, then swallowed hard. No. The man was delusional. His answer made no sense. Had to be his injury talking. "And how old are you now?"

"This winter will be my thirtieth year on this earth."

Her mouth went so dry she nearly choked. Without asking, she snatched the cup out of his hand and downed the rest of his water. "I shall get more," she said as she stumbled toward the stream.

What he insinuated could not be true. It was not possible. She knelt beside the water, filled the cup, and threw it in her face. This could not be the year 1296. He was just a confused re-enactor, and the blow to his head had him believing this really was the thirteenth century.

She scooped up a handful of water and splashed her face again, trying to silence her analytical mind that demanded an explanation for all the changes to the landscape. "Breathe deep," she whispered, closing her eyes and rocking back on her heels. No. This could not possibly be 1296. "Just keep breathing, and it'll all be fine. There's a data-driven reason for everything."

"Evie?" His calm deep voice with its rumbling brogue jarred through her misery and made her jump. "Saint's bones, lass. What is it?" He caught hold of her. His rich, dark eyes reflected the genuine concern echoing in his tone. "Are ye unwell? Are ye hurting?"

"I...uh." She paused, swallowed hard, and scrambled for something—anything sane to say. "Dizzy spell," she finally blurted out. "Happens when I only have tea and nothing to eat."

He scooped her up into his arms and carried her back to their seats of tree roots. As gentle as any mother laying down a sleeping child, he settled her on the root, then fetched her bag. "Which part holds yer bars of power?"

Joints locked to keep from crumbling into a sobbing lump, she concentrated on pulling in one deep breath at a time. She must not fall to pieces and reveal all her fears. Not in front of poor Quinn. She had already shocked the man too many times as it was. Besides, this just could not be the thirteenth century.

"Lass?" Kneeling at her feet, he peered up at her, waiting.

She pointed at one of the zippers. "That one."

He frowned down at the black zipper pull, rubbing his fingers together as if trying to work up the courage to touch it. "That one?"

"Grab hold and slide it downward," she said, closing her eyes at a sudden trembling taking over. Shock. She was going into shock because Quinn didn't know what a zipper was nor how to use it. No. Her body and mind were about to overheat and shut down from trying to figure out this mess.

"Evie—Heaven help ye, lass. Ye're shaking like a leaf in a wind-storm." He eased her down to the ground before she toppled off her seat. Closing her fingers around the power bar, he leaned so close his nose nearly touched hers. "The blanket, Evie, which part of yer wee bag holds the blanket?"

"I don't remember," she whispered. She locked her gaze on the bag as if it was her last hold on sanity. Her trusty backpack. Her supplies. Together, they had survived wars, third world countries, and data-driven hospital administrators who sucked up to government officials and didn't give a rat's ass about patients. She would damn well survive this and figure it out. Somehow.

Harder, uncontrollable trembling rattled her, forcing her to curl into a tighter ball. Yes. She would survive, but for now, a bit of a breakdown was definitely in order before returning to her old, resourceful self.

Quinn found the blanket and tucked it around her. "There now. Rest a spell and eat yer bar of power, ye ken? All will be well. I promise."

"What is today's date?" she forced out.

"The date?"

"Yes." She braced herself for what she hoped he wouldn't say.

"Last day of July, I believe." He pursed his lips as if unsure. "Or maybe the thirtieth. I canna say for certain since I seem to be missing a sizable chunk of my memories."

"And the year?" she whispered, squeezing the power bar so tightly it squished.

"Year of our Lord 1296."

"I see," she said more to herself than him—over seven hundred years into the past. Seven hundred and twenty-three, to be exact. She clutched the blanket closer and concentrated on controlled breaths. In. Out. Her heart rate was off the charts, which was actually quite normal, considering her circumstances.

"Ye've crushed yer wee treat, lass." He gently pried her hand open, removed the bar, and tore away the wrapper. Breaking off a tiny chunk, he pressed it to her lips. "A bite for ye, Evie. For me, aye? Ye're scaring the living hell out of me." He gave a soft laugh. "Ye're the fiercest woman I've ever met. Even though I've known ye but a day, I've not seen ye like this." Leaning closer, he treated her to a gentle smile and nudged the melting chocolate against her mouth again. "Where's the fearless lady who saved my life?"

She managed the bite for his sake. To quiet him. She needed to think. Not eat.

"Another?"

With a shake of her head, she pushed his hand away. "I can't right now. But, thank you. You eat it. It'll melt into a useless mess if you don't."

He sat beside her and leaned back against the root. After wolfing down the rest of the chocolate mess, he wiped his hands on his trews. "What happened there at the stream, Evie? Ye were well before then."

She didn't answer. What might she say? He already thought her a witch or one of the Fae.

"Are ye with child?"

"Definitely not." For one who remained silent most of yesterday, he certainly didn't possess the ability to be quiet now. Glad for his healing, she wished he would close his mouth. At least for a little while. She needed quiet to think and sort through this mess.

"Well, that's fine then," he said, apparently determined to keep the conversation going. "I just wondered, ye understand. My wife had such spells when she found herself in such a state."

It struck her as odd that he spoke about his departed wife with so little emotion. A defense mechanism, perhaps? She didn't comment.

"She died bringing the child into the world." His eyes narrowed the slightest bit as he stared off into the distance. "Good enough, woman, I suppose. Kind enough most of the time. I hope she rests in peace, along with the bairn."

Even with her head swimming, it still struck her odd that he spoke about his family as though idly passing the time of day. "Were the two of you married long?"

He shook his head. "Nay. Less than a year."

"I'm sorry." Even though she wished to, she didn't ask why he didn't sound sad about the loss of his wife or child. People mourned in different ways, and from what she remembered from her history classes, the thirteenth century provided plenty of opportunities. She'd best just concentrate on what she might do to reverse her own issues and get back to where she belonged. Then it came to her that everything went to pot after she came out from behind that waterfall.

Pushing aside the blanket and sitting straighter, she gave Quinn a reassuring smile she didn't feel. "I'm much better now. And here in the shade, you seem better, too. Are you?" She had to play this just right to avoid arousing any suspicions.

"Aye." His smile was genuine and pain-free. "The sunlight's a bugger. The shade helps."

"Do you think you might make it back to where we were without too much suffering? I'm afraid I pushed you too hard too soon. We should've camped there longer to give you more time to heal." She had to convince him to get back to that waterfall.

He propped his forearms on his bent knees. "Why not stay here? Plenty of water. Shade. Shelter beside this old tree."

Fair enough question. How might she counter such logic? On to Plan B. "We can stay here if you like."

With any luck, he'd nap, and she'd nick back to the waterfall, shoot in behind it, and hopefully, come out where she belonged. Quinn would be fine without her. In a few days, he'd be right as rain. She'd used absorbable stitches, so even those wouldn't be a problem for him.

Apprehension like she'd never felt before pushed her to her feet. "I'm much steadier now. Why don't you stretch out on the sleeping bag here in the shade, while I gather some wood for later? For the fire and all. I missed my afternoon tea yesterday. I'll not tolerate missing it today." She hated her mindless babbling, but it didn't matter. As long as it kept him distracted. Before he answered, she unbuckled the bag and spread it out. Happy to sacrifice both the sleeping bag and her backpack if it meant getting back to the twenty-first century.

"I'm nay tired. It's just the aching in my head with the bright sun and all." Suspicion put an edge in his voice. "What is it, Evie? Ye're nay yerself of a sudden."

"What do you mean I'm nay—not myself?" She snorted out a laugh that sounded fake even to her. "We just met yesterday. You hardly know me."

"I know enough," he said with conviction. "And ye're nay yerself."

Time to adapt and shift to Plan C. "I'm certain I forgot something back at the waterfall and can't rest easy until I go check."

"What did ye forget?" He wasn't biting off on Plan C. She saw it in his eyes.

"I don't know for certain. All I know is I need to look." She shrugged and gave a nonchalant flip of a hand. "Surely, you've felt that way before? No? Then it must be a silly woman thing, I suppose. I'll just nick over there. Take a quick look 'round, then be back here before you know it."

He rose to his feet and squared his shoulders. The tilt to his head and arched brow shouted that he knew her for the liar she was. "I'll be going with ye."

"But the sunshine—"

"Sunshine be damned. I'll be going with ye, woman. I dinna ken what ye're up to, but I know 'tis something. Do ye deny it?"

As long as she got back to those falls, she didn't care if he came with her or not. "I just need to get back there. Come with me if you like or stay here. It makes no difference to me." She slung her pack onto her shoulders. The sleeping bag and blanket could stay here in the past, as a souvenir of her visit.

He scooped them up and slung them across one arm. "Allow me to carry these for ye, m'lady. So, ye dinna get over there and feel like ye've forgotten something. Again."

So, the nosy chieftain excelled in sarcasm? Well met. "Why, thank you, good sir. Here's to recovering what I lost." She prayed her century would be as easy to fall into as his had been.

CHAPTER FOUR

T HE SUN DIDN'T pain him as much this time. Perhaps because it glared on his back instead of his face. Or more likely, because he was so distracted, trying to sort out the truth of Evie's odd behavior. While he hadn't known the lass for long, he had a lifetime of experience with liars. Her tale about leaving something behind was just that. A lie. A weak one, but still a lie.

They made it back to the pool quicker than the journey from it. At one point, he wondered if the anxious woman would break into a hard run and race him. He spread the pallet and blanket back in place beside the cold, wet ashes of last night's fire, alert to whatever strange plot this curious lady intended. He waited, no longer fearing her but watchful. She might be English but had proven herself a kind and caring soul. But something troubled her, and he stood poised to discover what her next move might be.

With the fidgetiness seen in unruly children and thieves about to be sentenced, she paced around the rim of the pool. Her knuckles whitened against the dark green shoulder straps of her bag. He counted three times that she glanced up at the source of the falls. What in Heaven's name did she see up there? Or hope to see?

"Do ye see what ye missed?" he asked, baiting her to reveal the truth of their return to the campsite.

After another fretful glance all around, she licked her lips, wetting them to unleash another lie. "No. No." She shot him a nervous smile. "I think I'll check up there. Be right back."

As she passed, he snagged hold of her backpack and stopped her. "Leave yer bag here, aye? No sense in toting it up the hillside, is there? Just to look around?"

With a strained, huffing laugh, she shook her head. "No. You're right. How silly of me." Her tone crackled with uneasiness. After forcing another tense smile, she slipped off the bag and swung it to the ground. "Be right back." Then bolted up the hillside.

Quinn strode closer to the water's edge, his attention pinned on her fine, taut arse as she scrambled upward. A sense of befuddlement made him tilt his head. As she stepped out onto the stone ledge partially hidden by the tumbling waters, startled realization took hold and shocked him into motion. What the hell did she mean to do? Jump? Did she plan to end her life?

Ignoring the grinding ache in his head, he charged up after her. "Evie! Woman, ye must stop!"

She cast back an apologetic flip of a hand, then slipped behind the waters.

If she meant to jump and survived it, he would save her from drowning. He thundered back down the hillside and waded in, never taking his eyes from the source of the falls. "Dinna let her die," he prayed. "If ye let her live, I willna thrash her arse for her. I swear it."

Her gurgling scream shattered the peacefulness of the clearing as she broke through the wall of cascading water, arms and legs thrashing. Several large slabs of stone fell alongside her, tumbling downward at a faster speed. He lurched backward, dodged the falling rocks, then dove forward as the churning surface swallowed her.

Even though the calm part of the pool was clear enough to see everything in it, the swirling froth at the base of the falls blocked everything from view. But fate granted him a boon. He caught sight of her shadowy form, grabbed hold, and kicked them both back up to the surface.

Limp in his arms, her head rolled against his shoulder as he swam back to the shallows. He scooped her up and held her. "Fool woman. What the hell were ye thinking?" He had promised God he wouldn't thrash her arse, but he'd not said he wouldn't scold her 'til kingdom come.

Head pounding with the same beating of his heart, he lowered her onto the sleeping pallet and hovered over her. "Dinna ye dare die on me, Evie. I'll be sorely cross if ye rob me of the pleasure of ranting at ye for giving me such a scare." He blinked hard to clear away an onrush of nauseating dizziness. "And ye made my head hurt worse, ye foolish lass!"

Determined to ignore the sickly feeling, he gently squeezed her arms and legs, checking for breaks. She appeared whole. No blood anywhere either. Her neck and back looked straight enough. She had hit the water at a twisting turn, entering right shoulder first. That side of her face was deeper red than his sister Fern's best roses. It looked to be swelling, too. He rolled her to her side, remembering how he had awakened on his side after she pulled him from the water.

"I wish I knew what else ye did to save me," he whispered, resting his aching head on her shoulder. She must live. He would consider nothing else.

He stretched over her and pressed an ear to her chest, praying for the sound of life. A faint thumping echoed, but he couldn't hear any wind moving inside her. With her face framed between his hands, he held her nose to nose. "Evie!" He was determined to yank her back among the living by the sheer force of his will alone. "Evie Wortham, ye bloody Sassenach! Dinna ye dare die on me! I forbid it!" This blessed woman had saved him. He'd be damned if she'd deny him the satisfaction of returning the favor.

She shook with sudden coughing and choking, spitting in his face. But he didn't care. At least she breathed, wheezing and sputtering, but she breathed.

He gathered her up and hugged her, smoothing away the hair plastered to her face as he rocked her. "That's it, lass. Pull that air in and spit out the pool. Hard as ye hit, ye probably gulped in half of it."

"The ledge," she rasped out with a weak thump of her fist against his chest. "The ledge gave way."

"Aye, those were the rocks that fell with ye. Ye're lucky they hit first."

"I can't get back now." She hit him again. "I can never get back." Face turning into his chest, her muffled moaning grew louder. She jerked with hiccupping sobs.

"Get back?" He rubbed and patted her back, at a loss as to how to console her. "Course we can get ye to the other side. All we must do is take the long way around the water. We'll do it once ye've rested, aye?"

"You don't understand," she argued, her tone so bleak and pitiful his heart swelled. Her hiccupping gulps faded, but she still snuffled and eked out despondent cries. Occasionally, she shuddered in a deep breath and beat on him again as she whimpered, "I can never get back now."

So he held her. Not knowing what else to do, since the poor thing seemed too distraught to explain it. She had saved him without question, and he felt sure she would hold him, too, if he needed it.

"It will be all right, lass," he said softly, then without thinking, kissed the top of her head. "I dinna ken what's happened here, but I swear to make it right for ye. 'Twill all be fine, m'wee hen. I promise."

If not for his worries about her, he would laugh out loud at himself for calling her his *wee hen*. His father had called his mother *wee hen* until the day she died. A loving pet name that always made Mam smile and give Da a kiss—even if the bairns were looking.

After what felt like a long while, she stirred in his arms and frowned up at him, her eyes red-rimmed from her tears. "You got your stitches wet."

Her quiet scolding dragged him from his pleasant daze. A warm woman in his arms. Gentle breeze cooling the ache in his head. Softly twittering birds harmonizing with the continuous splashing of the water. All had lulled him into a feeling of contentment he hadn't known in a long time. He smiled down at her, his gaze settling on her mouth and staying there, making him wonder how sweet her kisses might be. "What say ye, lass?"

"You got your stitches wet," she repeated, her voice still weak and quivering. "I told you I didn't want them wet. Remember?"

"Forgive me," he said. "I was a mite distracted and never gave them a thought when I dove in to snatch ye up before the kelpies took ye to the bottom and kept ye there."

She pushed herself out of his arms and wiped her face with her shirttail. "I'll need to change the dressing." Still sniffling, she went to her bag and rummaged through it. "Soggy bandages, especially those filled with bacteria riddled pond water, cause infection."

"It can wait, lass." He brushed away the wetness they'd dripped on the sleeping pallet, amazed how it beaded up on the tight weave of the strange slick cloth. "Come and rest beside me. Ye nearly drowned, and ye're soaked clean through."

"Your bandages cannot wait." She spoke as if trapped in a mild panic. As if she didn't change the wrappings on his head, she risked crumbling to pieces. Hands filled with all manner of oddities, some he recognized, some he didn't, she knelt beside him and arranged the things on a dry part of the pallet.

He caught hold of her wrist and forced her to look at him. "Ye need rest and drying out. It can wait. Sit here while I build a fire, aye?"

"No!" she said so loudly it echoed across the clearing. Ramrod straight, she yanked free of his hold. "I need to change your bandages."

The quiver in her voice told him she needed the task—badly. Somehow, tending his wound gave her a hold on survival. He had seen such a thing before in those mourning the loss of a loved one. Tasks busied the mind and kept inner demons at bay. "I understand. Do what ye must."

Her hands shook as she cut away the bandages with the strangest looking tool. Two blades hinged together and fashioned with loops for her fingers and thumb. As soon as she set it down, he snatched it up and examined it closer. When closed, the cutting tip of the thing bent at an angle, and the bottom blade was blunt and flattened on the end like a duck's bill.

"Bandage scissors," she said while peeling away the wet wrap and padding from his head.

"Bandage scissors," he repeated, placing his finger and thumb in the loops as he'd seen her do, then opened and closed them. "I've seen sewing shears, but none are bent like these."

"Protects the patient. Keeps them from getting gouged." She dabbed a cloth against the back of his head. It snagged in something and pulled, stinging like a fiend.

He dodged sideways. "Easy there, lass. Are ye ripping it back open?"

"Sorry. Caught the gauze in a stitch." But she didn't sound sorry. Her voice was dull and cold. Dead. She sounded as though her heart and soul had already departed. "I think we should leave the dressing off for a bit. Let it dry out and air."

Well enough. He didn't much care for anything wrapped around his head, anyway. "Sounds fine. Now sit yerself down, and I'll build a fire so our clothes can dry."

"No." She jumped back as if the suggestion burned her. "I'll do it. You stay here and rest. I'll get wood and get a fire going."

"Ye can fix some of yer tea to warm yerself, aye?" He hoped the prospect of a cup of that stuff she liked so well might help calm her.

It didn't.

Instead, the shaking in her hands spread. Her entire body trembled until she dropped to the ground and hugged her knees. "Tea," she repeated, rocking in place while staring downward. "No more tea once mine is gone."

"Of course, there will be tea." He pried her hands loose from her panicked hugging of her knees and held them. Their iciness concerned him. 'Twas a balmy day. Even with her drenching, she shouldn't be so cold. "I shall tell Mrs. Dingwall to add the stuff to the larder. We will never be without yer tea."

"But I don't think you can." A forlorn hopelessness filled her voice. Her tears welled and spilled over again. "Black tea hasn't made it to Scotland yet. Probably have to send someone to bloody China, and I'm not even sure the kind I like even exists there yet."

That made no sense. She had the tea. Where had she gotten it? "Ye visited China to get yer tea?"

She jerked as though startled, staring at him as if he'd threatened to strike her. "No."

"However ye got yer tea, then Mrs. Dingwall can do the same."

"A friend sent it to me." She stared down at her hands. "A friend who no longer exists."

"I am verra sorry, lass." He wanted to hold her, console her again, but she seemed so fragile. "I've heard China can be a dangerous place." He hadn't. In fact, he knew nothing of the country. But it seemed like the proper thing to say.

With a trembling dip of her chin, she agreed with a faint nod.

"We will find ye something else to brew." He was determined to make her feel better. "Ye soak dried leaves in boiling water, aye?" After another of her hesitant nods, he continued, "There must be something in Cook's garden ye can boil. My sister will help ye. Ye will relish whatever she finds. I promise."

She stumbled to her feet and backed away. "I'm going for a walk."

Everything in him shouted not to let her leave alone. Even though the queasiness still churned within him, he forced himself to his feet. "I shall walk with ye."

She gave him a loathsome glare. 'Twas a wonder he didn't burst into flames. Still shaking like a tree in a windstorm, she bared her teeth and spoke with them clenched tight. "Let me alone, Quinn. You have no bloody idea what I need right now. Just leave me alone. Please."

"I willna leave ye alone, Evie. Not now. Not ever." He had already decided Mistress Evie Wortham was under his protection. He'd toyed with the idea before. Might as well make it clear to her now. "From this day onward, ye are under the protection of Clan MacTaggart— and more importantly, *my* protection."

She held up a hand as though to stop his words, spun away, and stormed back up the hillside to the source of the falls. Back to the same spot where she had stepped out onto that ledge and scared the living shite out of him.

He trudged up after her. She might be stubborn as the devil, but he so was he, and she'd do well to learn that about him straight off. When he reached her side, she didn't acknowledge his presence. Just stared at the water cascading over the edge of the cliff. Even he noticed a difference in the arc of the falling deluge. With the breaking away of the ledge, the stream tumbled flush against the remaining stones, swift and wicked as any fast-flowing river.

"It really is gone. There is no space left at all." Her shoulders sagged, and she stumbled back a step.

He caught her up against him. "What is gone, lass?"

"The space. The ledge." She made a weak motion toward the water. "The way I got here."

"Ye came through behind the falls?" Few had the courage to attempt such. Too many myths and lore about cruel trickery from water spirits.

She nodded, then shifted with a deep inhale. "For the first time in my life, I have no idea what to do."

He held her for a moment longer, then turned them away from the water. Ever so gently, he walked her back down the hillside to the pallet. "For now, ye shall sit and rest whilst I build a fire. Then ye shall dry out. We both will."

"And then?" She didn't look at him. Just stared at the burnt earth and ashes from last night's fire.

"We shall see to *then* when then gets here, aye? Battle one moment at a time, lass. One moment at a time."

She didn't answer. Just went silent again and stared off into space. He liked it better when she argued with him. Nagged him. Told him things he didn't understand. At least then, the fire flashed in her eyes. A fire sorely missing from her now.

He kept her in sight as he gathered wood, not trusting her alone. It occurred to him she mourned for something. But what? He had no idea. All he knew was she had somehow suffered a significant loss that sent her reeling. Mourning folk sometimes harmed themselves. He prayed she didn't have that in mind.

"Evie?"

She didn't move.

"Evie, lass?" He crouched down in front of her, blocking her view of anything else.

Her hazel eyes, greener than gold this time, finally focused on him. "Yes?"

"I've laid the wood. If ye'll show me how to work yer wee tinder-box, I'll get the fire going, aye?" He had to get her engaged in some sort of activity, connected with something other than the pain inside her. Teaching him how to light a fire as if he hadn't done it thousands of times before seemed like a good place to start. "Ye need drying out, lass. We're both soaked to the bone."

She cast a disinterested look at the wood he'd prepared, then went to her bag and rummaged through the pockets until she found the small shiny box of metal.

"Here." She held it out.

Instead of accepting it, he took hold of her hand and gently pulled her closer. "Show me," he said, tugging her down to kneel with him beside the wood.

She shot him an irritated glare, but at least she reacted. A hopeful start to her journey back to herself. With the metal box held out to him, she opened its lid and revealed a small wheel inside that nudged against a smaller bit of metal with blackened holes. "You put your thumb here and spin the wheel with a downward rub. That strikes the flint and makes the flame." She demonstrated, then slapped the lid shut to douse the flame and flipped it open again. "You try."

"The lid snuffs out the flame?"

"Yes." She sounded weary enough to drop. He needed to get the fire going and get some of her tea into her.

He studied the thing. Smelled it. Its stench reminded him of pitch. When he rubbed his thumb on the wheel, nothing happened.

"Rub it hard and fast," she said, showing him a second time.

"Hard and fast," he repeated, closing the lid to douse her flame and give it a try. He did as instructed. The thing made the same crunching sort of sound as it had with her, and the elusive fire returned. "I did it!"

A hint of a smile teased across her mouth, then disappeared as quick as a wisp of smoke. That pleased him more than learning an easier way to make fire.

"Well done, you," she said quietly with an approving nod. "You are now a fully trained fire starter." A wistfulness filled her eyes. "At least while the flints and fluid hold out." She stood and meandered over to the pool. With a despondent huff, she lowered herself to sit cross-legged at the water's edge.

Quinn had never been one to tiptoe around a problem. Hence the reason he went through so many advisors, and few survived his trusted inner circle. Time to unravel the mystery of Evie's sorrow. He joined her, picked up a stick, and started drawing in the mud. "Why did ye try to pass behind the falls, Evie? Were ye trying to end yer life?"

"You wouldn't understand." She squinted at the sunlight bouncing off the ripples. The dappling of lights danced across her face like glowing spirits trying to soothe her. "I still haven't wrapped my head around it."

"I canna help ye if I dinna understand what ye need help with," he said, keeping his tone low and gentle. "Ye can trust me, Evie. Tell me so I can help."

She snorted out a bitter laugh. "I appreciate the offer, Quinn. But this is a proper cock-up. I don't think there's anything anyone can do."

"Cock-up?" he repeated slowly. "What does that mean?"

"A massive failure that no one can fix." She picked up a stick of her own and wrote in the mud *Here ended Evaline Indiana Wortham's life. May it ever Rest in Peace.* She smeared the words away with her hand, but not before he read it. It confirmed what he feared.

"I willna allow ye to take yer life." He took hold of her chin and forced her to look him in the eyes. "Do ye understand me? I dinna ken what's causing yer pain, but I mean to find out and help ye."

"You are a kind man." Her half-hearted smile eased him very little. "Don't worry. I haven't given up completely." When he released her chin, her gaze dropped. "At least not yet."

"What is yer pain, Evie? Tell me." He felt for this distraught woman who had done so much for him. Perhaps he could help her if she would but allow it. "Evie—please. Share yer pain. Tell me what ye mourn?"

"A lifetime lost," she said softly, as though talking to herself. "Not a perfect lifetime. But one I worked hard for and enjoyed most of the time."

"Yer banishment?" She had mentioned it before but hadn't seemed as upset about it as she did now. Had she remembered something she would never see again? Someone she loved? "Is yer banishment what torments ye?"

She stared out across the water, half-smiling but still wrestling with a terrible sadness. "Yes. My banishment. I have lost…a lot." A tear streaked down her cheek, but she batted it away and blinked hard to stop any more from escaping.

He scooted closer and hugged an arm around her shoulders. "Ye have every right to mourn all ye have lost, lass. Weep if ye wish. There is no shame in it."

"Maybe not, but I'm afraid if I start crying again, I won't be able to stop. I'm not normally a weeper. Hate the way it makes me feel." She picked up a pebble and tossed it in the water. "The big ripples swallow the little ones."

"What?" He suddenly felt ill-equipped to do as he had promised, but one way or another, he would find a way to help her. "What say ye?

She nodded toward the pool. "The heavy ripples created by the falling water swallow up my poor attempt at making a place in the pond with a rock." A heavy sigh escaped her as she tipped her head to one side. "I'm afraid any effort to restart my life here will fail just as easily." She huffed out another bitter laugh. "And no one I ever knew, not a single soul who might have ever given a damn about me, will even be here to notice."

He gently turned her to face him. "I give a damn, Evie, and ye will have a life here. I swear it." Then he kissed her. Perhaps he shouldn't have, but what better way to seal an oath? She tasted as sweet as he had known she would. Even better. He gladly accepted the challenge.

At first, she hesitated, then her lips parted, joining with him completely. She clung to him with a wonderful fierceness, then pushed away and stared up into his face as if making up her mind. "I need to sort out a lot of things without adding more complications." She rolled out of his hold, stood, and stepped back, massaging the back of her neck as her gaze settled anywhere but on him. "There should be a few hot coals by now. I think I'll get that tea going."

"Praise the Lord Almighty! Yer alive!" a familiar voice boomed from the high embankment on the far side of the waters.

Quinn jumped to his feet and threw up a hand. "Dugan!" Cousin and trusted friend, the sight of Dugan MacTaggart with his horse tied behind his, filled him with renewed energy. "And glad I am that ye found my horse."

"Yer beastie returned to the keep without ye," Dugan said as he led the mounts down to the pool. "All of us feared ye dead or captured by the English." The man rumbled out a deep laugh loud as thunder. "And here I find ye dallying in a secluded glen." He clapped a hand on Quinn's shoulder and shook him hard. "Why am I nay surprised?"

A sudden loss of balance made Quinn stumble sideways a few steps. He widened his stance to keep from landing on his arse.

"Do not jostle him!" Evie charged forward and pushed between them. "He has a severe concussion and hasn't been resting as he should. Through no fault of his own, I admit, but he's still quite overextended himself today." With a guilty look, she twitched a shoulder. "However, that is now over."

She gave him a sharp glance that almost made him laugh, then she turned to Dugan. "Now, I'll thank you to lower your volume and exuberance." With a firm tug on Quinn's arm, she pulled him away. "Come. Sit on the pallet and rest. Your friend can visit with you there." With another stern glare back over her shoulder, she added in a louder voice, "If he can talk quietly and control the urge to shake you."

"Well, well." With a rumbling chuckle, Dugan hooked his thumbs in his belt and puffed out his chest. "That's me put in my place, I reckon."

"This is Lady Evaline Wortham," Quinn said, turning Evie to face Dugan. "Without her, ye wouldha either found me floating face down in that pond or not at all. At least not until the weather changed and my bloated carcass floated back to the top."

Dugan gave a formal bow. "It is an honor to meet the savior of my chieftain. Dugan MacTaggart. at yer service, m'lady."

She granted him a tip of her head but still bore a pained expression. "Pleasure." With another tug on Quinn's arm, she edged toward the pallet and fire. "Please come and sit. I am quite serious when I said you've done entirely too much today."

He motioned for Dugan to follow. "Come, cousin. Let us rest and visit a while before we start back to the keep. Ye can tell me which of my fine clansman mourned my loss and which prepared to celebrate." He learned long ago that no matter what he said or did, never would every single one of his people love him. 'Twas impossible to please everyone.

Dugan flashed a toothy grin. "Let me settle the horses, and then we shall speak of those who love to hate ye."

CHAPTER FIVE

E VIE COULDN'T DECIDE if she liked Dugan or not. The man laughed and talked with such an abrasive loudness, she wondered if he suffered from poor hearing. With his barrel chest and even rounder middle, she sympathized with his horse, too. A smidge shorter than Quinn's towering six foot seven, when Dugan walked or strutted with his boisterous, arm-swinging gait, the earth shook. Or seemed to anyway. But Quinn acted as if he trusted the man, so she supposed she should give the bellowing mountain the benefit of the doubt.

She also wasn't all that keen on Quinn dubbing her with the title of a *lady*. How in the world could she manage a title in the thirteenth century when she didn't even know how to behave like a commoner?

"Would you like a power bar, Mr. MacTaggart?" Even though she only had a few left, she couldn't very well leave him out.

He took it from her with a quizzical drawing in of his bushy black brows. When the packet crackled, he frowned and rubbed his thumb across the shiny wrapper. "I…uhm…thank ye, m'lady."

"It's nay poison, man," Quinn teased. "Try it. With yer love of all things sweet, I promise ye will like it."

The man shrugged and went to shove it into his mouth, paper and all.

"No!" She barely snatched it away before he bit down. "We have to unwrap it first. I don't think you'd be too keen on chewing through that paper." She stripped away the foil and handed the bar back to him. "Now try."

The longer he chewed, the faster his head bobbed up and down. "Ye're right, cousin. Verra tasty indeed." With a jolly wink, he patted his enormous belly with both hands. "But it'll take more than that wee drop to fill this oversized bucket." He rolled to his feet. "I'll fetch us some hares for supper. Or mayhap a ptarmigan or whatever else comes within range." He laughed big and loud, making nearby birds take flight. "I'll bring back all I can gather so's we can enjoy a proper meal to celebrate today's tidings." After a polite bow in Evie's direction, he headed for his horse. "Fetching our meal will take no time at all with my bow," he bellowed back over his shoulder. "Tell her what a wonder I am, cousin. Impress her with me, aye?"

Quinn rolled his eyes before giving her a grudging nod. "He is fair enough." He stretched out on the pallet, then flinched as he folded his hands behind his head. "Feckin' scratch. I hit it every time." He rolled to his side and patted the place beside him. "Ye need rest too, lass. If ye dinna think I can balance well enough to ride today, the least ye can do is make me feel better by taking yer ease, too. After all, ye nearly drowned." His smile took on a mischievous slant. "Ye can keep me warm, ye ken?"

"It is July, and we have a fire." She folded the thermal blanket, doubling it to make a softer seat an arm's length away. Hugging her knees, she propped her chin atop them and stared into the crackling flames. "I hope he doesn't want me to cook whatever he kills. I order take out whenever I'm not on shift and find myself at home." She cringed as soon as the words left her mouth. If she expected to survive in this century, she must stop saying things that related to the future. "Take out is a fish," she lied to cover her error. "You eat it raw."

Quinn wrinkled his nose. "I reckon if ye're hungry enough, ye will eat anything."

"Too true," she quickly agreed, relieved he'd accepted the tale. She didn't lie well. Never had and sorely missed that skill set now. And while she wasn't an expert on the thirteenth century, she felt sure men of this time preferred their women powerless and unopinionated. Heaven help her mouth. It certainly kept her in hot water enough in the twenty-first century. "So, will he expect me to cook his catch?"

"Are ye saying ye *canna* cook? Or *willna* cook?"

She gave him a sharp glance but relaxed when his concerned demeanor assured her the question held no malice. "I'm saying if I cook, that piece of burnt wood will be tastier than whatever I prepare." She shrugged. "I am a damn fine surgeon, but as far as cooking or keeping house, it's low marks all around."

"Low marks?"

"Enormous fails. Epic proportions, in fact." She always took meticulous care of her patients. Drove her peers to distraction with her attention to the smallest medical detail. But in her personal life? She excelled in untidiness and ordering takeout.

She rose, too anxious to sit any longer. Perhaps a wash would clear her head enough to sort out a plan of surviving this mucked-up mess. "I'm feeling a bit gamey." She gathered up her only change of clothes and small bag of toiletries she'd possessed the foresight to bring along. "I'm going downstream for a wash." With the stern look she always used on those she wished to intimidate, she aimed the toiletry bag at Quinn. "Do I have your word that you and Mr. MacTaggart will stay here in the clearing and respect my privacy?"

He rested a hand over his heart. "Ye have my word, lass, but dinna go far. A woman alone is never safe." His relaxed manner disappeared, and he gave her a stern look of his own. "Promise ye willna go far nor tarry verra long, aye?"

A sound and reasonable request since they still did not know who attacked him. "I promise."

He nodded, then resettled himself on the pallet and closed his eyes. "Ye may go then."

"I may go then?" She kicked his boot with enough force to make him grunt and open his eyes. "I wasn't asking your permission. I merely extended you the courtesy of sharing what I intended to do." Thirteenth-century or not, she would not be treated like a child or a possession.

With a disgruntled frown, he pushed himself to a sitting position. "I've granted ye my protection, lass. I'll thank ye to treat that gesture with the gratitude and respect it deserves."

Even though she knew Quinn's manners and attitude hadn't evolved to twenty-first-century standards, she couldn't keep quiet on this. She just couldn't. "While I am grateful to have you as an ally, that does not mean you are my keeper, nor by any means does it grant you the right to order me around as if I'm your pet."

His eyes narrowed as he studied her. "I'm beginning to understand why ye were banished." Head tipping to one side, his intense scrutiny made her back up a step. "Of course, most healers are hard-headed and outspoken." He jabbed a finger at her. "But ye would do well to remember I am the chieftain, and my orders are to be obeyed, ye ken?"

The back of her neck always tingled whenever she said more than she should. It currently stung like fire. If she intended to survive, instinct told her to get control of her tongue and edit her thoughts before they came out of her mouth. "Forgive me. I am well aware you are chieftain."

His expression immediately softened. "I just want ye safe, lass. That is all. I would never treat ye with disrespect."

"And for that, I am grateful. By the way, you might dry yourself better while I'm gone. I'm sure your boots are still a bit damp." She hugged her change of clothes and hurried downstream, silently cursing Maggie and Finchcrest's admins for discovering a way to rid themselves of her permanently.

Distracted by whirling thoughts and storming emotions, she found herself back at the second set of falls before she realized it. She hadn't planned to go that far, but at least the stream looked deeper here, deep enough to wade in and submerge for a thorough scrubbing. With any luck, the cold water would shock her back to the future.

Perched on the mossy bank, she unlaced her wet boots and yanked them off. It would take forever to dry the things out, even if she propped them open and left them close to the fire. Socks, then jeans came next, all of them still quite damp as well. Right before pulling her t-shirt off over her head, a stick snapped behind her.

"Who's there?" She picked up a boot and prepared to throw it. It was the closest thing to a weapon within reach.

"Dinna fash yerself, yer ladyship." Dugan exploded out of the bushes with a broad smile. His eyes shot open wide, then he whirled around and gave her his back. "Beg pardon, m'lady. I didna see anything. I mean, I didna realize…beg pardon. I beg yer forgiveness for the intrusion. I swear I wasna spying on ye. I'm nay the sort of ill-bred cur who would dare do such a thing. 'Specially not to the fine lady who saved Himself."

She crouched behind a boulder and peered over it. "Well then, I suggest you carry on with your hunting in another area since I'll be here for a while longer." However, she wasn't all that sure about removing the rest of her clothes.

"Aye, m'lady." He held up a pair of birds. "I've already got us these so far."

"Well done, you." She wished he would leave and be done with it.

"Ye're certain the MacTaggart isna well enough to ride?" he continued, seemingly at ease with carrying on a conversation with his back to her.

"I am quite certain." She smacked at a stinging fly high on her flank. "Can we discuss this back at camp? These flies are eating me alive."

"Absolutely, m'lady. Forgive me." He dipped with a shallow squat, apparently meaning that as a respectful backward bow. "I shall get these to roasting, then head out for whatever else I can find."

"Good man," she encouraged, relieved when he charged off at a fast clip. She batted at the cloud of midges gathering. Apparently, the bugs had heard that a fresh buffet of naked Englishwoman stood beside the stream. The burning bites took priority over any worries about being watched. She stripped off the rest of her clothes, waded in neck-deep, then submerged and stayed there as long as her breath would hold. Every time she rose, she emerged enough to breathe and peer around like a pale, furless otter. When it seemed the midges finally gave up, she retrieved her soap and scrubbed, lamenting that soon, her favorite soap and shampoo would be a fond memory of the future, too.

"And deodorant," she muttered, emerging from the stream and slaking off the water with a push of her hands. Apparently, the midges either hadn't cared for the scent of her soap or had been too hungry to wait for her to step out of the water. Either way, they left her in peace as she rationed out the least amount of deodorant and lotion that would still be effective. She wondered if there would be someone in Quinn's clan who might teach her about local herbs. Soaps, lotions, and deodorant might be concocted from whatever Scotland provided.

Dry clothes felt better. She had forgotten her comb, so she raked her fingers through her tangled tresses until the wavy mess fell into some semblance of order. Wet boots and clothes in hand, she headed back to camp, barefoot and somewhat readier to battle whatever else life threw in her face. Always a fighter, she never backed down. Somewhat of a loner. Definitely a survivor. "Lookout thirteenth century. Ready or not. Here I come."

"IF SHE'S NAY one of Maggie's new girls—"

Quinn leapt up from the pallet and grabbed hold of Dugan by the front of his léine. "Lady Evaline is nay a whore, and if ye ever hint at such again, I'll gut ye quicker than ye dressed those birds, ye ken?"

Dugan lifted both hands high. "I meant no disrespect. It's just that—"

"It's just that nothing," Quinn cut him off again. "That woman saved my life. Ye will treat her with every respect."

"Aye, Quinn." Dugan smiled and waggled a brow. "If ye had let me finish, ye wouldha heard I dinna speak with disrespect. May I finish speaking, my hot-headed chieftain?"

Only Dugan got away with such name-calling. He had saved Quinn's life. Many times. "Ye may finish." Quinn released the bear of a man with a shove. "But tread carefully, cousin."

"Earlier, we spoke of who might have attacked ye." Dugan adjusted the birds on the spit and hung them across the fire. "And came up with a long list of possibilities, I might add."

"Aye. True enough." Quinn knew he had enemies within the clan, as well as outsiders who might wish him dead.

After wiping his hands on the seat of his pants, Dugan gave him a rare scowl. "But we didna speak of yer Lady Evaline." He shrugged. "Mainly 'cause she was right here, but still. Her presence begs a verra important question. What's an Englishwoman doing this far north of Hadrian's Wall? A lady alone? Or at least, appearing to be alone? Especially after that coward Balliol surrendered to Edward." He spit on the ground. "English bastard. He's a feckin' thief. I'll never bow to that bastard. Never!"

Dugan had a habit of losing himself in rants. Especially valid ones dealing with England. The only way to get him back to the crux of the matter was act as if he never veered off.

"She spoke of being banished," Quinn said. He glanced around to be certain Evie hadn't returned, found his flask, and treated himself to a hearty swig. She had refused to give him whisky yesterday. Said they did not recommend it for his sort of wound. Silly woman. Whisky helped with countless pains. He offered the tidy leather flask to Dugan. "I dinna ken if they brought her here and left her, or if she found the place on her own. All she said was she angered a person of power and couldna return home."

After a long draw on the flask, Dugan handed it back, his smile brighter than usual. "Even better! Can I have her then?"

"What the hell do ye mean *can I have her then?*" Before Dugan could answer, Quinn landed a solid blow on the man's jaw, knocking him back several steps. "Are ye deaf, man? I willna have her disrespected. She's nay some camp harlot to be passed about from man to man."

"Dammit, man." One eye squinted shut, Dugan worked his jaw. "I meant as a wife. Ye said she had no one, and my wee Mairi needs a mother. Ye said that verra thing a fortnight ago when my darling beastie got caught climbing trees in the orchard with the lads."

"It wasna her climbing the trees that was the problem." Quinn rubbed the side of his head at the memory. "Yer vicious minx inherited yer aim. Made my eyes cross when she pegged me with that green apple."

"She said sorry."

"Aye, and the both of us know she didna mean it."

Dugan chuckled. "Probably not." He poked Quinn in the chest. "That's why I could marry Lady Evaline. Give her a home, and she could teach my Mairi womanly manners." Bushy black brows waggling in time with his double chin, he poked Quinn again. "See? No disrespect at all."

None except that the idea of Evie becoming Dugan's wife set him afire with a sudden jealous fury. "Nay," was all he would trust himself to say, still wrestling with the possessiveness churning within.

"What do ye mean *nay?*" Dugan skewered a rabbit on another spit and placed it alongside the roasting birds. "If they sent her here alone, she canna be married to anyone else, can she?"

"I dinna ken if she's married or not." Quinn's attention drifted to her pack. A sudden urge to look through it made him glance to see if she was anywhere near. He had been so concerned about not upsetting her, he hadn't pried and asked too many questions. Perhaps he should have. "I suppose she could be married even though she's alone. What if the English imprisoned her husband?"

"Or hanged him," Dugan offered with a solemn nod.

"Then she would be a widow."

"Even better." Dugan slapped his shoulder. "Betwixt me and yerself, virgins are more trouble than what they're worth." His face puckered as if he'd just eaten something sour. "And I dinna think an inexperienced lass would survive Mairi."

While Quinn agreed, he'd be damned if he handed Evie over to the likes of Dugan MacTaggart and his wee demon spawn. "I willna allow ye to marry her."

His cousin darkened with a rare scowl. "And why not?"

"She is under my protection."

"That is nay an answer," Dugan argued, his fierceness hardening. "Ye refuse to give yer own cousin yer blessing? That wounds me clear to the bone, Quinn. What have I done to deserve such callous treatment?"

"I intend to marry her." The words came out without a moment's hesitation. Dugan wanted what he had decided was most certainly his, and he wouldn't allow it. "What better way to ensure she is safe even if something happens to me?"

"Well, that is disappointing." Dugan frowned. "I ken well enough that the clan's nagging ye to take another wife and sire an heir, but God help me, I dinna ken what the blazes to do with Mairi." With a slow shake of his head, he snorted out a heavy sigh. "I promised Leah I would never send her away."

"Send her away?" Quinn recoiled at the idea of anyone sending away their child.

"To a convent or some such place to train her up as a proper female."

"Ah, I see." He handed the flask back to Dugan. "Perhaps, Lady Evaline might still help with Mairi. Just not as yer wife."

"Aww...now that would be grand, cousin. Do ye think she might agree to it?"

"I dinna ken for certain if she will even agree to marry in order to keep herself safe," Quinn said, pondering how he would share this opportunity with the stubborn woman whose kiss had inflamed him.

"Well, here she comes. Reckon ye might ask her?" Dugan leaned closer. "And ye're nay going to let her keep wearing those clothes, are ye? They're nay entirely proper, ye ken?"

"These are all the clothes I possess, gentlemen." Evie came to a halt at the edge of the clearing, looking ready to kill them both. "Mr. MacTaggart, your voice is louder than Big Ben."

"Is that yer husband?" Dugan asked, much to Quinn's relief because he wondered the same.

Evie pressed her lips together, flattening them tight as though she wished them permanently sealed. After an uncomfortable moment of silence, she gave a light cough, then gave a modest nod. "Yes. He was my husband. I am widowed."

Dugan elbowed Quinn and whispered, "Lucky bastard."

"Shut yer maw," Quinn warned through clenched teeth.

After draping her things to dry, she propped her boots beside the fire. Her nose wrinkled when she spotted the carcasses sizzling over the flames. Slowly, she pulled her focus away from the meat and leveled it on them. "Who is this Mairi person, and why does she need me as her keeper?"

"My dear sweet daughter," Dugan said, tucking his thumbs into his belt. "Loving child. All I've got since my precious Leah left us nigh on three years ago."

"I assume Leah is—or was, your wife?"

"Aye." With a deep sigh, he bobbed his head.

"And she left you and your daughter?" She eyed the man as though trying to decide whether or not he lied.

"Fever took her. Mairi and me got down with it, too but survived." He twitched a shoulder and dropped his gaze. "My Leah always was a bit on the frail side. She nearly died bringing our Mairi into the world."

Quinn stepped forward. "Dugan thought ye might help with Mairi. Soften the wee lass's rough edges." He chose his words with care, knowing if he portrayed the child as an innocent cherub, he would pay for it later. "She's naught but eight years old."

Evie shifted with a flinching shrug. "Actually, I don't have that much experience with children. I've opera…uhm…healed several but have never dealt with them on a daily basis." As she edged around the fire, she kept glancing back at the roasting meat as if afraid it might come after her. "I'm afraid I've never known many children other than if they're sick or hurt. I have no siblings, and my parents traveled quite a bit, so they hired an older lady to watch over me until I was old enough for boarding school."

"Boarding school?" Dugan repeated, then gave Quinn a quizzical frown.

"Lady Evaline knows of many things that we do not." And he still hadn't decided if that was a good thing or bad. "But ye would meet the child? Maybe talk to her?"

"Aye," Dugan chimed in before Evie answered. "Convince my sweet lass that running and playing like a lad is no way for a lady to behave." After an ashamed shaking of his head, he rumbled out a huffing groan. "Climbs trees like a wee squirrel, tickles fish, and chases down sheep so she can ride them. My wee one needs a woman who'll teach her to act proper." His gaze slid to her clothing drying by the fire. "Course, ye willna wear those things around her, aye? Her skirts are about the only ladylike thing the wee minx does. If she sees ye in trews, she'll set up a howl to wear them herself."

"So, you're displeased that she's a tomboy?" Evie folded her arms and leveled a hard gaze at him.

"God help ye, man." Quinn clapped a hand on his cousin's shoulder as he stepped back. Dugan always let his mouth dig his grave. Quinn wasn't sure what a tomboy was but felt certain Evie was about to educate them both. That might be good. Or very unpleasant.

"I dinna ken what a *tomboy* is, m'lady." Dugan backed farther away than Quinn, seeming to realize he had overstepped his bounds.

"A *tomboy* is a girl fearless enough to stand firm and prove herself as bright as any boy." Evie advanced a step, looking ready to charge. "Brave. Courageous. Doesn't shrink from anything. Would you prefer your daughter be helpless?"

"I dinna ken what to say to her now," Dugan whispered, edging behind Quinn and peering around at Evie.

"Hell's fire, man, I do believe that's the first time I've ever heard ye whisper." Quinn turned back to Evie. "Congratulations, lass. Ye quieted the brute."

She smiled and seemed to relax. "I would be happy to be Mairi's friend, Mr. MacTaggart, but you might want to rethink that. I doubt I'm what you need or expect for your daughter." Her tone softened, and her gaze fell. "And I wouldn't wish to cause your little girl any problems by being associated with me."

Dugan's broad smile returned. "Dinna fash yerself about that, m'lady. Once ye become the chieftain's wife, none would dare tease her."

Her head shot up, and she marched a step closer. "What did you just say?" The woman's tone almost hit the sharpness of a shriek.

Quinn scrubbed his face with both hands, then pointed at the woods. "Go."

Dugan stared at him. "What?"

"Go. I dinna care where, just go." He hoped to quiet the approaching storm, but by the look on Evie's face…

"How long?" Dugan asked. "The meat'll need turnin' soon."

"I will turn the feckin' meat," Quinn growled. "Dinna come back 'til sunset, ye ken?"

Head bowed, Dugan edged away. "Aye, my chieftain." Then he slipped through the foliage without disturbing a single leaf, a rare feat for one so large.

Evie directed the full force of her scowl on him. "Would you care to explain why Mr. MacTaggart thinks I am going to become the chieftain's wife?"

"Call him Dugan instead of Mr. MacTaggart, aye? That just doesna sound right." Quinn shifted in place, stalling for time and praying for the wisdom to make Evie see sense. Not only did he need a wife, but the union would keep her safer. It helped them both. And dammit, he wanted her.

She swiped a hand across her mouth as though doing her best to control her words. Her flashing eyes and the high color to her cheeks sounded the charge to battle. He hoped he survived her fury. Because he saw it coming, sure as lightning from an approaching storm. She lifted her chin but didn't answer. Just glared at him.

"As my wife, ye would be safer. An Englishwoman living alone in the Highlands?" He gave her a dubious shake of his head. "Surely, ye understand that?"

No response. Just a tightening of her eyes as her scowl darkened more.

Might as well grab the beastie by the horns and hang on. "They would respect ye as Lady Evaline, ye ken? We could even say I sent for ye as a favor to Clan Ross and Philip after Balliol's failure. Ye've nay got any legitimate titles to yer name, have ye? That might help, too." The more he thought about it, the more the details fell into place.

Mouth open, she slowly shook her head. She lifted both hands, then let them drop. "Philip who? And why Clan Ross?"

"Philip IV of France. Their king."

"Why would the king of France care about who you married? Why would Clan Ross care?"

"Because William, the Earl of Ross, was captured at the Battle of Dunbar back in April. So, the clan shifted their backing to England to keep him alive in the Tower of London. And King Philip enjoys anything that gives that bastard Edward a case of the red arse and distracts him from his fiefs in southwestern France." While it was true Clan MacTaggart was smaller than some, his connection to Clan Ross through his mother was strong, and he was also an earl in his own right. Had she forgotten? "So, what say ye? Do ye agree?"

"I do not agree." She stared at him as if trees grew out of his nose. "I don't even know you, and trust me when I say you know absolutely nothing about me."

"I know you pulled me from that water before I drowned." He risked a step closer. "I know ye probably frightened off whoever clubbed me and left me for dead." Another step, this time close enough that her warm sweet scent wafted across him. He scooped up her hand before she could flee and dropped to one knee. "I know ye sewed my flesh and wrapped my head in yer strange bandages. Fed me. Dried me. Kept me warm. I know how ye watched over me and kept feeling for my heartbeat through the night. I know enough, Evie. Ye're a tender woman, a healer, a stubborn hellcat, and a terrible liar. What else need I know? Other than will ye accept my offer and become my wife?" He gave her hand a gentle squeeze, wishing he could scare away the fear in her eyes. "Let me protect ye, Evie. Let me save ye, as ye saved me."

"This is insanity."

"Nay, this is the Highlands of Scotland. A dangerous place, especially for a woman. But I would live in no other place because it feeds my heart and soul. What say ye, Evie? Will ye share this life with me?

Take the Highlands and me for yer own?" With a teasing tip of his head and his best smile, he tugged her closer. "I swear to protect ye and treat ye with the respect ye deserve." He added a shrug. "I'm nay such a bad man, and if ye marry me, ye willna have to spurn Dugan."

"Spurn Dugan?" The poor lass looked ready to faint. "What is that supposed to mean?"

"He thought to marry ye, so he would have a mother for his daughter."

She yanked free of him and backed up several steps. "You men act like getting a wife is no different from buying a horse! Or a wagon. Or whatever else you need to make life easier in this godforsaken place."

"I need a wife and an heir." Quinn didn't move toward her. Nay, she looked ready to run. "Ye need safety. A roof. Food." He glanced over at her pack. "I ken well enough that ye've survived this long into yer banishment, but how much longer do ye really think ye can live here in the wild with no help? And if ye happen upon a settlement, do ye truly believe any other Scots will risk helping a strange English-woman dressed like a man? How much longer will yer wee bars of power sustain ye, Evie? Can ye hunt? Fish? Build a shelter? I offer ye all of that and more." He lifted his chin, daring her to challenge him. "Is that such a terrible thing, lass?"

With a forlorn mix of fear and hopelessness draining the color from her cheeks, she stared at her pack. Hugging herself. Not even blinking.

Quinn smelled victory. She was so close to agreeing. "Answer me, Evie. I think ye will find I'm nay such a terrible man. Is the protection I offer ye so verra awful?"

"No," she finally said, so softly he almost missed it. "I suppose it's not awful at all when you consider everything."

"So, ye will be my wife?"

Head bowed, she rubbed her eyes. "I will consider it," she said with such weariness it filled him with guilt for pushing her. She looked up at him but didn't bother to smile. "This has been a trying day, you understand. Epic proportions, actually. I need time to adjust." After a hard swallow, she continued, "Just allow me to think about it. Please."

Quinn learned long ago to never leave a timeline for a decision open-ended. "Will ye give me yer answer before we reach the keep tomorrow?"

As she nodded, she closed her eyes and massaged her temples. "Yes. When I see your keep on the horizon, I will give you an answer."

"Fair enough." He risked easing closer and held out both hands. "Come, lass. Rest yerself while I turn the meat. If we let Dugan's supper burn, he'll go to greetin' like a spoiled bairn."

She allowed him to seat her on the pallet where she hugged her knees and stared into the fire. Just as she did right after she failed to cross behind the waterfall.

With one eye on her, he turned the spits until the blackened part of the meat was well away from the coals. He fanned the mouthwatering aroma toward her. "I know Dugan can be as annoying as a midge, but ye will never go hungry around him. Our supper smells fine, aye?"

"It smells bloody awful," she mumbled.

"Awful?" He couldn't believe she didn't relish the hearty smokiness and the rich smell of fat sizzling. "Ye dinna like hares or ptarmigans?"

With a pained expression, she twitched with a pitiful shrug. "I never have before, but I suppose there are a lot of things I better learn to like if I intend to survive here."

CHAPTER SIX

S HE HAD NEVER ridden a horse before, and the longer they rode, the more she wondered about the ability to walk afterward.

"Relax, Evie," Quinn said as he adjusted her seating by nudging her back against him for a third time.

"I never relax." And she didn't. Or never had before, and considering her current situation, doubted she ever would again.

"Yer set for a trying ride then." The slightest flexing of his muscular thighs made the horse trot faster. The uncomfortable bouncing got worse with the speedier gait, but she didn't blame the animal. Those hard thighs rubbing against her made everything faster. Her heart rate. Breathing. Thoughts. Everything.

Her unyielding sense of logic scolded her. The last thing she needed right now was that sort of distraction. Her starving libido needed to stay out of this. Determined to get her mind on something constructive, she studied her surroundings but came up empty. Clusters of trees, rough terrain, then open meadows green as emeralds. Gorgeous countryside, but not intriguing enough to pull her awareness from the strong protective embrace of Quinn's powerful arms and the warmth of his rock-hard chest against her back.

Riding horses. That's what she would think about. What did she know about riding horses? Very little. Somewhere, she didn't remember where, she had heard or read that riders and their horses learned each other's body signals. She'd never thought about it 'til now. Hadn't needed to. She either took the Tube, hailed a cab, or rented a car. "What are those reins for if you control him with your legs?"

"Lets him know when to turn or halt, but ole Fenn's a canny lad. I dinna use the reins verra much at all with him." He hugged her back against him again. "If ye wouldna keep edging up onto the rise of the saddle, ye wouldna be so uncomfortable." His low chuckling tickled up her spine. "Ye'd think ye were a wee bird trying to find a perch."

"I'll try to stop scooting up." It was his fault. His closeness disturbed her in a pleasant way she preferred to avoid. His heat, the play of his muscles rippling against her, all of it nagged her to go on and give in. Admit she had no other choice but to accept his offer of marriage and learn to live with it. Enjoy it. Adapt to the role...somehow.

Her head had cleared some since yesterday. Not much. But some. With some difficulty, she had removed her emotions from the equation and forced herself to think *forward* rather than bemoan the past. She could do nothing about what had already happened. All she could do was handle the reality of now. Adapt, improvise, and overcome. One of her American marine patients had shared that motto with her. She clung to it now, claiming it as her own mantra.

"What happens if I refuse your offer?" she blurted, wondering why she hadn't asked that yesterday.

"And why would ye do that, lass?" The horse slowed as if quietening its gait so it could eavesdrop.

"Because I don't know you. You don't know me. Wouldn't you prefer to marry someone you loved? I always thought to marry for love." Heaven help her. Could she not stop babbling and just speak like a sane individual?

She had always hoped to marry for love. If she married at all. Her schedule allowed little time to meet any prospects, much less invest in nurturing a romance. She almost huffed out a bitter laugh because her schedule had now cleared completely.

"We went over that yesterday. We know enough to start with each other. Many a successful union starts with even less." His legs shifted again, and the beast returned to its clip-clopping pace.

"You make marriage sound like a business proposition." She had heard of arranged marriages, but wasn't that for royals? And did those really go all that well? How many stories about infidelities filled the gossip columns? "Have you never hoped to fall in love and marry the woman your heart wants?"

An uncomfortable pause made her wonder if he had chosen to ignore her. He would soon learn she let nothing go. Especially not something this important. "Well?"

"I felt somewhat of an interest in my first wife," he said, sounding as though he balked at digging up the memory. "At least in the beginning." The warmth of his heavy exhale tickled across the hairs on the back of her neck. "But it went verra bad. She avoided me as much as possible the short time we were married. Said she loved another and had only married me to obey her father. In fact, I feel sure the babe she bore belonged to her lover."

"How awful." All of it. Not just the way the woman had treated Quinn, but that her father had forced her into an arranged marriage when she loved another.

"It was not a pleasant time at the keep," he admitted, his knuckles whitening with a tighter grip on the slack reins.

"I'm sorry." But her question remained. What would happen if she declined his offer? "You never said what would happen if I decided not to marry you."

He tensed against her. The corded muscles of his arms flexed and hardened. "I suppose ye might become our clan healer, but I canna say if that would keep ye as safe as bearing my name."

"Why?"

"Yer English. Yer strange ways and unseemly clothes. I'm still none too sure ye're not one of the Fae." He drew in another deep breath and resettled his powerful arms as if trying to relax. "Or a witch."

"You know very well I am not a witch." She frowned, trying to hone her argument. "Or one of the Fae," she lamely added when she remembered he had accused her of that first.

But she couldn't deny he still jumped when she used her penlight to check his eyes and had also warned her to never use it around anyone else. From what she remembered about her history lessons, this century, especially in the Highlands, was filled with a superstitious lot. Truth be told, twenty-first century Scots hadn't evolved all that much. Most were still as superstitious as their ancestors.

"But ye are most definitely English, and ye do wear unseemly clothes. At least, for now."

"Do you and your people truly hate the English all that much?"

"We hate anyone who tries to rob us of our identity and beliefs." He paused, then added, "Would ye not feel the same?"

"I suppose I would." She hadn't thought that much about Scotland's wish to be independent. It could still be a volatile topic in the twenty-first century. The issue obviously raged hot and strong right now. Especially since Scotland's first war for independence was no longer a mere page in a history book but a very active reality in her present timeline. "I would hope they'd give me a chance. You know—get to know me?"

His arms shifted with a shrug. "Decline my offer and try yer hand at getting the clan to accept ye."

She bristled at his poor attempt at reverse psychology. "Behaving like an ass does not further your cause."

He laughed out loud. "I love yer fire, m'wee hen. We two are a fine match. Trust me."

Dugan rode closer, a wide grin splitting his round face. "'Tis a day for merriment, indeed. They shall hail me a hero for returning with our chieftain alive and well."

"At least some will hail ye a hero," Quinn corrected.

"Nay, cousin." Dugan gave Evie a wink, then shook a finger as though scolding them. "Ye are beloved to most in the clan, and those who do hate ye dinna have the spine to do anything about it."

"Someone gave him quite a bash," Evie argued, wishing Dugan would stop attempting to sugarcoat everything in front of her. When a man spoke as loudly as he did, any confidences he shared could be heard clear to London, and he needed to realize that. She had overheard him ask Quinn if he remembered who in the clan rode out with him on the day of the failed attack. "Was anyone in the keep able to tell you who left with him that day?"

Dugan's bushy black brows arched to his hairline. "Ye've got the ears of a bat, m'lady."

"And you have the voice of a bellowing cow." It was the loudest thing she could think of in this era that he might understand.

"She has a point, Dugan. Ye ken we've told ye that before." Quinn smoothed the reins through his hands. "And no one in the keep knew anything, Evie. Or at least no one admitted to knowing anything."

"Well, they wouldn't now, would they?" Neither man asked her opinion, but it needed saying. "If you committed a murder, would you admit to it or confess anything?"

"Nay, but ye would think those true to the MacTaggart would share anything that might help reveal the traitor." Dugan wagged a finger in the air again. "Not a single soul remembered who rode out with our fine chieftain that day."

"Who usually accompanies you?" Surely, this wasn't the first time the man had left his keep. Had they even thought of that? She jabbed a thumb in Dugan's direction. "Other than this man, whom you seem to trust immensely, who else do you allow close? Don't chieftains have bodyguards who go with them whenever they travel?"

Dugan cut a scolding glare over at Quinn. "I dinna ken what a bodyguard is, but I will say we have suggested he never travel alone. Even so, the bullheaded man still does so on many occasions."

"Dinna yammer on about my behavior as if I'm nay here." Quinn tightened the reins and brought both the conversation and the horse to a halt. "We shall stop here for a while, I think."

"We're nearly there, man. Can ye nay make it any farther?" Dugan urged his sturdy mount closer, peering at Quinn as if he feared him about to fall from the saddle.

"Is the sunlight bothering you again?" Concerned that his head ached worse, Evie twisted around and studied his pupils.

"We are within a stone's throw of the keep, lass," he said quietly. "Ye promised me an answer. Remember?"

"I said I would give you an answer when I saw your keep on the horizon." The butterflies in her stomach multiplied into a herd of thousands, spread their wings and flapped hard. Thank goodness she hadn't eaten anything today.

His smugness grew to epic proportions as his gaze slid to the right. "Look."

There it was. Still a distance away, but visible. Leering at her above the treetops on the other end of the glen. The tip of a stone tower and a red flag fluttering in the breeze.

He dismounted, helped her down, then nodded at Dugan. "Water the horses, aye?"

Dugan frowned and made a wide sweep of his arm. "Where?"

"Find a place. Just go, aye?" Quinn's stare hardened until Dugan jerked as if his chieftain's true intent jabbed him in the ribs.

"I'll walk them through yon wood for a while. Give a shout when ye're ready to move on." He meandered away with the beasts in tow.

The knot in Evie's throat grew even larger when Quinn turned back to her. He crossed his arms over his chest and waited. Silent.

Smug. A sleek black brow cocked at an angle that spoke volumes. Her mind raced, trying to figure a better solution than marrying a man she hardly knew or attempting to endear herself to what might be a hostile clan. She wasn't talented at endearing. Not in the least. A professor had even dubbed her a bitter pill to swallow in front of a large class of peers. Of course, the instructor had been gracious enough to soften the blow by also informing the entire auditorium that it had nothing to do with her looks.

Her appearance he found acceptable. No. He had stated in a clear, damning tone that her difficult personality would be the wall that always separated her from the rest of humanity. Always. That had been psych class during her first year at university. She almost dropped out after that dressing down. But instead of letting that old bugger get the better of her, she had excelled at all her studies and graduated with honors.

Quinn cleared his throat but didn't say a word.

She shifted in place and looked at everything but him.

"This isna that difficult a decision, lass."

"Maybe not for you," she sputtered. "In my opinion, settling on who I marry is one of the most important choices of my life." She gave a nervous jerk of a shoulder. "It's not that I don't find you attractive, but I like to get to know someone before I have sex with them." Mimicking his stance, she popped her arms into a tensed fold across her chest. "And I take issue with forced marital relations." She twitched another shrug. "You know—to consummate things?"

That won her one of his befuddled frowns.

"I would never force myself upon ye. Surely, ye know that about me by now?" Then his frown disappeared, and his eyes widened as if he suddenly remembered something. "And rest assured, my clan no longer tolerates the bedding ceremony. I stopped that barbaric custom once I became chieftain." He tipped his chin to a daring angle. "Of course, I do allow the blessing of the marriage bed by the priest." With a sharp nod, he added, "For future bairns, ye understand."

She needed to get him back on track. He must understand her point. "You said your first wife didn't like you and avoided you whenever possible, right?"

"Aye."

"If you didn't force yourself on her, how did the two of you ever conceive a child?"

A muscle ticked in his check; his jaw tensed as though he ground his teeth. He stared at her for a long moment before answering. "She laid there 'til I finished." Disgust colored his tone. "She made it quite clear she would do her wifely duty but never enjoy it." His pained glare drifted to a point off in the distance. "The first time she agreed to the act because her father said if she didna produce the bloody sheet of a pierced maidenhead, she could never come home and visit her mother." He shifted in place, and his voice grew colder. "I caught her pouring a vial of sheep's blood where we had lain. It was then I understood it wasna her mother she wished to visit. 'Twas her lover. A myriad of emotions flashed in his dark eyes. Pain. Resentment. Embarrassment. His focus riveted back to her, held her trapped in all he relived. "As soon as she told me she was with child, I never touched her again." After a bitter snort, he added, "'Twas naught but a fortnight after our wedding. She thought me too stupid to realize the babe in her belly was seeded before we married."

She hurt for him. With everything he shared, she realized he wasn't some barbaric Highlander intent on bedding wenches whether they wished it or not. And how in Heaven's name had such an image ever gotten into her head? Too many movies overheard from her flatmate's laptop, most likely. She scrubbed her face, then let her hands drop. "I need to walk a bit. It helps me think. Will you grant me that?"

He took hold of her shoulders and kept her from looking away. "Yer wasting time, lass. What difference will it make if ye wait until the sun climbs a bit higher in the sky?"

"Fair point," she admitted. What difference would it make? Was she going to pluck some unseen solution out of thin air? She hated dawdlers, and now she had become one. Head held high, she locked eyes with him. "Yes. I will be your wife."

With a gentle pull, he enclosed her in his embrace until the heat of him scorched through her. His warm lips brushed across her mouth, nibbling with a hesitant tenderness. The chaste kiss set her blood on fire while, at the same time, reminding her of what she had just said. She could almost hear the door to her past life swinging shut, its hinges creaking with resounding finality like the closing of a tomb.

She had just agreed to marry a man she hardly knew. May God have mercy on both their souls. Uncontrollable giddiness took hold of another part of her. That tiny part she always kept hidden. The part of her that had always longed to draw closer to someone and have that same closeness, that need to be needed returned. She felt herself rising to the challenge and making a silent vow to turn this choice into a thrilling means of thriving—not just a way of surviving. As his hands slid from her shoulders, she leaned in and hugged him tighter. If his horse understood body language, maybe he would, too.

"That's my fine wee hen," he said softly, cradling her closer. "I swear ye willna regret yer choice."

A nervous giggle escaped her, and his quizzical look made it worse. She snorted out a very unladylike laugh. "Forgive me." Fingers pressed across her lips, she held her breath in a feeble attempt at regaining control. "I promise I wasn't laughing at you or what you said."

"Then what?" He looked as if he couldn't decide whether to smile or frown.

"You swore I would never regret my choice?"

"Aye?"

"My immediate thought was that *you* might regret my choice." She eased back a step. "It bears noting that I am not the easiest of persons to get along with."

He grinned. "Nor am I, lass." With a teasing wink, he wrapped an arm around her and led her back to where they had separated from Dugan. "That means our lives will never be dull or without passion.

Evie hoped he was right. She never much cared for dull, and if things kept going like they had for the past few days, she sincerely doubted she would ever see it again.

"Dugan!" Quinn's bellow blasted through the trees.

The man reappeared much too fast for her liking, and judging by his smile, he had overheard every word. "Here I be, cousin. Ready to lead yerself and yer lovely bride home."

"Subtlety is not your strong suit, is it, Dugan?" She stepped forward, not relishing the idea of getting back on the horse. With a hand resting on the smooth leather of the saddle, she glanced back at Quinn. "As your wife, will I be required to ride?"

With a devilish grin, he lifted her into the saddle. "I leave that entirely up to yerself, m'lady. Whatever pleasures ye the most."

"That is not what I meant, and you know it." Her cheeks burned like hot coals. That was twice he had managed to make her blush. "I was referring to horses?"

"Ahh, yes." He smiled, flashing that powerful dimple yet again. "It depends on whether we choose to travel. It would serve ye well to learn how to ride. Ye might be more comfortable on yer own mount. Eventually."

She doubted she would ever be comfortable in the saddle, but she would try. Horses seemed nice enough. As long as they put her on a meek one, she might survive it.

Quinn pulled her back against him and looped an arm around her waist. She vowed to stay put this time. After all, why not? She had made her choice. And besides—it wasn't as though resting against that wall of muscle was unpleasant. To distract herself from the warmth of him pressed against her back, she decided to learn what she could about her new home before they arrived. "Tell me about your keep.

Your clan."

He kept the horse at an ambling pace, as if sensing her need to immerse herself in all that lay ahead. "Some might think us a small clan, but we're fierce and allied with the Rosses. A favorite, in fact. My mother was a Ross, and my sister married one."

His mother was a Ross, and his sister married one? Possible genetic defects begged to be addressed, but she didn't dare voice her concerns. The thirteenth-century had yet to realize the dangers of intermarrying.

"I see," was all she allowed herself to comment. "Does your sister still live here, or did she leave when she married a Ross?" She wondered if the couple had children yet, and if so, would they need whatever medical assistance she could attempt to provide?

"Fern begged Gilbert to remain here." Both his pride and the smile she couldn't see echoed in his voice. "She's a sweet lass, my sister, but doesna tolerate any type of change well. She gets..." His words trailed off as if he struggled to describe her accurately.

"So upset she can't breathe? Trembles? Loses control?" Evie wondered if Fern suffered from metathesiophobia, the fear of change. Some stricken with the malady found it debilitating.

"Nay. She rages like a sore-tailed wolf, and the devil himself couldna get along with her if he tried. Do ye ken of an herb that might calm her and protect the rest of us?"

"I'm afraid not." If she knew how to handle anger issues, she wouldn't be in the thirteenth century. "It sounds as though her husband is understanding since he agreed to stay at MacTaggart keep." Fern sounded like a strong-willed woman. A kindred soul and a possible friend. "Do you and her husband get on well?"

"About as well as two dogs pissing on each other's trees." His grim tone rang with alpha maleness and the need to lead the pack.

"But you tolerate him for the sake of your sister."

"Aye. He treats her well. As long as he keeps her happy, I keep the peace between us."

"Good man." She patted his arm, then tensed. Her fate was at hand.

The multi-towered fortress loomed tall and foreboding on a point of land jutting out into frothy blue waters sparkling in the sun. It might be the North Sea or Moray Firth. Or Cromarty Firth even. She had lost her bearings since she didn't know how far north they had traveled. For all she knew, it could be a large loch if they had veered westward. The vast fortification of stone dominated her view, blocking all else in front of them. "What body of water is that?"

"Depends which direction ye turn. West is Cromarty Firth. East is the North Sea, or some might say the mouth of Moray Firth." He patted her arm. "Is it not a fine keep?"

"Grand," she said softly because the place commanded the reverence of quiet. The impressive skirting wall of chiseled stone blocks appeared cold and unforgiving; its weathered sides riddled with arrow slits. The barricade glared down at her, daring her to reveal that in a little over seven hundred years, nothing more than an overgrown patch of scattered rubble, barely discernible from the shoreline's mottled stones, would remain. MacTaggart keep would be forgotten. Returned to the earth from whence it came. She teared up at the thought. Or perhaps it was the brisk wind, briny and fresh, blowing in from the sea.

Before they reached the entrance, the iron portcullis, its jagged teeth rusty from the salt air, slowly raised with the jarring rattle of heavy chains and groaning gears. It made Evie think of a monster's gaping maw. "Unleash the Kraken," she whispered. The eeriness grew stronger when she realized not a single soul walked atop the wall or peeped out from the guard tower. It was as if the fortification itself recognized its master and welcomed him home.

The cobblestoned bailey magnified every echoing clippity-clop of the horses' hooves, wearing on Evie's straining nerves. If she had ever mastered the proverbial *stiff upper lip*, now was the time to shield herself with the famed British fortitude. She could do this. Of course, she had no choice but to do this or—Never mind, she didn't even want to think about all that could go wrong if she didn't have some sort of sanctuary in the thirteenth century.

Men, women, and children, as well as a noisy cluster of chickens and geese, milled about the enormous courtyard lined with both large and small dwellings built against the inner side of the protective curtain wall. The main keep reigned supreme in the center of the mighty fortress like the community building at the hub of a small town.

A medieval habitat. Re-enactments of the past dimmed in comparison to reality. She noted the smithy in one corner and what looked to be a barracks or armory built against the easterly wall. The sudden awareness that the individuals residing in the place proceeded to press in uncomfortably close interrupted her analytical study of the place. She scooted back, sinking deeper into the protective arc of Quinn's embrace.

"Our chieftain has returned to us hale and hearty thanks to this woman!" Dugan boomed in a voice loud enough to shake the cornerstone free of the foundation. "His—"

"My betrothed," Quinn interrupted. "The Lady Evaline Indiana Wortham."

He had remembered her full name. Even that accursed middle name her father had dubbed her with, according to her mother. The simple act warmed her heart. People remembered things about you if you weren't invisible to them. If you mattered. If you didn't fall through the cracks and disappear into their lint trap of nobodies easily forgotten. She hazarded a smile at the stares, picking her apart piece by piece. "It is my honor to meet you all."

A collective intake of breath at her British accent made her heart stutter and struck fear deep within her. Quinn hadn't exaggerated. These simple folk despised the English. She leaned tighter against him, wishing she could disappear back to her own time.

Quinn didn't hesitate, merely sat taller and tightened his hold around her waist. "This woman dragged me out from the waterfalls close to Rosemarkie. Kept me from drowning and tended the gash in my head. A wound from a blow intended to kill me. An attack by a cowardly blackguard too weak to battle me face to face."

People edged forward, enraptured by the tale. The women either clutched their hands to their hearts or pulled their children closer. The men's hands tightened into fists.

Quinn gave her a gentle squeeze, a silent reassurance that he knew how to motivate his people. "Lady Evaline shared her food. Her blankets. Built a fire and watched over me through the night. She told me England had banished her. Their harsh treatment of this remarkable woman is our gain of a tender-hearted healer who has agreed to be my wife."

The crowd cheered, and what had been glowering, suspicious glares became welcoming smiles.

"Aye," Dugan boomed again. "To the return of our chieftain!"

The men, women, even the children shouted again, stirred by Quinn's speech and Dugan's enthusiasm.

He played them well. Both men did. She released the breath she held, reassured and grateful that such a cunning ally paved her way into the thirteenth century rather than someone much worse. And now that ally was to be her husband.

Improvise, adapt, overcome, she repeated to herself in an effort to stoke her flagging determination. She could do this. Somehow.

CHAPTER SEVEN

E VEN THOUGH QUINN had appeared to win over the crowd, Evie couldn't shake the feeling that their stares pelted into her like tiny darts. She didn't begrudge them their curiosity, but did they have to make her feel like the newest addition to the zoo?

A glance at the women's modest dresses and hair coverings of white linen made her as self-conscious as a prepubescent teenager with glasses and a mouthful of braces. Her favorite jeans, t-shirt, and field jacket decorated with patches from all the medical units she had aided didn't fit in—just as Quinn had warned. She swiped her sweating palms across the seat of her jeans. Maybe someone could loan her some appropriate clothing.

As she bent to hoist her backpack to her shoulders, Quinn stopped her. "Nay, m'lady," he quietly corrected. "Maidservants will fetch yer things and take them to yer room."

"But—"

He cut her off with a look, then softened it with an indulgent smile. "It is yer right, my English lass. As future lady of this keep and the new Countess of Ardross, yer maidservants shall tend ye."

"I see." She released her backpack to a pair of smiling young women who kept dipping their heads and bobbing shy curtsies as they gathered the rest of the bundles from behind the saddle. Sidling closer to Quinn, she whispered, "Am I supposed to follow them?"

"Nay, I would have ye meet my sister first. Fern will help ye settle in and feel at home. Come, I wager she's in the garden with her roses." He offered his arm, although it took her a moment to realize what he meant. Heaven help her. If her clothing and accent didn't do her in, her ignorance of thirteenth-century etiquette would. Now she wished she had paid closer attention to those historical movies her flatmate always streamed on her laptop.

Through an assortment of brazen stares, welcoming nods, and hesitant glances, they followed a defined path of dark flagstones that led around the western corner of the keep. The walkway took them to yet another stone wall, this one much shorter, that adjoined the fortress's main protective barrier towering around them. This barricade was of smooth round stones mudded together. Their thin edges reminded Evie of odd-sized saucers stacked in a pile. An arched gate of iron bars marked its midpoint. A burly man, quietly snoring, stood guard or actually *leaned* against the wall beside the entrance. One boot planted in front of him, the other propped against the wall, he kept himself in place with a double-fisted grip on his spear.

"Berin!" Quinn barked.

The man almost dropped his weapon, fumbling as he straightened and stood at attention.

"My chieftain!" He bumped a fist against his chest and jerked his gaze downward. "Forgive me, m'lord. My weariness comes from a lack of sleep. Worried sick about yerself, m'lord. Feared ye lost to us forever."

Evie bit the inside of her cheek to keep from laughing and maintained the reserved expression she always adopted whenever dealing with the Human Resource Department at Finchcrest.

"Rest assured, I am quite well, Berin." Quinn patted Evie's hand where it rested on his forearm. "This is Lady Evaline. She is to be my wife. Ye may pledge yer fealty to her for saving yer chieftain so ye might again experience a peaceful night's rest."

Head still bowed, Berin grunted and labored down to one knee while pulling a dagger from its sheath. He offered it up to her like a cross, then placed the blade between his uplifted palms pressed together as though in prayer. "Ye have my solemn vow to serve ye, m'lady, and my gratitude for saving my chieftain."

"Thank you," she said, but the man remained on the ground, his gray head bent and hands extended in the prayerful pose. Was she supposed to do something else? She hadn't a clue.

"Ye must accept his fealty," Quinn whispered against her ear. "Cover his hands with yers and touch the dagger's edge."

With a quick nod, she clasped her hands over Berin's, making sure she touched the blade as if she were the one with the power. "Thank you, Berin. I am honored to accept your fealty."

"M'lady." He dipped his head again, kissed the haft of the dagger, then sheathed it. With another pained grunt, he struggled back to his feet, then favored them both with a broad smile that revealed the only three teeth he had. "Welcome home, m'lord. Welcome home, indeed." As his pleased focus shifted to Evie, she noticed his left eye had a milky blue-white coating clouded over it. His right eye appeared bright and alert, albeit watery. Its blue vividness rivaled the summer sky even though Berin looked to be well on in years.

"Ye will like it here verra much, m'lady," he said with a gallant sweep of a hand that appeared so disfigured by arthritis, he couldn't open his fingers. "Welcome to yer garden. Lady Fern's roses will be a joy to ye." He thumped his chest again. "I am the guard what keeps out anyone ye dinna wish to see. Ye can count on me, m'lady." His one-eyed gaze swiveled to Quinn. "Dinna that be true, m'lord?"

"Aye, Berin. True indeed." Quinn smiled down at her as Berin unlocked the gate and pushed it open. "Berin is one of my most experienced warriors. Even fought at my granddad's side when he was naught but a lad half-grown." He gave the man an approving nod as they passed through the gate. "Loyal and true. Ye are my most valiant warrior, Berin."

"Thank ye, my chieftain. Yer kind words are worth more than gold." If the man puffed out his chest any further, he would explode.

Evie understood Quinn's tactic. Berin might be old, almost tooth-less, and half-blind, but the man had his pride and had served the family well in the past. To ensure he knew his value, Quinn assigned him the post of the inner garden gate. It doubtless received little activity. But Berin still had a job. A responsibility. Worth.

"You are a good man, Quinn." She couldn't ignore the need to praise him. Her heart ached with memories of the future where valuing the aged had somehow gotten lost, and those individuals, with all their wisdom and worth, had become a dispensable burden to be ignored until they did society a favor and died. She squeezed his arm. "An honorable man, indeed."

"I am glad ye think so, but what prompted ye to say such a thing?"

"Because even though Berin is getting on in years and might not be the fastest or the best, you still make him feel appreciated."

"Every man, woman, and child has worth," he said, as if unable to understand why anyone would think otherwise. "Why else would the Almighty place them here?"

Fair point. She smiled and nodded but said nothing else. Care needed to be taken on how much she shared. Quinn might be a kind, understanding man, but she doubted he would ever believe or accept where she had truly come from.

They passed a circle of benches surrounding a small shallow pool bordered with rounded stones of a soft gray coloring. Long square patches of herbs and vegetables grew closer to the wall of the keep itself. Evie recognized the tall spikes of rosemary, pinkish-purple spears of lavender, and vibrant green leaves of mint. Someone must have recently cut some of the mint because its pleasant, clean scent filled the air. As for the other plants thriving in the well-tended beds, she didn't have a clue what they might be, but they looked healthy. Whoever tended this garden had quite the green thumb.

Then they came to the flowers. An abundance of roses in varying shades of red. Delicate pink carnations trellised in earthenware pots to keep them from falling over. Bluebells. Primrose. White clusters of Queen Anne's lace. Larger trellises overgrown with ivy created a maze of walls that separated the flowers from the fruit trees beyond. But Quinn's sister had yet to show herself. Then a low moan came somewhere from within the maze of ivy and hedging.

"Fern!" Quinn charged into the mass of green.

Evie followed, wishing she had her bag at her side. From the sound of that moan, someone was in pain. She rounded another corner of the maze and came up short, almost tumbling over Quinn, who crouched beside a pregnant woman.

"Fern, lass, is it yer time?" He pulled her up against him, supporting her shoulders as she clutched his hand and buried her face in his chest. "Fern—speak to me, I beg ye."

"Satan's bollocks, ye smell like a goat, Quinn." She whipped her head away and made a face. "When was the last time ye bathed? 'Tis summer, man, and no excuse for such a stench."

Quinn's eyes flexed to slits. He clamped his mouth shut for a moment before forcing a strained smile. "These past few days have been a mite busy, dear sister, and might I also add, I'm pleased my absence didna trouble ye."

"I knew ye'd be fine. Ye always win the day." She paused and eked out another long, low groan. "I wasna worried for a whit." She balled up tighter, and her face shifted to a darker red. "I am nay ready for this. It canna be my time. Old Merdrid promised it wouldna happen 'til the full moon."

Evie scooted around and crouched on her other side. The woman's coloring, as well as the state of her hands and ankles, concerned her. Fern had passed the point of a little puffiness. Her extremities had swollen a great deal. Evie felt sure the woman's blood pressure had reached a dangerous level as well. "When did the pains start?" she asked, taking hold of the woman's wrist to confirm what she knew would be a racing pulse.

"Who are ye?" The red-faced beauty snatched her arm away, glaring at Evie as though she were the devil himself.

"Calm yerself, Fern." Quinn tipped his head toward Evie. "This is my betrothed, Lady Evaline Indiana Wortham. She saved my life and—"

"Call me Evie," Evie interrupted. Proper introductions could wait. "I'm a doc—a healer, and I've helped bring quite a few babies into this world."

"Betrothed?" Fern beamed up at Quinn, then twisted with another labor spasm. She clutched her belly and drew up her legs. "I canna bear this. I fear for certain I'm dying." She snatched hold of Evie's hand. "If I die, please take care of my babe. If Quinn trusts ye, then so do I."

"Now, there shall be no talk of dying," Evie scolded in a gentle tone. "I intend to take care of both you and your baby, but we must get you inside since your pains seem quite close." She locked eyes with Quinn. "Does the keep have a litter or some way of transporting her to her rooms? We must get her somewhere comfortable."

He scowled at her as if she had just insulted his ancestors.

"Oh, ye've done it now," Fern said with a roll of her eyes. "Ye've insulted his strength and manhood. He'll pout for a week and a day if ye dinna take it back. Quite the sullen pet, he can be when he thinks ye dinna admire him."

"I dinna pout," he growled through clenched teeth, then scooped his large sister into his arms and stood. "I shall carry ye to yer rooms."

Evie doubted he could manage it but waved him on. "Whatever it takes. Just mind your step, and don't drop her."

Fern laughed, then bared her teeth and grabbed her stomach again.

"Heaven help me, no one said there would be so much pain. Mark my words, from this day forward, Gilbert is barred from my chambers! He might as well find himself a mistress."

By the time they reached the first landing of the narrow stone staircase that had started at the back of the kitchen, Evie noticed Quinn's pallor and labored breathing. Sweat poured down the sides of his face. Carrying a heavily pregnant woman up these devilish stairs would wind a hearty man in the best of times. Quinn needed to realize he had not yet fully healed from his concussion.

"Set her down here," she ordered in her sternest take-charge voice. "Now!"

He didn't lower Fern to the steps but relented and leaned back against the wall, struggling to catch his breath. "I can—"

"You cannot. You are not fully recovered. Now set her down and get help while she and I get better acquainted." Evie gave Fern an encouraging smile that the woman took to heart.

"Listen to her, brother," she said. "Please run and tell my maids to prepare my bed." She closed her eyes and tensed, then forced them open and fixed him with a pleading frown. "And fetch Gilbert so I can curse him for doing this to me."

"I am not a messenger boy," he weakly argued while blinking at the sweat running into his eyes

"Please, Quinn," Fern said softly. "Ye dinna seem well, and I do worry after ye. I lied when I said I dinna."

Evie decided to chime in with a language he might understand. "Are you so eager to make me a widow before you even make me your wife?"

He stared at her, his chest still heaving. Those dark eyes of his grabbed hold of her soul as if daring her to toy with him. She would pay if she dared such. And pay dearly. She heard the vow as if he had spoken it aloud.

"Get a sturdy blanket and two of your most trusted men. We'll get her the rest of the way by all of us carrying her. It will be easier for her."

He eased Fern down to the steps, then strode up them, taking them two at a time now that he no longer carried the heavy burden of his beloved sister.

Evie patted Fern's damp brow with a diner napkin she found in her jacket pocket. "How much farther to your rooms?"

"Next floor," Fern whispered, curling against Evie, and clutching her hand. "Please help me. I canna bear this pain any longer."

"I'm going to help you all I can. I promise." Evie prayed it would be a birth with no complications. As hard and fast as the pains were coming, Fern still hadn't mentioned the need to push or acted as if she even felt the urge. She hoped it was a matter of Fern not knowing how painful childbearing could be and that the woman had a low pain threshold. If not, she worried about a difficult birth ahead with none of the twenty-first-century technology that protected mother and child. "Breathe with me, Fern. It will help." If she distracted the poor girl, that would help, too. "Tell me about this man I have promised to marry."

"My dear twin acts the ruthless, hard-hearted braggart but dinna be fooled." Her advice trailed off into a whining groan as she clutched at her middle. "If ye let him," she panted, "he will grow to love ye more than life itself. All the way to the grave. Maybe even beyond." She lifted her head, her deep brown eyes riddled with shadows. "His first wife hurt him. Not by dying when she birthed her bairn, but by swearing to anyone who would listen that she loved another. But he wouldna admit it. Nor act as though anything she said mattered." Fern managed a rueful nod. "But if ye ask me, I think he was relieved when the Almighty took her and her lover's child."

The thunder of hurried footsteps grew closer. Quinn and his men had returned.

"I need you to scooch over onto the blanket and lie as still as you can. We'll have you to your bed in no time." Evie motioned for them to spread the cloth beside Fern. It took some maneuvering, but they got her set, lifted her by the corners of the heavy blanket, and made it to her chambers much easier than if Quinn had attempted to forge onward.

Her maids had already stripped the bed and covered it and her pillows with old linen. As soon as the men settled Fern onto her bed, her maids surrounded her, preparing her to be as comfortable as possible in what could be an extended battle.

Evie stepped away, pulling Quinn into the adjoining sitting room. "I need my bag. Can you have someone fetch it?" As he turned to do as she bade, she yanked him back and pressed a hand to his pale cheek. "You don't appear well at all. Never mind about fetching the bag. You must lie down."

"I will be damned if I lie down and leave my sister to face this alone." He shot a hateful glance at the door leading out into the hallway. "I couldna find that feckin' husband of hers. Dugan is searching for him now."

Evie took hold of his fists and tugged him toward a long bench covered in cushions and pillows. "Please sit and rest. You know Fern would wish it. I'll send a maid for my bag. Then I'll make sure your sister knows you're cheering her on right here in the next room. I promise."

He raked his dark hair out of his face, wincing as he brushed against his wound. "Ye swear ye will call me to her side if aught goes awry? Ye willna let her pass without my seeing her one last time?"

She prayed it wouldn't come to that but understood his fears. Childbirth could be perilous in any century but especially brutal here in the past. "I swear it. I would never deny you the right to say goodbye."

With a stiff nod, he relented. Perched on the bench, he sagged forward and held his head in his hands. Evie's heart went out to him.

The torment of his fears joined forces with the physical pain of his injury, doing its best to beat him into submission.

"Now, I'm going to see what I can do about getting your new niece or nephew into this world," she said in as cheerful a tone as possible.

As soon as she crossed the threshold into the bedchamber, the commanding, bullheaded persona that had earned her hatred from her peers and adoration from her patients surfaced. "More pillows behind her," she ordered, noting Fern's labored breathing. She pointed to a maid at the end of the bed. "You. Go to my room and fetch my bag. STAT."

"Stat?" the young girl squeaked, her eyes rounding with fear. "What is stat?"

"As fast as you can run," Evie said without a backward glance. Then she remembered Quinn had mentioned they would unpack her things and put them away. She whirled about just as the maid reached the door. "Wait," she shouted, halting the girl. "If they unpacked it, I need every single item from my bag brought to this room. Do not forget a single thing. Understand?"

"Aye, m'lady." The servant dipped a hasty curtsy and charged away.

"Her name is Reah," Fern said, her voice sluggish with weariness. She pushed herself higher among the additional pillows. "And this is Janet." She managed a smile at an older maid piling linens on a table beside the bed.

"You never mentioned when your pains started," Evie said, ignoring the introductions. Her concern was Fern and the baby. Nothing else.

Fern made a face that had nothing to do with pain but more a distinct look of guilt. "Last night, I'm afraid." She shifted a shoulder with a defeated shrug. "I thought it a bad case of the winds because I ate so many baked apples."

No wonder the pains kept hitting fast and fierce. It was a miracle the child hadn't made its appearance in the garden. Evie didn't scold. Fern was a first-time mother. With no guidance or prenatal care, she would have no idea what to expect.

Evie strode to the steaming bowl of water beside the linens and submerged her hands. "Any soap?" she asked the dubious-looking Janet.

"Soap?" the maid repeated. "Whatever for?"

"I want clean hands to welcome this baby into the world." She returned the old woman's scowl. "And get a move on, will you?"

"Do her bidding, Janet," Fern said as she curled to her side and hugged her middle. "She's soon to be the lady of this keep."

Janet's demeanor immediately shifted. She rummaged through a drawer, then held out a pale, waxy sliver. "Beg pardon, m'lady. Yer soap."

Evie scrubbed from fingernails to elbows as well as she could without a brush. The distinct eye-burning aroma of lye pleased her. Strong soap meant less bacteria.

After another glance back at the door, she perched on the foot of the bed and gave Fern a reassuring smile. "I need to see how far along you are so I can know when we'll meet baby. Can you roll to your back for me?"

"Aye." Fern eked out another groan as she shifted to her back, bent her knees, and planted her feet on either side of Evie. "Get this child out of me so the pain will stop. I beg ye."

"I'm going to do my best, Fern, I promise." The examination increased Evie's concerns. Even after hours of labor, Fern's cervix had barely dilated. "You said your pains started right after supper?" she asked in a calm tone as she palpated Fern's stomach with both hands. Additional complications telegraphed themselves into her hands. The baby had not positioned itself head down. As near as she could tell, there seemed to be only one. At least, she prayed so. For her smaller bone structure, Fern seemed quite large for a single newborn. Huge, in fact, and it wasn't fluid or fat. "Right after supper?" she repeated when Fern didn't stop groaning long enough to answer. "Fern?"

"Before, actually," the girl said, struggling to catch her breath. "Closer to just after midday yesterday. But I had eaten three apples whilst I tended my roses, so I didna think anything about it. Merdrid promised the babe wouldna come 'til the full moon, and that's a sennight away."

"Only baby and your body know when the time is right." She wished this Merdrid person had kept her wives' tales to herself. She had done Fern more harm than good. If Quinn's sister had started labor early yesterday afternoon, she had endured the pains for nearly twenty-four hours now and failed to progress in dilation. Evie admired the level of strength and fight left in her. The dear woman had to be exhausted. "Janet!"

"Yes, m'lady?" The older woman looked ready to jump at Evie's command. "I need you to see what's keeping Reah. I need my things to help your mistress."

"Yes, m'lady." The maid turned to go.

"And Janet! While you're at it, please see if Lady Fern's husband has been found." She slipped off the bed and walked part way to the door with the servant, counting off her thoughts on her fingers. "I also need an unopened bottle of whisky. Two would be even better. Your sharpest kitchen knives, and have Quinn...I mean...the chieftain come in here as well." She didn't know how she was going to accomplish it, but if she didn't perform a cesarean section, the odds of Fern and the child surviving were doubtful.

"I shall take care of it all, m'lady. I swear it." The matron tipped a quick nod, then steamed out the door.

Evie returned to Fern's side, wet a cloth in cool water, and dabbed it across her forehead. "I have a plan, Fern, but I'll need you to be braver than you have ever been before."

"Do what ye must, sister. I trust ye." Fern didn't open her eyes, just kept them squeezed tightly shut against her misery. "This may be my first bairn, but I ken well enough that things are nay as they should be. Please dinna let my baby die."

Evie never lied to a patient, but she never over-shared her fears, either. She folded the cool, damp cloth and placed it over Fern's eyes. Another pain would hit soon since they came in rapid succession. The woman needed to breathe easy while she could.

The squeak of door hinges made her turn. Quinn eased in first, pale with fear and eyes stricken with dread. A man followed close at his heels. Evie didn't recognize him but wondered if this was the infamous brother-in-law Quinn didn't like. Tall as Quinn but not even close to being as muscular, the ruddy-haired chap took the lead and charged to the bedside.

"Fern, m'love. Dinna leave me. I beg ye." He knelt beside her and cradled her hand to his cheek.

"Let her rest while she can," Evie said. Husband or not, he didn't need to upset her by acting a pitiful fool.

The man's face flashed a furious red. He rose and charged toward her. "Insolent servant!" he growled with a hand lifted to backhand her.

Quinn stepped between them. "Strike my betrothed and die where ye stand."

Fern cried out and rolled to her side.

Evie rushed to her, took hold of both her hands, and brought herself nose to nose with the struggling woman. "Breathe, Fern. Concentrate on my voice and breathe. As soon as I tell your husband and brother what I plan to do, we'll get the baby into this world. Breathe and see yourself holding your little one soon."

"Tell us then," Fern begged. "I canna bear this any longer."

The two maids rushed into the room, Janet with two bottles of whisky and Reah with her bag.

"Thank Heavens." Evie gave Gilbert a stern nod. "Either keep her spirits up or get out."

"She and my child are dying," he said. "Are ye blind? A priest should be fetched. Now."

"Get him out of here," she ordered. Quinn grabbed the man, shoved him out the door, then barred it shut.

He hurried back to his sister's side, grabbed her hands, and grinned. "I enjoyed that, Fernie. Ye ken I always thought him an arse, even before ye married the bastard."

Fern managed a weak smile through her pain.

"Good enough." Evie grabbed her stethoscope. First, she listened to Fern's chest, then to the baby's heartbeat. She closed her eyes and concentrated. "Oh, bloody hell," she swore under her breath, then listened again to make sure she wasn't mistaken.

"Evie?" Quinn sat back against the headboard and supported his sister.

"Two." And she had to get them out as soon as possible.

"Twins?" Fern repeated in a weary whisper. "Two *babies*?"

"Yes." She scrubbed a hand across her face. What was that concoction she and a couple of second-year anesthetists had mixed to knock a pair of cocky first years on their ass? It hadn't done the students any harm but had well ensured they slept through an entire day of classes that they couldn't afford to miss. She hated using anything that would affect the babies, but Fern needed it for her surgery.

She racked her brain and counted off on her fingers. Whisky. Cheap stuff. It was all they could afford at the time. What else? One of her partners in crime had been an avid herbalist before university. What had he added to the alcohol, and would it be available here?

If all else failed, whisky alone would do, but it was unstable and downright dangerous for the babies. But how else could she perform a caesarian section in the thirteenth century without over-traumatizing her patient?

CHAPTER EIGHT

QUINN HELD HIS sister, fighting to remain strong and not reveal he already mourned for her. She and her sweet bairns would die. Just like their mother and unborn brothers had died when he and Fern were wee ones themselves. He bowed his head. Fernie couldn't leave him. She was more than his twin. He trusted her, confided in her. Fernie was his best friend.

"Hemlock? Opium? Henbane?" Evie broke through his pain with her odd babbling, then dismissed him with a wave when he didn't answer. He couldn't. He didn't have a feckin' clue what she wanted.

She turned to Reah and Janet. "Do you have any of those? Or this Merdrid person—does she? What sorts of herbs might she have? Or a midwife. Is there a midwife here?"

"Merdrid was our midwife. She died," Reah said.

Janet bobbed her head in agreement. "Aye, m'lady, a fortnight ago."

"Well, damn and blast." Evie eyed the table piled with linens, gave Fern a worried glance, then turned back to the maids. "What about Merdrid's things? Or those herbs I asked about?" She marched back and forth in a frenzied pacing. "Poppy! Do you have poppy? I mistakenly called it opium."

"Evie, why?" Quinn stared at her as he replaced the cool rag Fern had knocked away with her thrashing.

"I need to make an anesth—something to put Fern into a deep sleep." The look she gave him chilled him to the bone. "If I don't open her up and take the babies, both Fern and her children will die."

"Open her up?" What she suggested horrified him. The babes would live, but Fern would die.

"Do it," Fern moaned, writhing back and forth. "Save my bairns and let me go on in peace."

Evie moved closer and rested a hand on his shoulder. "I can save the babies, and barring any complications, I can save Fern, too."

"Do it!" Fern shouted, then fell back against Quinn, sobbing. "I can bear this no longer, brother. Please let her do it."

"Give her whisky. Now." Evie's jaw hardened with familiar determination. He recognized that look, and it gave him hope. "I hate to use it because of the babies, but I've no choice. There's no time to brew a dwale, anyway."

"Dwale?" Janet stepped forward. "Cook saved all of Merdrid's dwales in case another of her teeth went black and started paining her."

Evie perked like a dog begging for scraps. "Did Merdrid use the dwale on Cook so she could pull a rotten tooth without it hurting her?"

"Aye." Janet nodded. "Snored through the whole thing. Didna feel a bit of it."

"Fetch it. Quick now. Run like the wind." Evie scrubbed her hands together, acting giddy as a child about to get treats.

"Aye, m'lady!" Reah took off at a dead run. Janet barred the door behind her.

Evie rushed to her pack and snatched out all manner of things. She dipped the strange metal pieces in the whisky she had sloshed into a bowl, then lined them up on the table. During her preparations, she glanced over at Quinn. "I will need your help, and I need you to trust that I am doing my best to save your sister's life and her babies. Can you do that?"

Even though he barely knew this woman, something in her tone and her eyes convinced him that if anyone could save Fernie, she could. Aye. He trusted her. With his sister's life and his own. At least, for now. His sister's life and the lives of her children hung in the balance.

Banging on the door interrupted them. "Let me in to say goodbye and grieve my wife and child! I command ye!"

Quinn nodded at Janet. "Take to the tunnels to lead Reah back to us. I dinna trust that fool bastard to let her through, and for Fern's sake, I dinna wish to kill him. Yet."

"Aye, m'lord." The elderly maid disappeared behind a colorful tapestry of a unicorn in a field of flowers that hung beside the head of the bed. Quinn hated that tapestry, but it was Fern's favorite.

Evie handed him a large cup of whisky and then the bottle. "Not for you. Get her to drink it. Then another. And another. Until she passes out. I'd bet my favorite scalpel that's the chief ingredient in Merdrid's dwale, anyway. We need to get a head start and get those babies born. Their heartbeats concern me."

Quinn put the cup to Fern's lips. "Drink, lass. 'Twill take the edge off." Even if it didn't save her, at least it would dull her pain. After she got that down, he refilled the cup and urged her to drink again, just as Evie instructed.

Fern turned her head aside at the second glass. "Nay, brother," she slurred. "Ye know Da will thrash us for getting into his whisky."

"I'll take the thrashing for ye, Fernie. Drink away so ye might rest, aye?" Quinn lifted her head and turned her toward him, sloshing the golden liquid against her lips. "Please, Fernie. For me." When she still refused, he switched tactics. "So ye meant to let me out do ye in this? Wait 'til I tell one and all that I bested Fernie at something."

Fern smiled and swallowed a big gulp. "I'll sh-show ye, brother."

"I'm afraid to wait any longer." Evie snapped on a pair of strange gloves. The things were pale and thin like an extra layer of skin. She picked up a deadly looking thin strip of metal. Its edge glinted in the candlelight. She gave him a fierce look, then nodded toward the pile of linens. "If you feel sure she won't move, soak one of those in whisky and be ready."

He did as she asked, but when he held it out to her, she shook her head. "Wait and use it to staunch the bleeding if I tell you to do so. For now, hand me the bottle."

Reah and Janet appeared out from behind the tapestry just as Evie doused Fern's bared stomach with whisky. Fern giggled. "That's verra cold."

"Make her drink," Evie ordered.

He did as best he could, but doubted he got more than a few spoonfuls down her.

"We brought both bottles of dwale and another two of whisky," Janet announced as she and Reah clunked them down on the table.

"Good," Evie said without looking up from where she hovered over Fern's stomach. "Let me smell the dwale." She made a face and shook her head. "Pure whisky. Just as I thought." As she leaned back over Fern's stomach, she nodded at the maids. "One of you hold the candle closer. The other, help Quinn hold her in case she moves. She's had enough whisky to numb her somewhat. Let's do this. I've risked the babies long enough."

"Do as she says," Quinn ordered as he clamped hold of Fern's arms. Reah laid across her legs, and Janet held the candlestick high, shining the golden light where Evie directed. He flinched as this woman who had promised to save his sister's life took the thin strip of metal and ran it low across Fern's stomach, reached inside, and lifted out a wriggling baby covered in its mother's blood. She tied two strips of linen around the cord, then cut it.

"Well, hello, sweet miss," she said as she held the baby in the crook of her arm. "Can you cry for me so I can hear your lovely voice?" Evie patted the bottoms of the wee bairn's feet until the wee one squalled like a Highland storm. "Well done, you! Now, let's meet your sibling, shall we?" She handed the howling mite to Reah, who had scrambled off Fern's legs to help her.

A chill froze him to the bone as he glanced down at his sister's lifeless features. "Evie, I dinna think she's breathing."

Evie pressed the disk of her strange black and silver necklace to Fern's chest. When she smiled and nodded, his knotted muscles eased a notch. "She's passed out. But we do need to hurry."

He nodded, maintaining his hold on his sister's arms just in case. His heart clenched again at Evie's grim expression as she lifted the second bairn from the womb.

"Come now, my little man. You don't want your sister outdoing you, now do you?" She held out a hand. "Dry linen. Now."

Quinn slapped it into her hand.

She rubbed the wee laddie all over, then covered his nose and mouth with her mouth. Quinn couldn't tell what she did. All he knew was that she massaged the mite's chest while she held her mouth against his face, then turned and spit and started all over again.

"Come on, dear boy, come on now. I got all the muck out of you. Take in some air for me. Don't be stubborn."

The tiny arms and legs remained still far too long, and their coloring had a bluish tint. Evie glanced back at Reah. "Hand her to Quinn and come here."

Reah placed the tiny babe in his arms. He had held a bairn this small only one time before. His wife's child as the boy took its last breath. Red-faced and squirming, this wee lassie required skill and focus to hold her. With half his attention on the fussing baby in his arms, he watched Evie show Reah what to do for the wee laddie while she took care of Fern.

"Gently blow in two breaths, press his chest thirty times like so, then two additional breaths. Over and over. Just like this. Understand?"

As soon as Evie had stitched his sister's stomach closed better than the finest seamstress, she returned her attention to Fern's son, who had yet to respond. "Young man, I need you to perk up immediately. I do not tolerate losing patients. I don't care what century it is." She draped him longways across her forearm and massaged his back.

A bittersweet sadness crept into Quinn's heart. Fiona and her daughter lived, but her wee son did not. He knew his sister. She would be both overjoyed and heartbroken when she awoke, and nothing he could say or do would ease her pain.

"He moved!" A fragile wail followed Evie's exclamation. "Shame on you for giving us such a scare, young man!" She laughed as the cry strengthened.

"Is he all right?" Quinn asked after a glance down at his tiny niece, who had quieted. The red-faced lassie gazed up at him with the darkest blue eyes he had ever seen.

"He is alive," Evie said quietly. The joy lighting her eyes faded. "I'm afraid that's all I can promise you for now."

"Where there is life, there is hope," Janet proclaimed, smiling at the wee ones as though they were her grandchildren. "And what is the best way to care for the mistress and her fine children? We dinna wish for aught to go awry."

"Lady Fern needs the care and attention of one who has just fought a valiant battle." Evie nodded at Fern as she handed the wee laddie back to Reah. "Clean bed. Fresh shift. We must not allow infection. As soon as she comes around, plenty of broth and water to flush the whisky out of her. She doesn't need to nurse these two until the alcohol is completely out of her system."

"The pebbles?" Quinn suggested, remembering how Evie's small white pebbles had helped him with his pain.

Evie smiled. "Yes. The pebbles will help her, too. I'm just not sure how many I have left." She pressed the disk of her odd necklace to each babe, tucked her chin, and seemed deep in thought before pulling it away. "Hold them for a bit and gently rub their backs. At least until we see if they're able to latch hold and nurse. I'll feel better once I see how they respond at the breast. Our little lady appears quite hearty, but this gentleman has some catching up to do. I don't want them left in a cradle just yet."

"Fetch Isla," Janet told Reah, taking the babe from her. "She said she'd be proud to help and wet nurse our lady's bairns."

Reah scurried to the door, then paused before lifting the bar. "Shall I let him in?"

As much as Quinn hated it, Gilbert had the right to know that his wife and children lived. But before he could answer, Evie replied, "Not yet. Better take the tapestry tunnel again for now. We need everything cleaned up properly before we admit him. I don't think he would understand all the blood."

Quinn smiled, and immense pride filled him. He had chosen wisely. Picked a fine woman to lead the clan at his side. A life bringer. A protector of those he loved. Perhaps the attack on him at the pool was the hand of Fate turning him in the right direction.

She made a sideways glance at the door as she reached for the wee one in his arms. "I'll hold your fine niece while you have a proper word with your brother-in-law." She paused and locked eyes with him. "A proper word, now. Civil. Your Fern needs calm even if she isn't aware of everything just yet." Her voice changed to a singsong croon as she briskly patted the babe's back. "We shall let your Daddy in for a visit once Miss Janet and I have Mummy and your brother all cleaned up." She turned and addressed him with an arched brow. "You agree to be on your best behavior?"

Relief, joy, and an intense awareness of being extremely blessed awakened a rare benevolence in him. "Aye, my bossy wee hen. Peace shall reign. I swear it." He eased out from behind Fern, carefully adjusted her pillows, then straightened and turned to Evie. "Ye're a rare woman, Evie." Without hesitation, he cupped her face between his hands and gave her the gentlest of kisses. "Mere words could never explain what ye did for me this day." He pressed his forehead to hers. "I shall spend the rest of my years thanking ye."

She stepped away with a faint smile, babe in her arms, a finger caught in the wee one's grasp. "I'm glad I could help." Her voice had softened until almost breathless. She inclined her head toward the door again. "Best see to your brother-in-law now. Janet and I have much to do."

"Aye, lass."

"And be nice," she called after him, making him smile.

Not even married yet and already giving orders. He held the pleasure of it close as he unbarred the door and shoved into the sitting room without allowing Gilbert entry.

The irrational man, his ruddy hair sticking out in every direction, looked like an angry hedgehog. He charged forward and grabbed hold of Quinn by the front of his tunic. "I knew ye hated me, but I didna think even Quinn MacTaggart would sink so low as to refuse a man a last goodbye to his beloved wife."

The promise to behave still ringing in his ears, Quinn clamped hold of Gilbert's wrists, yanked the man loose, and shoved him away for his own safety. Promise or not, he had never done well at holding his temper. Wickedly hoping the fool would jump him again, he stood ready. "Yer wife lives. As do yer son and daughter."

Noting Gilbert's disheveled appearance, he headed to the sidebar and poured two glasses of whisky. The fool looked like highwaymen had jumped him. Wild hair. Scraped shoulder oozing blood. Tunic ripped, and a sleeve almost gone. "Pull yerself together, man. Ye look a mess."

Drink part-way to his lips, Quinn paused. "By the way, how the hell did ye mangle yer sleeve?" Out of the corner of his eye, a caved-in dent of splintered boards about shoulder high in the bedchamber door caught his attention. For the life of him, he couldn't remember any loud thuds. Of course, the unusual birthing of his niece and nephew had commanded his full attention at the time. He held up the other glass and wiggled it as if it were bait. "Well? Can ye nay speak? Do ye nay wish to drink to yer family's health?"

"This is some cruel trickery of yers." Gilbert spat at him, then wiped his mouth with the back of his hand. Pure hatred gleamed in his eyes. "I know she is gone. I saw her at death's door."

"Ye're a damn fool." Quinn refilled his glass, then lifted it high, the golden liquid sparkling in the glow from the day candles lighting the darkest corners of the room. "If ye willna toast yer wife and bairns, then I shall. Here's to their good health, long lives, and happiness—I daresay they'll need the Almighty's best guardian angels with yerself as husband and father."

"Ye swear on yer own soul that my Fern lives?"

"Think, man. Ye know how much I love my sister." Quinn sauntered forward, one slow step at a time. "Do ye truly think I would jest about her death? That I'd be calm and drinking to her health if she had left us both?"

"Ye're covered in blood." Gilbert stared at him, pale but unyielding. The man's fears had pushed him beyond reason. "'Tis her blood, is it not?"

"It takes verra little blood to make a large stain." Quinn moved closer. "Ye would know that if ye ever fought to defend yer clan."

"I have defended my clan by ensuring agreements are right and fair." Gilbert tamed his unusually short hair with a few jerking swipes of his hand. "Swords and spears are nay the only weapons that protect a people." He tapped his temple, then shot Quinn a foul sneer. "Ye should ken that well enough after the mess ye made over the Ross cows. I sorted that for ye, did I not?"

Quinn kept his teeth clenched and didn't rise to the bait. He had promised to maintain peace, so he ignored his brother-in-law's barbs. Instead, he returned to the waist-high cabinet laden with decanters and fetched Gilbert's untouched glass, clutching it so tightly it should have shattered. He almost laughed out loud when the sniveling coward backed up a step when he tried to hand it to him. "Here. Ye need it."

His long, thin fingers trembling, Gilbert accepted the drink, then lowered himself into a chair. "Ye swear she lives?"

"Aye," Quinn replied in an even tone, determined, for Fern's sake, to be civil to this worthless shite she had married. "Ye may see her and yer bairns once they're sorted proper and comfortable." He shot Gilbert a hard look. "Birthing can be a grueling ordeal."

"And I have a son?"

"And a daughter, as well." Quinn shifted in place, already finished with nursemaiding this fool. "The wee lassie is yer first born by a brief span of time."

"A son and a daughter," Gilbert repeated, then turned and stared at the door. "A miracle. Truly. By the grace of Almighty God."

"Aye, and with the help of my betrothed," Quinn added. "If not for Lady Evaline, we would be preparing my sister and her bairns for the grave."

Gilbert's eyes twitched, wrinkling at the corners as his attention slid back to the bedchamber door. He seemed either nervous, plotting, or guilty of something. Quinn had always felt the man had a greasiness about him. Like a rat fresh from raiding the larder. He never would've believed it possible for his brother-in-law to appear even more dishonest, but today, he did. Gilbert was about to say something that would earn him a thrashing. But Quinn swore to keep his promise. At least for today.

"Forgive me for mistaking Lady Evaline for a servant," Gilbert said with a thoughtless shrug that showed how little he meant it. "But her dress, ye understand—or the lack thereof."

As much as Quinn hated to admit it, the useless churl made a fair point. "I would imagine running from oppressors is easier in trews than a dress." He jutted his chin higher, daring Gilbert to respond wrongly.

"Oppressors?"

"Bloody Sassenachs banished her from her homeland. Chased her all the way to the Highlands." Perhaps he embellished a bit on the chasing part. Evie had never mentioned that. But a wee bit of butter added to any story merely made it tastier.

"I see." Gilbert emptied his glass, then rose and poured himself another. Before sliding the decanter back in its place, he found the decency to wave it toward Quinn. "Another?"

"Later." The day had wearied him something fierce, and the pain pounding inside his skull was getting stronger. As much as he liked whisky, for once, he knew it wouldn't make the situation any better if he over-indulged.

"And where is yer talented Lady Evaline from?" Gilbert meandered closer to the bedchamber door.

Quinn cut him off and blocked the entrance. Did the man think him that easily out maneuvered? He allowed himself a victorious smile as he folded his arms across his chest. "Lady Evaline is from London." At least, he thought she had mentioned London. Memories from the past few days were still a bit muddled. Some came to him clear and quick. Others remained as murky as shifting shadows. With a haughty dip of his chin, he silently dared his brother-in-law to say the wrong thing. The man had a talent for it. "I'd say she's quite the woman to make it this far into the Highlands on her own. Canny. Strong. Fearless—would ye not agree?"

"Known her naught but a few days, and yet ye've already offered this Englishwoman yer name?" Gilbert gave him an insulting, squinty-eyed leer. "Ever consider she could be a spy for Edward?"

"She saved my life." Quinn forced an even tone. "Saved me from drowning. Treated my wounds. Watched over me when I couldna watch over m'self." He popped his knuckles with a grinding twist of his fist into his palm. "I trust her a damn sight better than I ever trusted Annag. The union ye swore would be so beneficial to this clan."

"It *was* beneficial." Gilbert downed the rest of his drink, then plunked the glass onto a nearby table. "Have ye not audited yer books lately, my chieftain? Annag's dowry filled yer coffers quite nicely." He shifted with another nonchalant shrug. "I promised ye financial gain— not a blissful union. At least she did ye the courtesy of dying and making room for another."

"Dinna disrespect the dead." Quinn staunched the urge to cross himself. Such talk exposed the keep to ill-wishes and curses from those beyond the grave.

Gilbert laughed as he plucked splinters from the scrape on his shoulder. "Dinna disrespect the dead," he muttered. "Ye couldna stand the wench, nor could she stand the sight of ye. 'Twas a wonder she didna try to kill ye in yer sleep." He jutted his chin upward. "Dinna go all holier than thou on me. I know ye too well."

Quinn couldn't continue this cold politeness any longer. As he started toward Gilbert, the bedchamber door opened and saved him from breaking his oath.

"You can both come in now but be quiet. Fern is still asleep and needs her rest." Evie motioned them forward, opening the door wide.

Quinn stepped aside and gave Gilbert a nod. "After ye. I met the precious ones earlier."

Once Gilbert crossed the threshold, Quinn reached into the room, snagged hold of Evie's arm, and tugged her out into the sitting room beside him. "Ye must never trust that man," he warned soft and low. "Fernie loves him. I canna fathom why, but she does." He peered through the open door at his despised brother-in-law cradling a bairn in each arm. "Be wary of anything ye say to him. The bastard twists yer words into dangerous lies that benefit no one but himself."

Evie eyed the man. The longer she studied him, the harder her gaze became. "I look forward to the challenge." Then she turned back to Quinn and brushed stray tendrils out of her face. "Would you mind showing me to my room? Janet and Reah have promised to fetch me if Fern or the babies have any issues. I believe the wet nurse should be here soon, and they'll report if the infants fail to latch on. I've got my bag all sorted. Soon as I grab it, we can go." A weary smile curved the sweet lips he had barely tasted and looked forward to tasting again. She reached inside the door and scooped the strap of her bag up onto her shoulder. "I'd love a wash and a nap if that could be arranged. Is there someone particular I should ask for to arrange for some heated water?"

He took her bag and hefted it onto his own shoulder. "What did I tell ye about carrying yer own things?"

"I am too tired to wait for some poor maidservant to run up two flights of stairs to carry a bag I have carried since university." She gave him another weary smile. "I'll do better at remembering decorum once I'm rested. I promise."

While he didn't agree with her penchant to do everything for herself, he understood it. She would learn soon enough. "What is *university*? I believe ye've mentioned it before."

Her eyes flared wide, and she caught her bottom lip between her teeth. A sure sign she was working on a lie. Fern did the same thing right before she blurted out an untruth. He waited. If a liar was given enough rope, they would eventually hang themselves.

"Uhm...surely you've heard of the University of Oxford? Established in 1096, maybe even earlier." She lengthened her stride to keep up with him, swinging her arms as though she didn't know what to do with her hands. "I studied there. Years and years ago, really." With a teasing tip of her head in his direction, she gave a tensed laugh. "Not everyone can afford private tutors and such, now, can they?"

"I wouldha thought ye learned yer healing at an abbey." He

stepped back and waved her toward the stairwell leading to the third floor. Their private floor. Solar. Bedchambers. And with any hope, someday, a nursery full of bairns. "Or mastered yer arts at a monastery, even. Although I'm none too sure monks would tutor a woman."

"Oxford gave me my foundation. London the rest." She climbed the narrow stone steps faster, as if distancing herself would end the conversation. "So, you think I'll be able to have a good scrub? Maybe enjoy some hot water?"

She was changing the subject again. A thing he noticed she did quite often. He'd leave off about her education for now. They had all their lives to sort through the truths and lies of their pasts. God help him, he had enough regrets of his own. If she could accept his mistakes, he would accept hers.

CHAPTER NINE

E VIE EXHALED, HER shoulders sagging in relief when Quinn left her in what he called *the lady of the keep's chamber.* Ever since agreeing to marry the man, a tense edginess took over whenever she found herself alone with him. Kind of like a spring wound too tight. Thank goodness his sister Fern had supplied the temporary distraction of a complicated birth.

"Cripe's sake, I'm full-on knackered." She raked her fingers back through her hair and refreshed her ponytail, securing the loose strands determined to flutter around her face. She didn't need to be near anyone until she'd rested. Weariness always dulled her sharpness, increasing the risk of her saying something she shouldn't. The adrenaline rush she always enjoyed after a successful surgery had ebbed into a warm, satisfied glow, leaving little energy for anything other than breathing. Ensuring her words fit thirteenth-century vernacular was most definitely out of the question right now.

She meandered around the large, high-ceilinged room, waiting for whoever Quinn had assigned *to serve his lady,* as he had so proudly put it. Whoever it was, she hoped they brought hot water. Enough for tea and a good scrubbing. The thought of tea made her sad. Soon, it would run out. Life without her precious tea would not be pleasant.

But she had managed it before, and while she wouldn't like it, would somehow manage it again.

The room was pure dead brilliant. Gorgeous as one of those touristy displays in castles preserved by the National Trust. A massive, canopied bed drowning in pillows reigned supreme, centered between a pair of opulent tapestries wafting down from a beam snugged up where the roof met the stone wall. The rich, velvety bed curtains secured with gold cording were a vibrant navy embroidered with trailing vines and white roses. Identical wardrobes guarded either side of the bedchamber entrance like a pair of massive sentries. An assortment of heavy chests and a scattering of side tables, all crafted from dark mahogany, waited to be explored when she had recharged. The furniture gleamed from polishing, reflecting every flicker of the multiple candelabras strategically placed for the best lighting.

A bench beneath the arched window on the east wall caught her eye.

"Absolute aces." An appreciative sigh escaped her as she sank into the soft nest of cushions and closed her eyes. Unfortunately, she had reached the point of weariness where sleep refused to visit. Her mind kept shifting into overdrive and revving the gas. Wound too tight to drift off and escape the strangeness of this new life, her eyes popped back open. The tapestry on the opposite wall caught her attention. Elaborate gold tasseling and narrow rope braiding framed a burgundy field filled with a family of strange long-eared rabbits cavorting among a colorful mass of flowers and large green leaves. Garish for her tastes, but she supposed she could get used to it.

With a slow tilting of her head, she studied the odd hares with their vivid pink eyes. They looked angry. Or demon possessed. Not all cute and fluffy like bunnies should be. She rubbed her eyes. "I have hit delirium. Get a grip, Eves."

A sharp rap on the door pushed her to her feet.

"Yes?"

"Might we enter, m'lady?" inquired a mature voice from the other side.

"Yes. Of course." Evie braced herself, wiping her sweaty palms on her jeans. She had never had her own staff before. Well, not in private life anyway. She had commandeered many a team at Finchcrest and abroad, but she doubted that counted in this situation.

The door swung open, admitting a tall, thin stern-faced matron followed by the same two young girls who had commandeered her bags when she first arrived. With a click of her fingers, the older woman gave the girls a look that sent them bustling, then she marched forward with a polite dip of her chin. "I am Mrs. Dingwall. House-keeper here at MacTaggart Keep. It is an honor to serve ye, m'lady."

"Thank you, Mrs. Dingwall. It's a pleasure to meet you." Evie tried to focus on the housekeeper, but the dark-haired maid unpacking her bag and placing all her medical tools in a neat line across a low dressing table in the corner distracted her. She didn't like anyone touching her things but bit the inside of her cheek to keep from telling the girl to bugger off. No. She was overtired and needed to dial it back, else she'd look like a fool and overplay her hand.

"That is Lorna, m'lady." Mrs. Dingwall peered at her like a research scientist studying a rat running a maze. "Is anything amiss?"

"No," Evie hurried to say. "Forgive me. I am...tired." Unable to restrain herself any longer, she darted across the room and snatched up the small container holding her precious tea before Lorna reached for it. "Might I have some hot water?" She gave the housekeeper and both maids her politest smile. "Or perhaps a pot I could hang over the fire and heat some water in? Along with a cup. If it's not too much trouble?"

The other maid, her hair as bright as hot coals, crouched at the hearth tending the fire. She turned and eyed Evie as if she spouted silly gibberish. "Begging yer pardon, m'lady, but the lads are fetchin' Himself's verra own tub and all the water needed to fill it. Be that all right? Or are ye needing the water for something else?"

Mrs. Dingwall's thin lips twitched with a smugness enhanced by her overlarge nose that reminded Evie of a flamingo's beak. "And this is Agnes, m'lady," she noted with a gracious nod. "These two shall be yer closest maidservants tending to all of yer private needs. They will take fine care of ye. Whatever ye need, they shall see to it. If they do not..." She paused and assumed a hard-jawed expression that would make the mightiest warrior tremble. "I shall address it." With a decided squaring of her narrow shoulders, she stood taller. "But I daresay there will be no issues. Lorna and Agnes are my most efficient. Aye, girls?"

"Aye," both girls said in unison. They added a quick curtsy, then resumed their tasks.

Evie was both impressed and intimidated. Mrs. Dingwall made quite the formidable general, her haughty professionalism enhanced by the severity of her black clothing. Only a single item of her apparel wasn't dark. The stark white cloth covering her hair and wrapped under her chin.

The older woman touched a hand to her head covering and arched a brow. "Does her ladyship have issue with my fillet or the barbette?"

"Absolutely not." Evie scolded herself for staring. Hugging the tea container to her chest, she forced an apologetic smile. "Forgive me. I'm just a bit tired. Not rude. At least, not normally." She was babbling. Weariness did that to her. She cleared her throat and tried again. "I was just wondering if a small pot could be brought up so I might heat some water for te—a broth?" Tea. She needed tea. The caffeine and familiarity of her comfort drink would help her manage whatever they threw at her.

Mrs. Dingwall's sparse brows twitched together, then smoothed. "Of course, m'lady. If ye wish to prepare yer own pottage rather than Cook, we will be happy to provide whatever ye require."

"It's a broth I drink for my health," Evie explained. "Herbs."

The housekeeper bent her head, failing to hide an indulgent smile. "There is no need to explain yerself, m'lady. Whatever ye wish, is yer right. Ye are the lady of this keep."

Yes, well, she had yet to come to terms with that and was doing her best not to think about her upcoming role as wife. She blinked, forcing her focus back to the matter at hand. Her tea. "A pot of hot water and a cup would be grand." With a weary sigh, she lowered herself to the bench at the foot of the bed. "Just grand," she muttered while attempting to rub the burning grittiness from her eyes.

Agnes popped out from behind the door of the largest wardrobe with a gauzy white garment draped over one arm. "I shall fetch it, m'lady, and whilst I'm at it, I'll check on those lads. That tub and water should be here by now. Himself will skin'm alive if they dinna get a move on." She laid out what looked like a nightgown across the end of the bed, then rushed out the door.

Mrs. Dingwall, her thin hands primly clasped in front of her narrow waist, gave a subtle dip of her chin. "Is there anything else her ladyship requires? Cook is preparing a tray for ye to enjoy after yer bath, and Lorna has ensured all the pitchers and decanters both in this room and the sitting room are refreshed. We hope ye find the solar quite comfortable."

"I am sure I will," Evie said, wishing for hot water and some alone time. That's all she needed o right now to recharge. "You all are most kind, and I appreciate everything you have done."

Mrs. Dingwall accepted the compliment with the barest tilt of her head. "Then I shall leave her ladyship under Agnes and Lorna's excellent care. But if any need should arise, dinna hesitate to send for me, aye?" Before Evie could answer, the housekeeper gave another reserved nod and left.

"Will her ladyship wish to dress to go down to the great hall after bathing, or will she retire for the evening?" Lorna asked, pausing in her rummaging through a trunk. "Himself said ye was verra tired after saving Lady Fern and her new bairns." The girl gave a shy, excited smile, bouncing closer as if bubbling over with a happiness she couldn't contain. "'Tis truly an honor to serve one as wise as yerself, m'lady. If ye dinna mind me saying so."

"You're too kind, Lorna—and I'll be retiring as soon as I've had my te—broth." Evie pinched the bridge of her nose and rubbed the corners of her eyes again. Everyone addressing her as *her ladyship* and *m'lady* grated on her nerves, but she supposed there was no helping it. If she tried to correct them, they'd think that strange. She massaged her temples, wondering if she had remembered to pack ibuprofen as well as acetaminophen.

Another knock at the door sent Lorna to answer it. "'Tis about time ye two," she scolded as she swung the door open wide. "Ye've kept her ladyship waitin', and she's far gone weary."

A pair of gangly, barefooted lads shuffled in with a large metal tub and plunked it down in front of the hearth. Both wore pants that reached just below their knobby knees, and their dingy tunics billowed with every move. Neither young man responded to Lorna's scolding, but Evie could tell by the way they cut her a surly glare that the three of them would have words later. The tallest of the two made a curt bow in her direction. "Murphy and Ronic's got the water coming, m'lady. Beg pardon for the delay."

The second boy didn't bow. Instead, he tossed his disheveled blonde hair out of his eyes and grinned. "Aye, and me and Raibert here'll bring all we can carry, too, m'lady. There'll be enough hot water for whatever her ladyship wishes."

"And your name is?" She needed to keep everyone's name straight to let them know she appreciated everything they did. Heaven help her. As tired as she was, she barely remembered her own name.

"I be Liam, m'lady." He smiled, then elbowed his dark-haired partner. "Raibert here's none too talkative, but I'm happy to tell ye anything ye wish to know."

"Aye, he'll tell ye all right," Raibert muttered. "He'll have ye ready to cut out his tongue."

"Out wi' ye now." Lorna shooed them toward the door. "Get that water coming, aye? Yer mistress is bone-weary after helping Lady Fern get her babes safe into this world. On wi' ye now! Scat!"

After fixing Lorna with another serving of narrow-eyed glares, the young men lumbered out.

"I don't think they appreciate your dedication, Lorna." Evie scooted back on the bench, kicked off her boots, and sat cross-legged, wishing they'd hurry with the water for her tea.

"Raibert nay appreciates anything, m'lady." The girl hurried over and retrieved the boots, then glared back at the door. "He's me eldest brother and wishes himself a warrior instead of a servant."

Evie immediately saw the resemblance. Dark hair. Larger than usual eyes that were either hazel or brown, and both had the same long, angular faces. "Well, he's young. Maybe he can work his way up to be a part of Qui—Chieftain MacTaggart's guard."

The maid gave a polite smile but shook her head. "Nay, m'lady. Raibert and I were captured in a battle of sorts. Spoils of war, ye might say. We're blessed that our lot in life is as good as it is."

"Spoils of war?" If she wasn't so tired, she'd call for Quinn this minute and ask what that was about.

"Not exactly spoils of war, m'lady." Lorna's bouncing sparkle disappeared. She stared down at Evie's boots, picking at the laces. "Our Da challenged the chieftain, made a poor bet, and lost us."

"Your father wagered you and your brother?" Maybe she wouldn't be so hard on Quinn. Apparently, the plot of this story had a twist.

"Aye, m'lady." Head still bowed, Lorna twitched a shoulder in an embarrassed shrug. "Da never wanted us anyway, so it worked out all right." She lifted her head and managed a trembling smile. "And our lives are much better here. Truly, they are. Raibert wishes to be a warrior for..."

"For vengeance," Evie finished.

"Aye."

"Revenge can be a bitter pill." Evie undid her ponytail and scrubbed her scalp, fluffing out her long curls. "It poisons the one serving it up as badly as the one receiving it." A weary, mirthless laugh escaped her. "And sometimes, even when you have your revenge, it doesn't help. The pain remains."

The bedchamber door swung open again, admitting a beaming Agnes and two young lads Evie hadn't met. The boys walked slowly, bent beneath the weight of steaming buckets swinging from the curved wooden yokes across their shoulders. They emptied the buckets into the tub, then fled the room after bobbing a hasty bow in Evie's direction.

Agnes clutched the cloth wrapped bale of a large iron kettle. Black from years of use, steam rose from its spout. The sight of it made Evie's heart sing. Balanced on her hip, the sturdy maid carried a tray holding a cup and several saucers covered in linen. "For yer herb broth, m'lady," she announced, taking the things to the table beside the window. "And Cook just pulled fresh bannocks from the oven, so she sent her ladyship some of those along with butter, honey, a fresh sliced apple from the orchard, and cheese that just ripened yesterday."

"My goodness, such a bounty." Evie hurried to the table and took in the lavish banquet for one. "I'll be properly spoiled by this fine treatment. Thank you so much."

"Ye're verra kind, m'lady," Agnes said with a shy curtsy.

For the first time since meeting the young maid, Evie noticed the puckered red scar starting high on the girl's right cheek and running down to her jawline. Agnes always kept a thick fringe of her tousled red curls loose around her face while the rest was pulled back in a braided bun. The stocky maid also stayed in perpetual motion. A closer look hadn't been possible until now. The scar appeared to be older. Poor thing must've fine-tuned the art of keeping the disfigurement concealed. Evie couldn't help but wonder what horror the dear girl had endured.

The crestfallen maid shied away while snatching her curls back in place over the scar. "Beg pardon, m'lady, if'n I've offended yer eyes. If ye dinna wish me in yer sight, Mrs. Dingwall will replace me. She said for me to tell ye."

Evie thumped the heavy kettle back on the pad and gave the girl her full attention. Tea could wait. "You do not offend me, Agnes, and I wouldn't dream of replacing you." With a sweep of her hand that encompassed the entire room, she gave the maid her kindest smile. "Look at all that you and Lorna have done to make me feel welcome." When Agnes didn't move, she gently turned the girl back to face her. "I judge people on what is in their hearts. Their outsides are just wrappings." With a stern nod, she added, "I do not judge anyone on their wrappings."

The maid's blue eyes welled with tears, and she ducked her head. "Thank ye ever so much, m'lady. I willna disappoint ye." She planted a hand over her heart. "I swear on me Mam's grave, I shall serve ye well."

"Seat yerself, m'lady. We'll prepare yer plate." Lorna gave Agnes an encouraging smile as she nudged between them, dragging a chair up to the table.

"Got more water, Lorna!" announced an irritated voice from the other side of the closed bedchamber door.

"Well, bring it in then," Evie bellowed without thinking.

Both maids turned and stared at her, their eyes wide.

To cover her embarrassment, she shooed them away. In future, she must remember not to shout. "I can handle making my plate. Done it for years. Help the boys so I can have a bath after I enjoy this proper feast you've brought me."

After exchanging dubious glances, Lorna and Agnes each dipped a quick curtsy, then scurried off.

Determination and the craving for caffeine set Evie in motion as she watched the others out of the corner of her eyes. She would never be a proper lady. At least not like they expected, and she had no intention of trying. To survive, she would align herself as closely with this century as possible, but other than that, she promised nothing.

What she *had* promised earlier in the day pushed through all the noise banging around in her head. Of course, the oath had nipped at the back of her mind all along. The daunting prospect of marrying Quinn gnawed at her like a puppy cutting teeth on a table leg. She shook her head again and reached for her tea, refusing to face this new reality just a bit longer.

The smooth warmth of the earthenware cup settled into her palms as if meant to be. She closed her eyes and inhaled the familiar, fragrant steam of strong black tea. Then she sipped, savoring the full rich flavor she would soon be without. How could she cope without her precious caffeine?

And be Quinn's wife. There it was again. Stark reality and the pact she had made. Whored herself out for a safe haven in this dangerous era. She plucked a golden corner off a crusty bannock and popped it in her mouth. It could be worse, she reasoned, trying to tamp down a rising wave of panic. She could've fallen into the hands of a corrupt, unseemly bloke bent on raping and pillaging. That thought nearly made her choke on her tea.

"Get a grip, Eves. For cripe's sake, you can't lose the plot now." She took another long slow sip and held the hot liquid in her mouth, then washed down another bite of bread. Quinn appeared to be a decent sort. Fine looking for certain. The physical part of her agreement would not be a chore at all. It was all the other bits and bobs that went along with wifery. Or what she *assumed* wifery included in the thirteenth century.

She plucked up a slice of apple and bit into it as if attacking what lay ahead. Then she stopped chewing. Birth control. What in bloody hell would she do about birth control? She had about a month's supply of pills and an old box of condoms that had probably dry rotted by now. After another hefty sip of tea, she set down the cup, bowed her head, and massaged her temples. As an elective at university, she had taken a course on do-it-yourself drugs—*herbal remedies*, she silently corrected. There had to be an herb that prevented pregnancy. But did it grow in Scotland?

"There has to be," she whispered. If not, they risked a population explosion. She closed her eyes and shook her head. No. No risk of a population explosion because of the high mortality rate for both infants and mothers in this era.

"I must not get pregnant," she muttered like a mantra, her eyes still shut.

"M'lady?"

Agnes's gentle call startled her. She sat bolt upright and popped her eyes open wide. "Yes?"

"Her ladyship's bath is ready." The maid eyed her as if watching for signs of demon possession. "Are ye well enough, m'lady? Did the food not sit right with her ladyship?"

"Must you speak to me in third person? Stop saying her ladyship this or that. I am right here in front of you." Her snappishness gave way to guilt the size of a boulder that sank to the pit of her stomach. Her lot in life was not Agnes's fault, and she shouldn't take it out on the poor girl. She managed an apologetic smile as she rose from the chair. "I am so sorry. Everything was quite nice, Agnes. Thank you. Please don't pay me any mind. I didn't mean to snap. It's just that I am...weary."

"A long soak will do her...ye...wonders, m'lady." Agnes bobbed her head and hazarded a smile.

Evie noticed the girl's strained attempt at cutting down on the *her ladyship*'s. As guilty as she felt for snapping at the maid, she hoped the trend continued.

"Aye," Lorna chimed in as she fell in step on Evie's other side. "If ye will stand in front of the fire, undressing will nay be as drafty."

Evie gently but firmly pushed their hands away. "I can undress and bathe all by myself, thank you. Why don't you two go on break?" She needed peace, quiet, a hot bath, but most importantly, solitude. A pair of maids fluttering about her like flies buzzing a carcass was not on the agenda. "Go on now. Get a cup of…" she paused. What did they drink besides wine, whisky, water, and ale? "Get a drink and go on break," she finally finished.

"Go on break?" the two repeated in unison.

"M'lady, we cannot," Lorna said. She shot a worried glance at the door as though Mrs. Dingwall might appear at any moment.

"It is not done," Agnes whispered as she pulled more curls over her scar with a nervous tug.

"Oh, for cripe's sake. Fine then." Arms up, she waited for them to pull her t-shirt off over her head. "Well? Get on with it? Water's getting cold." She sidled over in front of the fire as Lorna had requested. "Do what you must."

Both maids smiled as if she had just promised them extra pudding for their supper. But as soon as they stripped off her shirt, they stopped and stared.

"M'lady?" Agnes said softly. "What is that?" Both maids couldn't take their eyes off her sleek sports bra. In fact, she wondered if either of them possessed the ability to blink.

"Uhm…support," Evie finally answered, unable to fathom what sort of support wear they used in the thirteenth century. "A fitted bodice? For those finding themselves quite active?"

Neither young woman spoke, but they did manage a nod.

Evie pulled it off and held it out. The thing needed laundering. "If you could rinse it out. Gently, mind you. Then hang it to dry?"

"Yes, m'lady," Lorna agreed, holding the strap as if Evie had just handed her a poisonous snake.

Jeans and panties came next. The zipper and lacy elastic amazed them as well. Thank Heavens they recognized socks.

As she lowered herself into the scalding hot water, a sigh of relief escaped her. At least the comfort of a hot bath hadn't changed. It might take a team of servants to generate one, but the end effect was the same. Pure. Relaxing. Bliss. She slid down and sank beneath the surface, wishing she could stay there until reality went away.

CHAPTER TEN

E VIE HAD SENT word by her maid that she would be with him soon. Quinn paced the circumference of the wishing pool, his attention locked on the door that would bring her to him. He'd mulled this over all night and knew it to be the right thing to do. But now, he must convince Evie. A morning stroll through the flowers, the orchard, wherever she wished to go. The garden was the perfect place to make her see they should wed today. Why wait? She had spoken of no kin who needed to be informed, and as far as the clan was concerned, they were as good as married anyway. Even Father Gabriel had agreed with his reasoning.

"There ye be," called out a voice that didn't belong in the garden. At least, not on this day.

"Did I not send ye to secure our borders?" Quinn turned and glared at the hulking blonde warrior, second in command to his trusted war chief, Kendric Macwaters. Rosstan Corbett. One of the few men in this world he trusted with his life.

"Kendric called me back to protect ye. Ye wouldna have me ignore our war chief, now would ye?" Rosstan flashed a smile that didn't diminish the concern in his eyes. "I'd not even reached the border when the runner caught us and said yer horse had returned without ye."

"My horse wouldha needed a new master if not for the woman I plan to marry this day."

"Today?" Rosstan frowned and jerked a thumb toward the courtyard. "Not a soul mentioned a wedding feast this evening." He tipped his nose higher and pulled in a deep breath, nostrils flaring. "And I dinna smell the roasting pits. Cook always lights them well before dawn when preparing to feed a proper gathering. No boar? No fowl?" With a teasing wink, he tilted his head. "Dugan said ye had taken another blow to the head. Is this woman real, or is it time to lock ye in the tower for yer own safety?"

The soft thud of a door made Quinn smile. He shoved past Rosstan with a hand extended. "Good morning, my betrothed." He took in her new attire and heartily approved. The maids had done well. Transformed oddly dressed Evie into the lovely Lady Evaline. "Ye're lovelier than the dawn," he said as he brushed a kiss to her cheek.

She twitched away, as though startled by his greeting. A nervous frown creased her brow as she pressed a hand to her cheek. "Uhm...forgive me for keeping you waiting." She failed at a convincing smile. Instead, she nervously fiddled with the narrow belt of gold braiding resting low on her hips. "The girls and I had a slight disagreement about garments." Wincing, she adjusted the copper circlet shining at her crown. The headpiece, decorated with simple knots and whorls, accentuated the rich darkness of her hair. "This thing will be the death of me. A migraine for certain."

"Migraine?" Quinn repeated, thankful that her deep blue kirtle hid the cleft of her arse that her strange trews had displayed for all eyes to see. A possessiveness had taken hold of him when it came to Evie. No one deserved to enjoy anything about her other than himself.

"An ache in my head," she amended, her gaze lighting on Rosstan. She edged back toward the door. "Did I interrupt something? Would it be better if I came back later?"

"Absolutely not." He took hold of her hand and tugged her forward. "Rosstan Corbett—allow me to introduce ye to the fair Lady Evaline." Unable to resist, he added, "My betrothed, whom ye thought existed only in my head."

Rosstan stepped forward with a gallant bow and, much to Quinn's irritation, scooped up Evie's hand and kissed it. The only reason he didn't knock the man on his arse was because Rosstan took care not to touch Evie's fair skin. He kissed the air *above* her hand, as a loyal friend should.

"It is a pleasure to meet ye, Lady Evaline."

"Thank you, Mister Corbett. The pleasure is mine." Evie hitched a step closer to Quinn, as if seeking safety. He approved of that. Perhaps Rosstan's arrival wasn't such an annoyance after all.

"She saved my life," he explained, amused when her cheeks flushed a deeper red. "Pulled me from the fairy pools before I drowned. Mended my wound. Took care of me." He locked eyes with Rosstan. "And I know what ye're thinking."

"I verra much doubt that." Rosstan blew out a snort before returning his attention to Evie. "Forgive me, Lady Evaline, but how did an Englishwoman find herself this far north? Alone?"

"They banished her," Quinn answered before Evie could open her mouth.

"Yes," she confirmed, lifting her chin as though accepting Rosstan's challenge. "I said the wrong thing to the wrong person and was banished to Scotland." She appeared to force a hard swallow, then squared her shoulders. "Forever."

Rosstan's tight smile told Quinn the man didn't believe a word of it. "Then whoever banished ye did ye a favor by sending ye to spend the rest of yer days in God's own paradise."

"Yes." Evie's tensed smile revealed she had read Rosstan's true feelings as well. "Paradise."

Quinn gave Rosstan a pointed look, silently ordering the man to make himself scarce. He and Evie had much to discuss. "Perhaps, ye should see if Kendric still plans a visit to Kildary, ye ken? There was no time to speak with him yesterday."

The shadow of a smile softened Rosstan's suspiciousness as he lowered his chin in a submissive nod. "As ye wish, my chieftain." After another tip of his head in Evie's direction, he turned and strode away.

"He doesn't like me," Evie observed, her tone detached. Emotionless. "Or at the very least, doesn't trust me because I am English."

"Rosstan takes a while to warm to everyone." Quinn tucked her arm in his and headed toward the orchard. "Did ye rest well? Are yer chambers suitable?"

"Yes. My chambers are quite lovely, and Lorna and Agnes see to my every need." She kept her gaze lowered, as if unsure where to place her steps. After a moment of strained silence, she smiled and lifted her head. "I checked in on Fern and the babies before I came down. All are doing well. I am quite relieved that the little boy seems healthy despite the problems during his arrival." Her smile brightened. "He has a bit of catching up to do. His sister is bigger. Definitely the dominate twin."

"I dinna ken what names she has chosen." Quinn steered them to the path through the fruit trees. "I feel sure she'll allow Gilbert to name the boy. God help the child in that regard." He reached up and plucked an apple, then handed it to her. With a tap on the bright red offering, he leaned toward her and winked. "Did ye know if ye halve it through the thickest part of its middle, ye'll find a hidden star?"

She arched a sleek, dark brow and made no attempt to hide a disbelieving smirk. "No. I was not aware of that."

Rather than convince her with words, he took out his dagger, sliced the fruit in two, and showed her. "Yer stars, m'lady." He loved the way her eyes lit up at his proof.

"I stand corrected." She handed the halves back to him and eased away. When she reached the next tree, she rested a hand on its trunk. "Why did you ask me to meet you here, Quinn? What do you wish to talk about?" She bowed her head. "As if I didn't know."

Her mannerisms set him on edge. Sank the same weight into the pit of his stomach that his first marriage had created. "So, ye regret yer choice?" His past union with a woman who despised him filled him with bitter memories and a resentment he would never escape. Wounded his pride. Made him question himself as a man. He'd be damned if he'd go through that again. "If ye wish release, Evie, all ye must do is tell me."

She turned and stared at him for so long, he thought surely, she was about to do just that. After what seemed like forever, she gave the slightest shake of her head. "No, Quinn. I do not wish release, but I do request patience and understanding." After an uncomfortable shifting of her shoulders, she ran a finger under and around her neckline as if her maids had laced her kirtle too tightly. "I have not done well with relationships in the past." With a flustered flip of a hand, she continued. "And while I realize that what we are about to embark upon is an arrangement, I would hope we could find some middle ground somewhere. Where we can at least be friends and tolerate each other's company without wanting to kill each other."

He tossed away the apple and went to her. Ever so gently, he lifted her chin and forced her to look him in the eyes. "There are verra few whom I will ever trust." Sliding his fingertips along her jawline, he hesitantly cupped her cheek. "To find another, a friend and a help-mate, would please me more than ye could ever know." The velvet of her cheek slid so perfectly along the side of his thumb as he brushed it back and forth. Mesmerized, he surrendered to the golden green of her eyes. "A wife I could trust...and cherish...would be the finest blessing indeed."

When her lips parted as if to speak, he leaned forward and silenced her with a kiss that he couldn't, nor wouldn't stop. As urgency gave way to tender exploration, a silent plea for acceptance, she relaxed and welcomed him. Leaned into his embrace. Her soft mouth, flavored by the sweetness of morning mead, stoked his need for her. She slid a hand up his chest and teased a touch along his throat. The entire fit of her, mouth to mouth, curves to hard planes of muscle, all melded as though two long-lost halves had once again found each other to complete the whole. She shuddered in his arms, making him smile into the kiss. The consummation of this union would be no one-sided affair. Her passion begged to dance with his.

He lifted his head, kissed the tip of her nose, then pressed his brow to hers. "We will work this out between us," he whispered. "I think us well matched. Do ye not agree?"

"A Brit and a Scot," she murmured with a dryness that made him laugh.

"Aye, well, there is that." He drew back, giving her the breathing room he sensed she needed. But he held tight to her hand and brushed a kiss across her knuckles. He couldn't give her too much space. To do so would leave him aching. Whenever the warmth of her, the enticing scent of her, drew too far away, he sorely missed it. "And ye asked why I wished ye to meet me in the garden?" He paused, struggling to temper his words and choose wisely so she would agree.

"Yes," she prompted, her eyes flexing to slits. She read him too easily.

"We should speak our vows today." There was no other way to put it. He excelled at bluntness and prayed she would agree.

"Today?" She caught her bottom lip between her teeth.

"Aye." He returned her hand to the crook of his arm and led her deeper into the trees. "Ye have never spoken of kin, so I assumed ye didna have anyone who might wish to be here to see ye wed. Is there anyone?"

She stared off into space. Her jaw tightened, as if she braced herself against some sort of pain. "No. There is no one."

So many troubles she bore. He hoped someday she would trust him enough to share what caused her suffering. "I am sorry, lass. I didna mean to rub salt into an old wound."

Evie walked along beside him in silence for quite some time. So long, in fact, that he wondered if she would ever answer whether she would be willing to marry today or not.

"I don't suppose there is any reason to wait," she finally admitted. The despondency in her tone disappointed him. Did she find a union with him that difficult to accept?

She came to a halt and turned to him with a befuddled frown. "But don't you need time to gather the rest of your people? It's summer. I thought chiefs met with their clan during this time of year. Won't they expect the opportunity to attend your wedding?"

"Some might feel so, but if there is anything I have learned over the past few days, it's that there is nothing certain in this life." He gave a slow shake of his head. "I will no longer live my life according to others' expectations and put off 'til tomorrow what I should do today."

"Fair point." But she still looked troubled.

"What is it, lass? Tell me so I might help ye."

With a shake of her head, she gave him an unconvincing smile. "Nothing that I haven't already mentioned." She looked away and cleared her throat. "So, what do we do now? Find a priest? Sign some sort of papers?"

"All we must do is gather a few witnesses and join Father Gabriel in the kirk." He supposed he should warn her that MacTaggart Kirk was a modest chapel with an altar and a few pews, but Evie had never struck him as one who cared about such things.

"What sort of witnesses?" She slid her arm out of his and started fidgeting with her belt again. "I know Fern and her maids. Mrs. Dingwall. Lorna and Agnes. That's it."

It occurred to him she might be less ill at ease if her maids and Mrs. Dingwall attended. "I suppose it is too soon for Fern to be about, aye?"

"Absolutely not. Fern does *not* need to go anywhere near all those steps and can lift nothing heavier than her babies until I say so." She gave him a look that dared him to argue.

A snorting chuckle escaped him. "Yes, m'wee hen."

When she cut him another stern glare, he coughed to hide his mirth. "I shall have Mrs. Dingwall and yer maids fetched, as well as Cook informed a feast needs to be readied." Such short notice for a wedding celebration would make the already surly woman rage like a banshee, but it could nay be helped. He'd make sure she understood a small feast would do. "I shall get Rosstan, Kendric, and Dugan, aye? That will be six witnesses. A prosperous number."

Evie scrubbed her hands together, then wiped her palms on her gown. Her cheeks had lost their color, and she kept breathing deep as though trying not to lose her breakfast.

"Evie?" He caught hold of her arm. "Are ye all right, lass?"

"I'm sure I will be fine," she whispered, wetting her lips. "Just need to press on." She pulled in a deep breath and blew it out. "I can do this."

"If ye dinna wish it, ye dinna have to," he reminded, as much as he hoped she wouldn't change her mind now.

"No." With a jerky shake of her head, she held up a hand. "No. I am going to do this."

"Would ye care to lie down until everything is ready?"

"Perhaps, that might be best." She grabbed up her skirts and headed toward the keep at a hurried pace, leaving him staring after her. If clad in her trews, he felt sure she would've broken into a dead run.

"I'll send for ye, aye?" he called out.

She glanced back, gave a quick nod, then slipped inside the keep.

"M'LADY! ARE YE unwell?"

Evie pushed past Lorna, heading straight for the bench in front of the window. Today. He wanted to marry today. She clawed at the front lacing of the uncomfortable dress as she clambered up onto the bench. With a mighty shove of the iron bar, she forced the tall panes open as far as they would go. Air. She needed air.

"Let us help ye with the lacing, m'lady. Be yer kirtle too binding?" Agnes eased closer as if Evie were a cornered animal.

"Panic attack," Evie wheezed, finally succeeding in unknotting the ties and spreading open the front of the gown. She peeled it off her shoulders and shoved it down as far as the blasted tight sleeves would allow. With a death grip on her chemise's neckline, she fluttered the linen in a vain attempt at moving air. "So hot in here. Are the two of you not sweltering?"

"Nay, m'lady," Lorna said. The maids exchanged bewildered looks.

Evie pressed her cheek to the cool slab of the stone windowsill and concentrated on slowing her breathing. This wasn't like her, but considering how the past few days had played out, she had earned a full-blown panic attack for as long as she wished.

"Here, m'lady."

She opened her eyes to Lorna, who offered a small glass filled with a sparkling ruby liquid. Some sort of wine. She had never much cared for wines. Or whisky. Apparently, that preference needed to change since alcohol appeared to be her best option for anti-anxiety medication at present. The heady fumes warmed her nostrils, warning the liquid was not the gentle honeyed drink they had served her at breakfast. "What is this?" She sniffed at the strong fruity concoction again.

After a glance back at the door, then a warning glance at Agnes, Lorna leaned closer. "I canna remember what Lady Annag called it. But she drank it every day. A lot."

"And all the maids agreed the lady was much easier to deal with once she had a few glasses," Agnes added.

The first sip set Evie on fire worse than any whisky. "Cripe's sake, that is strong." She pushed it back toward Lorna and waved the girl away. "Send it back to Lady Annag with my blessings. She can have it."

Both maids remained rooted to the spot, staring at her.

"What now?"

Lorna and Agnes were transparent as glass, and Evie had already mastered reading them. When neither answered, she gave them the demeanor she reserved for junior surgical trainees struggling to understand procedures. "I have a lot going on today. Either tell me why you're looking at me like that or leave me be."

"Lady Annag was Himself's first wife," Lorna said in a conspiratorial whisper. She and Agnes crossed themselves and, in unison, murmured, "God rest her soul."

"I see." Evie drew up her knees and hugged them. "Did the two of you attend her as you do me?"

"I did," Lorna admitted.

Agnes didn't answer, just looked aside, as though attempting to make Evie forget her scar. The maid's actions spoke louder than words. Apparently, Annag suffered from the inability to see past Agnes's disfigurement.

Evie supposed being compared to the first mistress of the keep was inevitable, but she had never handled that sort of thing well at all. Too competitive. Too determined to make her own mark in the world. At least that's what her personnel file said—courtesy of her supervisor. "I assume this was her room?"

"Nay, m'lady." Lorna emptied the glass into the bucket of the morning's wash water and refilled it with fresh water from the pitcher. "The chieftain's quarters used to be on the ground floor, behind the great hall."

"Once Lady Annag died in there, Himself refused to dwell in those rooms again," Agnes said. "Put them to use for quarters when the Ross or his kin come to visit." With a shy smile, she offered a cloth she had dampened. "To help, m'lady. Yer coloring still isna right."

Evie found some small comfort in knowing that she didn't inhabit the same room as the first wife. But more importantly, she didn't sleep in the bed where the woman had died. She didn't believe in ghosts. Of course, she had never believed in time travel either. Until now.

After a gulp of water, she clapped the cool, damp linen over her eyes and sagged back down to the hard resting spot of the stone windowsill. "He wants to marry today," she said, then blew out a heavy sigh. "And I agreed."

"Today?" Agnes repeated, excitement pinging her voice an octave higher. "The dress, Lorna? Did the seamstress finish it?"

"I dinna ken. Mrs. Dingwall gave her but a short time, so I suppose it's possible. 'Twas a wonder Mistress Kemp finished the blue she's wearing right now."

"I am still here. Stop talking as though I am not." Evie lifted a corner of the wet cloth and peered at them both. "I can wear this to marry in. I really don't think the dress matters."

"But the other is such a lovely shade of the softest yellow." Lorna clasped her hands in a pleading pose and bent closer. "It will surely bring out the gold in m'lady's eyes," she wheedled.

"Himself will be dressed in his best," Agnes chimed in as she threw open the doors of both wardrobes. "I am nay so bad with a needle. I can stitch a bit of lace along the neckline of this chemise. Ye've yet to wear this one." She ducked her head and turned aside with a giggle. "I can make it ready for tonight, mind ye. After the feasting."

Evie covered her eyes again. If they kept this up, she would hyperventilate again. "I don't care what either of you do. All I know is that when he sends for me, I need you to come along, too. You're my witnesses, along with Mrs. Dingwall."

"We be most honored," Lorna said from what sounded like the

other side of the room.

Creaking hinges and slamming lids made Evie lift the cloth from her eyes again. "Agnes, what is she doing?"

Already seated on a low stool and threading a needle, Agnes leaned to one side and studied her counterpart. "Jewelry, I believe, m'lady. Hose and slippers, too, I'm sure. She's ensuring we have everything on hand so as ye can do Himself proud."

Evie covered her eyes again, wishing she hadn't given the overly strong wine back to Lorna.

A sharp rap on the door made her jump and sit upright. "What?" she snapped without thinking.

"I have brought the seamstress and the dress," Mrs. Dingwall called through the unopened door. "I shall leave her here while I attend to matters below, then I will return to fetch her ladyship. Himself has everything in place and is donning his best now."

Fingers pressed to the pulse point on her wrist, Evie counted off as she breathed in, held the breath, then exhaled. She had to calm down before she passed out. She gave her word. That meant everything. Besides, all her other choices seemed a lot less pleasant.

Lorna waited for her nod, then threw open the door and waved the seamstress inside. "Come, we've much to do, and her ladyship isna well at all."

The tiniest slip of a woman scurried inside, nearly hidden by the bundled yardage of cloth and lace in her arms. "Ready her ladyship for the gown," came her muffled order from deep within the folds of yellow. "I shall add the finishing buttons and trim once she has it on."

Lorna and Agnes headed toward Evie like vultures about to strip a carcass.

She held them off and walked them back by sheer force of her will alone. "We discussed this earlier. You may help with the difficult ties and things, but other than that, I undress and dress myself. Remember?"

"Yes, m'lady," the girls agreed in docile unison.

They had a habit of that, Evie noticed. Not entirely sure if that was a good thing or not. It was like they were in sync or something. Both of them stared at her with sad puppy eyes. But it couldn't be helped. She had tolerated being dressed and undressed like a favorite doll as long as she could stand.

With a great deal of twisting, silent cursing, and accidental popping of a few buttons on the snug sleeves, she relieved herself of the kirtle. What she wouldn't give for a comfortable set of surgical scrubs. Or jammies. Or better yet, her jeans. She draped the gown over the bench and turned back to the maids.

"Does this stay on?" she asked, plucking at the chemise.

"Nay, m'lady." Agnes charged forward as if unable to contain herself any longer. "A new shift is the order of the day. Did her ladysh…did ye not get over warm earlier?" She beamed a proud smile for correcting herself.

Come to think of it, the thin linen gown was still a bit damp from her sweaty panic attack. She gave herself a critical sniff. "Another wash wouldn't be amiss either."

"Here, m'lady. I've the water ready in the bowl." Lorna waved her toward the corner of the room partitioned off by a trio of wooden panels hinged together. Behind the ornately painted screen was the chamber pot stand, as well as a pitcher and bowl for washing. "Whilst ye were in the garden, I fetched the last of the rose oil from Merdrid's stores. I thought ye might enjoy it."

"I'll be right there." Evie went to the trunk holding her things from the future and retrieved her soap, body spray, and deodorant. She had thought to hoard the items for special occasions and, even then, use them sparingly. She thought it the best way to ease herself into the hygiene of the thirteenth century and its raw, earthy aromas. But this was her wedding day. She would not go to Quinn smelling like a goat, as his sister had so aptly put it.

As she passed the seamstress hunched over the gown, the wizened old woman squinted up at her. "Smaller waist," she mumbled, then bent back to her task. Her nimble fingers flew across the seams, nipping and tucking.

"Lovely color," Evie commented, feeling she should say something to acknowledge the woman's hard work.

"Silk," the seamstress replied without looking up. "Himself said must be the best. 'Tis the dearest I had on hand 'til Himself grants another trip to the port when the ships from the east arrive."

"It's gorgeous," Evie said, hoping the seamstress would somehow understand the compliment. The woman seemed absorbed in her world of sewing and nothing else. "I feel sure it will be perfect."

"M'lady?" Lorna called out from behind the screen.

Soap, deodorant, and body spray clutched to her chest, Evie forged ahead, determined to keep a level head and get through this. She set her precious items on the stand beside the bowl, then stripped off the chemise. Out of the corner of her eye, she caught Lorna tilting her head and frowning at the bottle of body spray.

As she lathered up a cloth and set to washing, she smiled at the maid. "Well, go on then. Pick it up and have a better look at it. I would've thought you'd given it a once over when you unpacked my things."

Lorna's eyes flew open wide. "Oh no, m'lady. That would be wrong."

Guilt swept across Evie. She'd meant the girl no harm. Such nosiness was completely natural. As she rinsed and scrubbed, she nodded toward the articles again. "I know I can trust you, Lorna. You and Agnes both. Go ahead. Have a look at them if you wish."

"What is it?" Lorna asked as she finally found the courage to pick up the body spray and examine the plastic bottle closer. She tilted it back and forth, frowning at the liquid sloshing inside.

"Uhm...fragrance." Evie doubted body spray would be a wise term to share. She popped the lid off her deodorant and applied it sparingly.

Lorna noticed and arched a brow. "Her ladyship rubs wax 'neath her arms?"

"Additional fragrance, you might say." Evie held it out. "Smell. Lilies of the valley. My favorite."

The maid sniffed it and smiled. "Verra nice." She held up the body spray. "And this?"

"White musk." Evie removed the cap, sprayed it all over, then handed it back. "You press down here, and it sprays. See?"

Lorna did as instructed, startling herself when it sprayed. She sniffed the air, then gave the bottle a wide-eyed look. "Such a wondrous scent it whooshes out into the air. Where did this amazing fragrance come from, m'lady?"

"France," Evie lied. Lorna would never understand about corner shops in London.

The girl placed it back on the table. "Verra nice, m'lady." She lifted her chin. "But we mustn't keep Himself waiting, and Mistress Kemp has the trimmings to finish once her ladyship dons the gown."

"I suppose so." Evie gave a heavy sigh. The inevitable could be delayed only so long. "I am washed and ready," she announced, stepping out from behind the screen completely nude. Shyness about her body had left long ago because of communal showers at boarding school.

"And you may dress me this one time," she added when she noticed hosiery, ribbons, combs, and pins laid out on the bed. She'd never figure all that out by herself.

Agnes and Lorna sprang into action like a pair of girls with a new doll on Christmas morning. First layer was a fresh chemise. This one a finer weave, with fitted sleeves and a low-cut neckline bordered in lacy frills. Then came the hose, which they secured above each of her knees with a ribbon tied so tight, she worried about blood flow. A pair of pointy-toed slippers made of leather so soft they turned out to be surprisingly comfortable. Agnes laced them so snug, Evie felt sure her toes would soon be numb.

"We're ready for the gown, Mistress Kemp," Lorna called out.

The seamstress pulled a stitch taut and bit through the thread. She rose from the bench, carrying her creation like a treasured child. "Dress her ladyship in it whilst I stand back and watch the folds. 'Tis a waist tuck I have never done before. The skirts should fall just so." The petite woman's hands chopped the air with every word, directing them like a conductor.

Evie held up her arms and bent forward, trying to remain as pliable as possible. Someone else dressing her took some getting used to. As they tugged it down into place, she straightened but kept her arms held aloft.

"This bodice fits much better than the blue," Agnes observed, yanking the snug piece into place. She took hold of the pale green ribbons and gave a warning look. "Breathe in, m'lady."

"Not too tight," Evie warned, inhaling until her ribcage expanded as far as it would go.

Jaw set with determination, Agnes tugged and pulled. Lorna helped by smoothing the material around Evie's ribcage and forcing the pieces closer.

Evie exhaled. "Do not make it any tighter," she warned after seeing the glint in Agnes's eyes. She glanced downward and held up both hands for a full-on stop. "You have pushed what little bustline I have clear up to my chin. My nipples are about to pop out."

"Nay, m'lady." Lorna adjusted the frill of the chemise peeping above the neckline. "This fine shift will keep everything properly covered. I'll pull the lace a wee bit higher to ensure nothing peeks out."

"Step away so I might see," Mistress Kemp ordered.

Both maids moved away, their focus locked on the tiny woman, while Evie stood on display.

The seamstress circled her, tugging here and there. All the while, she muttered under her breath. Occasionally, she clucked like a disgruntled chicken. After walking around her twice, she halted and nodded at the tight-fitting sleeves. "After ye've laced the sleeves better, I shall add the pearl buttons and finish the hem." She squinted up into Evie's face and gave another curt nod. "Jewelry. Hair. Her ladyship will then be ready to present herself."

"Ye do the sleeves, Aggie. I'll fetch the necklace." Lorna spun away and began pawing through what remained of the treasures spread across the bed. "The golden circlet with the green stone. Do ye nay think so, Aggie?"

Agnes beamed at Evie, then nodded. "Aye. It will crown her ladyship perfectly, and Himself will be verra pleased."

Evie stood there, the center of attention, but most definitely feeling ignored. Her opinion counted for nothing it seemed. The staff's primary concern was pleasing *Himself.*

"How much longer?" she asked, not caring that she sounded ratty. She felt ratty. Cross. Agitated. And all the other adjectives that didn't begin to cover the situation.

"I am finished," the seamstress announced, snapping the thread connecting her needle to a tiny button on Evie's right sleeve. She turned and left the room without another word.

"What an odd woman." Evie examined the fancy buttons and delicate lace the woman had added. Most decidedly an odd woman, but talented. She cringed as Agnes and Lorna combed out her curls, plaited them into a complicated braid, then coiled and pinned it to the back of her head.

"And now the circlet," Lorna said as she settled the headpiece in place and centered the jewel on Evie's forehead. "It belonged to Himself's mother," she added with a knowing smile. "Lady Annag never wore this. Himself ordered it brought to ye from the vault."

Evie wasn't certain if that was good or bad. All she knew was that the information made breathing difficult. "Will I do?" she asked as both maids stepped away and folded their hands.

"Better than do, m'lady," Agnes said.

"Aye," Lorna agreed. "Her ladyship looks grand, if ye dinna mind my saying."

She didn't feel grand, but she supposed looking the part was half the battle.

Another loud rap on the door sealed her doom. "It is time."

CHAPTER ELEVEN

QUINN STARED DOWN at his clasped hands, pondering all that was about to take place. The last time he waited for a woman in front of this altar, it turned out to be a curse rather than the blessing promised. This time would be different. Life with Evie would be all he hoped for in a marriage. He might not know the unusual lass well, but he knew enough. They had a future. All they need to do was embrace it and move forward.

The hinges of the heavy oak door to the modest kirk softly whined, drawing his attention to the entrance. Gilbert appeared, striding down the aisle with a gloating air. The man knew he wasn't wanted here. "Fern sent me," he said with an upward toss of his smirk, as if daring Quinn to oust him. "She wanted to ensure ye had plenty of witnesses." His leer softened to a congenial smile—almost. "And she instructed me to return with a detailed report since she couldna be here herself."

"Welcome, my brother." Quinn gave a curt nod, determined not to allow Gilbert to cast a shadow on the day.

"Reckon, they'll bring her in soon?" Dugan asked in a loud whisper. He cast a nervous glance around the candlelit room as if lightning might strike him at any moment.

"What's wrong with ye, man?" Rosstan asked. "Feel as though ye're about to burst into flames?"

"Father Gabriel." Clan war chief, Kendric Macwaters, jerked a thumb in Dugan's direction. "Might ye do an exorcism while we wait? Could prove verra entertaining, ye ken?"

"Settle down now," warned the diminutive man as he quietly flipped through the pages of his tattered book. He licked his thumb, gave them all a narrow-eyed scowl, then returned to perusing his Bible. "Dinna forget our Lord watches each and every one of ye."

Quinn tucked his chin and grinned to himself as all three of his friends glanced at each other like lads about to take a thrashing. Three hulking warriors bested by a wisp of a man backed by God Almighty.

"That includes yerself, my chieftain," Father Gabriel added without looking up from the pages.

"Aye, Father." Quinn resettled his stance and turned his focus back to the door. Surely, they would bring Evie soon. He had sent Mrs. Dingwall to fetch her hours ago. A distant rumble of thunder made him turn and look up at the large wooden cross hanging behind the altar. Well, perhaps he hadn't sent for her hours ago, but it had been a very long time.

The door gave another whine. Mrs. Dingwall, as fierce and unsmiling as ever, marched inside, followed by Evie's maids. They made their way to the front pew, then turned and looked back.

Quinn patted the pocket of his surcoat for the hundredth time, ensuring the ring still rested safely in its depths. Whether instinct or leeriness had stayed his hand, he would never know, but he had declined to offer Annag his mother's ring. And as it turned out, had been wise not to do so. But with Evie, he would share the precious memento and felt clear to his bones it the proper thing to do.

Then she appeared in the doorway, bright and welcome as the rising sun after a long dark night. God help him, he couldn't take his eyes from her, nor could he wait for her to join him at the altar. He charged down the aisle until close enough to feel her warmth and bask in her sweet fragrance. Without a word, he offered his arm to this captivating woman who, with each passing moment, made herself more impossible to live without.

"Weren't you supposed to wait up there?" she whispered, clutching his arm so tightly her fear pulsed through him like a heartbeat.

"I couldna wait for ye, my precious love." And there it was. He might not know her, but he did know he would come to love her if she would but allow it. Maybe he already did. "Ye are a beauty to behold, dear one. Stole my breath away."

She lowered her gaze in a failed attempt at hiding a shy smile. "Thank you. Your people worked very hard to make sure you would be pleased."

"It wouldna matter how much effort they gave if the loveliness wasna there to begin with."

As they walked slowly up the aisle, Quinn noticed the heather trembling in the small bundle she carried. "It will be all right, m'love." He didn't understand all her fears, but he supposed he understood some of her reservations. After all, they had no history together. Silently, he made an oath that she would never regret this choice.

By the time they reached the altar, all color had drained from her face. Her wee flowers shook so badly, petals broke free and fluttered to the floor. The leaves of ivy and stems of heather rustled as loud as bushes shaken by hunters.

Father Gabriel caught his eye, arched a brow, and gave the slightest tip of his head toward the rattling nosegay.

"Allow me, m'lady." Quinn gently pried the flowers out of her clenched hand and tossed them to Mrs. Dingwall. Turning back, he gave the priest a nod.

The holy man stood as tall as his short frame allowed, giving all in the chapel a long, slow, serious look. He cleared his throat and flipped to a page marked by a frayed red ribbon. "We gather here this day to unite this man and woman in holy matrimony."

Quinn stole a sideways glance at Evie while the priest talked. She had her attention so fixed on the man that she didn't blink. Her breathing made her delectable expanse of bare chest rise and fall at such a rapid rate that concern soon replaced his admiration. The poor lass was about to swoon. He held up a hand. "Stop, Father."

Father Gabriel halted mid-sentence, his mouth ajar.

Ever so carefully, Quinn turned Evie to face him. "I worry for ye, lass. Are ye certain this is what ye wish?"

She didn't speak. Just caught her bottom lip between her teeth and managed a quick nod.

He read uncertainty and fear in her eyes. Fear? Why in Heaven's name would she fear him? A fierce need to ease her every doubt filled him. With the greatest care, he pulled the ring from his pocket and held it between them. A deep green emerald surrounded by golden leaves of ivy. He remembered every word his mother had told him about this favorite gift from his father. Ivy. The symbol for eternity, fidelity, and loving attachment. Emerald for love and protection.

"This was the ring my father gave to my mother on the day they married. I have shared this ring with no other woman." He kept his gaze locked with hers as he took her left hand and lifted it higher. "No other woman deserved to wear it." He slid it onto her ring finger, smiling at the perfect fit. A prosperous omen, indeed. "No other woman deserved to wear it 'til now." Gently, so as not to frighten her, he cradled her face in his hand. "As long as I draw breath, I swear to protect ye, cherish ye, and make certain ye never regret this day. For better or worse. Richer or poorer. As God is my witness."

Her tears welled, then overflowed, tumbling down her pale cheeks, but the sweetest smile graced her mouth. She touched his chest, flattening her palm over his heart. "I fear I cannot wax as poetic as you, my fine Scotsman, but I will say, I am ever so thankful you are the one I discovered at the waterfall." She paused, almost wincing as if what she wished to say pained her. "I cannot promise to always be the wife you wanted, but I swear to be the best wife I can be. Faithful. Loyal." Her smile grew as she added, "Stubborn and opinionated. I pledge myself to you and you alone, and I shall do my best to make you happy. As God is my witness."

With an irritated snort, Father Gabriel snapped his book shut. "Well then—by the power vested in me by the Church and Scotland, I pronounce the two of ye are now as one. Man and wife. Let no man put asunder what God Himself hath joined." He waved them toward each other. "Go on then. Time for the kiss."

Quinn brushed his mouth across hers, then kissed the saltiness of her tears from her cheeks. "No tears, m'wee hen," he whispered. "Lest they be happy ones, aye?"

Evie nodded. "Aye."

"Well done!" Dugan boomed and clapped a hand to Quinn's shoulder with a resounding pop.

Father Gabriel shot the man a harsh glare and aimed his Bible at him. "Ten Hail Mary's for shouting in the church and startling the daylights out of me! Now!"

"Aye, Father." Dugan bowed his head, his lips moving as he began muttering his penance. The large man rocked back and forth with the rhythm of the prayer.

Rosstan and Kendric thumped Quinn on the back and winked but didn't say a word. Neither was fond of reciting prayers nor wished to incur Father Gabriel's wrath.

Quinn offered his arm to Evie. "Come, my lovely bride. Let us go to our seats in the great hall, so ye might meet yer clan properly."

She didn't answer. Just gave a nervous dip of her chin. Her tense smile had returned.

He halted and gently touched her hand where it rested in the crook of his elbow. "Would ye prefer to sit in the quiet of the garden until the feast is ready? We can do that instead if ye wish."

By the set of her shoulders and the renewed hope in her eyes, he felt sure she was about to accept his offer, but then she shook her head. "No. We should go to the hall."

He remained rooted to the spot, leaning closer until his nose nearly touched hers. "Only if ye wish it. I ken well enough this hasna been the easiest time for ye. We've the rest of our lives to meet the clan." He paused, toying with the words begging to be said. "I dinna wish to start off wrongly with ye, Evie. 'Tis my hope to make ye happy to have me as yer husband."

"You are a good man, Quinn." She touched his face with such tenderness it made him shiver. "And where I'm from, good men are in short supply."

"Then if ye are certain, let us go to the hall." He gave her an apologetic tip of his head. "I have no doubt word has spread, and folk are already gathering.

She squeezed his arm. "The girls and I looked in on the way here. It seemed quite busy already."

Several waited for them outside the kirk, clapping and cheering as soon as they opened the door. Children rushed forward to hand Evie wildflowers they had gathered from the meadow next to the wall.

"Ahh...now I smell the roasting pits," Rosstan said as he followed a few steps behind.

Kendric stepped around them and walked in front as though standing guard. He glanced back over his shoulder and gave a curt, unsmiling nod. "Kendric Macwaters, m'lady. War chief and head guardian of yer husband since the attacks."

"It's a pleasure to meet you, Mister Macwaters. I hope you're able to keep him safe." Evie glanced up at Quinn. Worry had replaced the doubt and fear in her eyes. "Still no memory of the other day? Before the bash on your head?"

All he remembered was a muddled mess of distorted sounds and pain, but he wasn't about to go into that on their wedding day. "Today is a day of celebration. Nothing else." He pointed Kendric's attention toward the double doors leading to the main hall. "If ye wish to protect me, see that enough drink is set and ready. If we run out of ale, it could be dire."

Kendric thumped a fist to his chest and made a slight bow. "Aye, my chieftain. Rosstan and I shall see to it."

As the two men ambled off and entered the hall first, Quinn caught Evie watching the men. A twinge of jealousy flared. He tried his best to ignore it but couldn't. His past wouldn't allow it. "What do ye think of them?" he asked, flinching at his own bluntness.

"I think they could pass for brothers," she said, oblivious to his jealousy. "Blonde. Same height and muscular build. I didn't notice the color of their eyes, but the shape of their faces even favor each other. Angular jaws. Both looked to have had their noses broken at some point in time. Last names are different though, yes?"

Her detached observations quelled the tightness in his chest. She sounded like Mrs. Dingwall inventorying the larder. "Aye. Cousins. Mine as well."

"Really?" She pondered the news with a dubious look, her gaze sweeping him from top to bottom. "Then they are the light to your dark. Interesting."

He halted at the base of the steps and tried to help her manage them. She seemed to be having trouble with her skirts. He caught her as she tripped and nearly tumbled forward. "Did the seamstress not hem yer gown properly?"

She made a face as she regained her balance after a second stumble. "Yes, she hemmed it properly. It's not the gown's fault. I'm just not used it, and going up steps is a lot trickier than coming down." After a perturbed jerk at the generous folds, she added, "Have you already forgotten what I wore the day I found you?"

"Nay, m'love," he said, then swept her up into his arms and carried her before she fell and did herself harm. "Trust me when I say I shall never forget ye in those trews."

As he pushed through the doors, she went silent, clinging to him like a frightened child. Her gaze darted all around the large gathering room, lighting on the servants as they passed out tankards to the many men and women already gathered. When his people noticed he had crossed the threshold with his bride in his arms, they cheered.

While he basked in their well wishes, he couldn't help but notice Evie's distress. The poor lass tensed and pulled herself higher in his arms. At this rate, she'd soon perch on his shoulders.

"I thought this was a small clan," she whispered as he gently peeled her free and set her on her feet.

He tucked her hand back into the crook of his arm. "It is. Not nearly the size of Clan Ross, but we are one of the largest septs." With a smile at those who parted and made a path for them through the long room, he continued, "But we are a wealthy clan. Well landed. Powerful. Coffers full." He patted her hand. "Ye should be filled with pride over all that is set before ye."

"Oh, I am filled all right," she whispered as though speaking to herself. She managed a weak smile as she turned and seated herself beside him at the head table. "Filled with the urge to run."

He kissed her hand, then held it tight. "Ye have nothing to fear, dear one. I promise ye." From the chief's table on the long dais, they could look upon all in the room. "All these folk know ye as the lady of the keep. None will harm ye."

She gave him a sideways glance and a doubtful arch of a brow. "I hope that's true."

A servant came and filled their glasses. He lifted his. "I raise my glass to the woman who saved my life and granted me the honor of giving me hers."

Evie picked up her goblet, touched it to his, then sipped. After pondering him for what seemed like a long while, she lifted her glass. "To the future."

Her words gave him hope. He clinked his glass to hers. "To *our* future," he corrected.

EVIE FORCED HERSELF to drink the wine even though she never much cared for the stuff. Another panic attack, here in front of everyone, simply would not do. With every swallow, it became more tolerable. She just wished it would hurry and kick in.

As she gave in to her habit of nervous twitching, the sparkle of the emerald ring caught her eye. His mother's ring. He said he hadn't given it to his first wife. In fact, every word he had said at the altar came back to her, replaying in a continuous loop that made her heart beat faster. No man had ever spoken to her like that before, nor held her captive within the storm of emotions thundering in his gaze. Thoughts of what was to come later this evening made her drain the goblet and hold it up for a refill.

She stole a glance at him as he laughed and talked to Kendric, who sat on his other side. He seemed happier and more relaxed than she had ever seen him. She almost laughed out loud at herself. Known the man but a few days and already an expert on him? Right. Well, as his wife, she supposed she would now be in a position to be just such an expert.

Wife. That called for another hefty sip of wine. She had actually done it. Kept her word and married the man. Last week, if anyone had told her she would be laced up in a silk gown and sitting at her own medieval wedding celebration, she would have ordered an MRI scan of their brain and a complete round of bloodwork.

Resettling herself in the cushioned chair, she slid her glass back to the table. "Slow down, Eves," she breathed to herself. She needed the alcohol to calm her—not make her toss all caution to the wind and say something she shouldn't—especially later.

She tucked her fists into her lap and tried to focus on the present, observing the chaos of the overfilled room without drawing too much attention to herself. Dear Heavens. If this was a small clan, she couldn't imagine a large one. The gathering hall reminded her of a fair-sized auditorium, albeit one fitted with huge columns, flickering torches, and a stone hearth large enough to roast an ox. And the place was packed. Not an empty seat remained on any of the long benches lining the walls and sitting between the rows of tables.

Those finding themselves without a seat either leaned against a column or loitered in the doorways. She glanced up at the gallery. The narrow second floor crowned the room like a halo with sturdy banisters decorated with tartan banners. That was full as well. Where had they all come from? And on such short notice? Surely, they all didn't live within the protective walls surrounding the keep.

Everyone looked happy and well on their way to inebriated bliss. Well, at least the men did. The women and children laughed and chattered away between stolen looks to size her up. Except for a trio of men in the farthest corner beside the entrance. They appeared almost surly and wore some sort of black leather armor and dark green cloaks, unlike any she had seen any of the other guards wear. Were they some sort of elite force or something?

She tugged on Quinn's sleeve, interrupting his conversation with Kendric. "Who are those three?"

He looked where she directed, his expression tensing when he spied the men. "Those are the last of Annag's kin living here at the keep," he explained. "Fighting men given to Clan MacTaggart as part of her dowry."

"You mean like slaves?" She didn't know how dowries worked in the thirteenth century. And making a gift of people?

"Nay, lass." He emptied his glass and thumped it back to the table. "I told them they could return to Clan Munro anytime they liked. They're nay prisoners or slaves." His jaw tightened. "They informed me they could not return home. If they did, Annag's father would have them killed. So, here they remain. A part of Clan MacTaggart for as long as they wish—barring any grievances."

Grievances? Maybe that explained why they looked as if someone had stolen their favorite toy. "What sort of grievances?" she asked before he turned back to Kendric.

"It is complicated," he said, then lifted her hand and kissed it. "Someday, I will explain. But not today. Forgive me for dividing my attention when I should be focused on my bride alone. Today is ours, ye ken?" He brightened and nodded at the archway closest to them. "And now for the feast. I am sure Cook has outdone herself, even with such short notice."

A seemingly endless string of servants entered, bearing platters and bowls piled high with all manner of food. Evie swallowed hard as they placed large oblong halves of dark bread in front of each guest at the head table. Smaller disks of either bread or wood, she couldn't tell for certain, were passed out to those at the other tables. Folk without a seat appeared to be waiting their turn, some with longing looks at the platters of food. Others appeared more content with their ale.

Quinn selected an assortment of fruits, cheeses, roasted vegetables, and a steaming hunk of gravy-drenched meat for the platter of bread between them. "Our first shared trencher," he said as he broke off a small chunk of cheese and held it to her lips.

She needed to eat but really didn't want to dilute the long-awaited numbness of the overly sweet wine. More from a sense of duty than anything else, she accepted the bite and forced it down. "Thank you." She followed it with a hefty swig that almost emptied her glass, determined to keep the alcohol to food ratio balanced to optimum buzz level.

He smiled at her and seemed to wait. For what? She hadn't a clue.

A quick glance at the others in the room revealed everyone waiting. They had stopped eating, drinking, and gone silent. All eyes glued on her. Watching. Was she supposed to feed him, too? She couldn't very well ask. Not with everyone staring. A juicy chunk of meat caught her eye. There. She would feed him that and pray it was the right thing to do. Without aid of a fork that she promised herself she would introduce at first opportunity, she picked up the gravy slathered bite and lifted it to his mouth.

He took in the bite and held her hand in place as he sucked the juiciness of the morsel off her fingers. She hitched in a quick breath, suddenly overcome with a heat that had nothing to do with alcohol. His thumb stroked across her palm in an intimate caress that made her shiver.

The hall erupted in cheers. Tankards banged on the tables, making her wish she could melt into oblivion. Quinn smiled and leaned in for a kiss. The long, slow tenderness of the connection made her forget the noise. Without realizing what she did, she slipped her arms around his neck and gave herself to this man who had become her anchor. Her safe harbor. Heaven help her. She suddenly realized just how much they each needed the other. Without him, she would be cut adrift in a strange time. Without her, he would continue to focus on the embarrassment of his first wife's infidelities. Perhaps this odd marriage of sorts wouldn't be so difficult after all.

"A toast!" Dugan boomed above the cheering. "Hush it now! I wish to make a toast."

Evie slowly eased her arms down from around Quinn's neck, hoping her décolletage hadn't flushed as red as her cheeks felt. Without thinking, she fanned herself. Social graces had always eluded her.

Quinn's proud look and devilish grin made her even warmer.

"A toast, I say!" Dugan shouted again. He slammed a fist on the table, making everything bounce. "Raise yer glasses to our fine chieftain and his lovely bride." He faced the two of them and gave a solemn nod. "May the best ye have ever seen be the worst ye ever see." Lifting his tankard higher, he continued, "To a long life blessed with good health, freedom from sorrow, and the keep ringing with the laughter of yer many children!"

The crowd responded with cheers and the cry for music.

Three musicians emerged from an archway to the left, filling the hall with song. The first beat a drum, a large bodhrán with bright blue dragons painted on its skin. The second drew a bow across the strings of his fiddle, and the last man swaggered forth with cheeks bulging and fingers flying as he coaxed a lively tune from his pipes.

A sense of wonder and eeriness filled Evie. The history books didn't do the past justice. She never realized the richness of these peoples' lives. Always before the information had been dry and stale. Names and dates memorized to pass a course. Cold dead pages that meant nothing. But this—

"Are ye ready to retire, m'love?"

The whispered words made her shiver. Such a simple question on the surface and yet so complex. She nodded and took his hand, not trusting herself to speak.

He helped her maneuver her skirts between the heavy chairs and down the steps of the low dais.

"Going down them is easy," she said as she managed the obstacles without a stumble.

"Aye." He smiled. "I suppose it would be." He led her to a large tapestry of red deer running from hounds. It covered most of the wall behind the head table. "After ye, m'lady." With the weave held aside, he motioned her through the hidden archway ahead of him. When he let the flap fall back in place, she was amazed at how well the heaviness of the cloth muted the noise from the other side.

"Is this a secret tunnel?"

"Nay, lass." He offered his arm, then proceeded down the narrow, torchlit hallway. "Merely a corridor that leads to our private stairwell."

"Are there secret tunnels throughout the entire keep? Like the one in Fern's room?" She had always heard that most castles used such things for safety measures.

As honeycombed as this place seemed, she wasn't so sure they needed them. It would take her quite a while to remember all the ins and outs of the stronghold. It took her a moment to realize he hadn't answered. She halted and looked up at him, noticing the strained lines in his face made even deeper by the shadows in the passage. "You don't trust me enough to tell me."

He stared down at her for a long moment, his internal war clear in his dark eyes. "No. I do not." His gaze dropped to the floor and stayed there. "At least, not fully as of yet."

"Because I'm a Brit?" She hoped that was the case and even understood. Up to a point anyway. It still stung to hear it after all they had shared the past few days. She thought they had forged the beginnings of a friendship—maybe even more. "Answer me, Quinn. Is it because I'm English?"

"Partly." He lifted his head, revealing a pensive expression. "Experience has taught me it can be quite painful to trust too fully...too quickly."

She assumed he meant his first wife, but something in his demeanor hinted otherwise. Her new husband appeared to be a complex man. "I understand," she said in the detached, emotionless tone perfected for use both professionally and privately when needed to protect herself. "I understand completely." She knew how to shield herself with an untouchable facade as well as he did. Had done it for years.

With a sad smile, he lowered his chin and motioned toward the stairwell at the end of passage. "There. Shall we?"

"Fine." She caught hold of her skirts, lifted them out of the way, and strode forward at a fast pace.

"Wait, lass. Best let me help. Those steps are narrow and steep."

"I will never learn if I don't do it myself." She grappled the yards of silk up to her knees and climbed. The effects of the wine must be dimming. The warm motivation from before, from all his flowery words, seemed...less. Pity that, to lose the impetus of looking forward to the consummation. Bloody fool had ruined the mood by admitting he didn't fully trust her. For cripe's sake, he had trusted her enough to let her cut his sister open and deliver his niece and nephew. Did that not count for anything? And if he thought her some sort of English spy sent to snipe out a few chieftains, wouldn't she have finished him back at the waterfall?

She understood his hatred of the English—but still. The longer she thought about it, the harder she stomped as she wound her way upward. She couldn't believe she had allowed him to hurt her feelings. "Bloody fool," she growled, taking the steps two at a time now.

"Evie!"

She ignored the call and the loud thud of boots against stone echoing up through the tower.

"Evie! Stop!"

She pulled up short. Not to obey his bidding, but because she was out of breath. Which was ridiculous. She ran the stairs every day at Finchcrest to work off stress. Of course, smooth, standard flights of stairs in a light pair of scrubs were a great deal easier to manage than these narrow, triangular death traps. Especially while swathed in half the silk in China. She sagged back against the wall and drew in deep breaths as she stared upward. Another floor. Maybe. With the winding staircase, figuring where a floor landing hit proved to be a challenge.

"Why are ye so angry?" he asked when he caught up with her.

"Why am I so angry?" Did he want the general version or the chapter exclusive to him? She decided to go for the exclusive chapter. Much shorter that way. "After all I've done to help you and your sister, you still don't trust me."

"Not fully, I said." He sucked in a deep breath and leaned against the wall. Apparently, he was winded, too. "But I am verra close."

"That is utter rubbish. Either you trust me, or you don't." She gathered up her skirts again and started to take off, but he snagged hold of her arm and held her in place. With a serious urge to kick him in the chest, she glared down at him. "Let go. You don't trust me, remember? Aren't you afraid I'll knock you backward?"

"I dinna fear a damn thing when it comes to ye," he growled as he closed the remaining distance between them. "Ye're nay a murderess. Ye've already proven that. But ye canna fault me for caution about the secrets protecting this keep. I have responsibilities. Have ye told me every one of yer secrets? Do ye trust me enough to tell me the real details of yer past instead of the vague answers and lies ye've already given me?"

As much as she hated to admit it, he made a fair point. But she didn't intend to tell him that. Instead, she tried to jerk her arm free of his hold. When that failed, she stared upward, refusing to look at him.

"Evie." The way he rumbled her name soft and deep made it sound like a great cat's purr. He joined her on the narrow step and pinned her against the wall. "I'll nay let ye go 'til ye look at me and tell me ye understand and forgive me."

"Then your guards will someday find two skeletons on this step." She glared at him, realizing that if either of them lost their footing now, they'd both tumble down and break their necks.

"Forgive me," he breathed against her ear with a nibbling of her earlobe that greatly strengthened his argument. "In time, we will win each other's complete trust." He pressed harder against her, making her uncomfortably aware of the growing heat between them. "Forgive me, my fiery lass, so we can enjoy our first night together."

CHAPTER TWELVE

ONCE AGAIN, HE might have chosen his words poorly, but at least he hadn't lied to her. Surely, someday, she would come to appreciate that about him. He pushed open the door to their solar. "Shall we tarry here in the sitting room for a bit? Yon window looks out upon the sea if ye would care to sit on the bench for a while."

She tossed him a side-eyed glare, marched into the room, and perched on the bench as if ready to bolt at any moment.

He suppressed a frustrated huff, determined to salvage what was supposed to be a special night. Rather than comment and risk inciting her anger further, he made his way to the sidebar. "Wine or whisky, m'love?"

"Wine. I won't do well if I mix my spirits."

At least she answered him. He drew some comfort from that, knowing other men who had complained of their wives punishing them with silence and sullen looks. After pouring wine for her and whisky for himself, he joined her on the cushioned seat in front of the open window. Perhaps the rhythmic shushing of the waves and the gentle breeze would calm the storm between them.

"I am sorry I offended ye." He offered her the drink, hoping she would believe he meant every word. "Please know that wasna my intent." When she accepted the glass, he noticed she avoided touching his fingers. This time, the frustrated huff escaped. "I say things I shouldn't. Or I say them wrong. But ye must know I would never intentionally hurt yer feelings."

"I know." She avoided meeting his gaze. Instead, she sipped her wine and shifted on the bench to stare out the window. "I understand you need to keep your people safe," she added in a grudging tone.

"And yerself," he gently reminded. "Even though we know much about each other, we still have a great deal to learn. Can ye honestly say ye trust me fully?"

"I am not certain trust would be the proper word." She spoke as if in a trance, her attention focused somewhere else. Far from the window in their solar.

He propped against the broad ledge of the windowsill and joined her in looking out at the night. Dark. Lonely. A starless void that mirrored the aching emptiness of his heart. "And now we are married," he mused quietly.

"Yes. We are married." She set her elbow on the ledge and rested her chin in her hand. With no thought to her gown or decorum, she settled both feet atop the cushions and hugged her bent knees.

Evie reminded him of a forlorn child searching for a star to wish upon. The utter simplicity of her ways. Her flagrant disregard of all things ladylike and proper. She captivated him. Made him need to know her better. He yearned to possess her and make her want to possess him. This rare woman was meant to be his—if only he could convince her.

The sound of the waves encouraged him. Made him as relentless as the sea. "It occurs to me a way to foster trust between us is if we share more about ourselves." He rose, sauntered across the room, and refilled their glasses. "Tell me one thing about yerself that ye have yet to share with me. Just one thing. If we share one thing every night, soon, we shall know each other better than anyone else ever could."

"You go first," she said as she accepted the fresh glass of wine. She sank back into the cushions, watching him like a wee beastie eyeing an adversary.

Her response brought him a grin. Somehow, he had expected her to say that. The one thing he wished to share came to him in an instant. "My father wasna chieftain before me."

Her eyes narrowed as if she struggled to sort through her thoughts. "Then how did you become clan chief? And how did he afford this?" She held up her left hand and flashed the ring.

"He was war chief, as was his father before him. Both were paid verra well for their battle prowess." Quinn rolled the glass between his hands. "The chief before me was Dugh MacTaggart. My father's brother. A cruel bastard feared by one and all."

"He had no children?" She watched him over the rim of her glass as she took another sip.

"One. A son. My cousin Fingal. As vile a man as his father." He downed the whisky and rose for another. "I killed him."

"You *killed* him?"

"Aye," he said. "I came upon him ravaging a young lass." The memory of it still unleashed enough rage and disgust within him that he wanted to roar, but he maintained a quiet tone. "She was little more than a child." With his glass refilled, he returned to his seat. "So, I killed him."

"Good."

That one word meant the world to him. Filled him with hope. She understood and agreed with what he had done.

"So, I suppose when his father, your uncle, found out, that didn't go well?" She rocked forward, still hugging her knees, like a child enraptured by a bedtime story.

"No. Not well at all." That day haunted him worse than his failed marriage. "The day after, while in the great hall, Dugh avenged his son by killing my father, overcoming him in a surprise attack." He set down his glass before he crushed it. "My father's last words were *kill the bastard*. So, I did." Overcome by the memory, he shifted and stared out into the darkness, calming himself and shuttering the dark memories back into oblivion. "Some in the clan agreed when I claimed the chieftainship. Others did not." He finished his drink but didn't rise for another. None for now. Not when his blood had heated with the memory of his rage that day. "That is one of the many reasons why I am verra careful with my trust. The waterfall wasna the first attack on my person. I have spent the past five years weeding out those in this clan who dinna willingly grant me their fealty." He slid his hand beneath hers, then lifted it for a kiss. "I protect those faithful to me. I banish those who are not."

She nodded, her gaze locked on their hands. "I understand."

"Now, it is yer turn to share something."

She pulled her hand away and returned to hugging her knees. With a nervous shifting and quick intake of breath, she stared out the window instead of looking at him. "I hadn't spoken to my parents in over a year when they were killed in a car—in an accident."

"In a carriage accident?" She had the oddest way of speaking sometimes. As if forced to interrupt herself for reasons unknown. It made him wonder if she had an ailment that befuddled her speech or if she was lying again.

"Yes. A carriage accident." She held out her glass. "Another, please."

"Did they live far from ye? Could ye nay write to them?" he asked as he refilled her glass.

"London," she said in such a sharp tone that he turned and looked at her. "We lived in London. Only separated by a few blocks."

"I take it ye didna get along with them, then?"

She gave a small laugh that held more bitterness than mirth. "It wasn't that we didn't get on with each other." She shrugged as she accepted her wine. "They created me, and then they were done. I guess you could say I was like a limited-edition doll. Placed on a shelf. Brought out when it served to make them look like fine, upstanding people. They had a child because that was what married people did. Then they went on and lived their lives. Too busy to be bothered by something as troublesome as raising a daughter."

"Then who looked after ye?"

Her head tipped to one side, and a thoughtfulness pulled at her face. "Nannies, boarding schools." She shrugged again. "Anyone they could pay to keep me out their hair."

"Out of their hair?" She said the oddest things sometimes. He hoped someday he would understand her fully.

"Out of the way. Seen but not heard." She took a long drink, then set the glass back on the ledge. "There. That was my one thing for tonight."

He sensed she held back, not yet ready or willing to share more. Taking her hands in his, he pulled her around and leaned her back against his chest, wrapping his arms around her as she settled. "I will never ignore ye," he whispered with a soft kiss to her temple.

She shifted with a heavy sigh. "That's what they all say."

Ever so gently, he lifted the circlet off her head and placed it on the ledge. She had complained the other one had made her head ache. He had no doubt this one did the same. With a firm but gentle touch, he massaged her temples. "Does yer head pain ye?"

"I should ask you that," she said but closed her eyes and went all loose, relaxing under his touch.

"My head is fine." He undid the ribbons and fastenings holding her braid in place, taking care not to pull or snag. He freed her lovely tresses and combed his fingers through the shimmering silkiness. "Is this better?"

"Most definitely." But she kept fidgeting as though uncomfortable.

"What is it, lass?"

"Agnes laced me up so tight, I can hardly breathe in this position."

She sat up and stared down at the tied panel running from her low neckline down to a point past her waist. "If Mistress Kemp hadn't worked so hard on this gown, I'd slice the bloody thing open, so I could pull in more air."

"Here. Let me help." He had unlaced a few dresses in his time but wasn't about to share that with her. Especially not when she seemed to be warming back up to him. "They always tuck the ends so no one will see them. There. She hid them at the base."

"Thank Heavens." Evie pushed his hands out of the way. She made quick work of the lacing and stretched open the front of the bodice as wide as it would go. With a blissful smile, she pulled in a deep breath and released it. "I can use the full expanse of my lungs now. You have no idea how wonderful that feels."

"Aye, I do. I broke my ribs once, and old Merdrid wrapped them so tight I could hardly draw a breath."

"That should never be done," Evie said as she reached for her wine. "The patient needs to breathe as deeply as possible to prevent pneumonia."

"What?" Where did she find these strange words? They weren't Latin. Latin he would understand.

She stared at him as though startled. "Uhm...the ague. Infection in the lungs that clogs them." She slid the half-full glass back to the ledge and folded her hands in her lap. "Perhaps, I've had enough wine for the evening."

"Are ye unwell?" Her cheeks had flared to a fiery red, and matching patches of scarlet trailed down her slender throat and spread across her chest.

"No. I'm just...nervous." Still plucking at the ribbons dangling from the front of her dress, she gave him a shy look. "I guess we should just get on with it, shall we?"

His heart sank. Was this going to be just a duty to her? Like Annag had treated it? He shook his head. "If ye dinna wish to share my bed tonight—or any other night for that matter, ye dinna have to, Evie. I will never force myself upon ye."

With the corner of her bottom lip caught between her teeth, she studied him for a long moment, then scooted closer, yanking impatiently at her gown as she tried to maneuver back into his arms. With an irritated growl, she jumped up, peeled the silk creation off her shoulders, and let it drop to the floor. "I am so done fighting with this thing."

Her action inflamed him. Made his trews entirely too tight. The outline of her lithe body silhouetted by the candelabras made it impossible to take his eyes away.

She stepped out of the circle of silk, scooped it up, and tossed it over a chair. "Please don't misunderstand. It's lovely and all. I'm just not used to all this." She plucked at her chemise, then bent to untie her shoes. The loose neckline of her shift gaped open, revealing her tempting breasts.

Heaven help him. He could remain still no longer. "Let me assist ye, m'love." He knelt at her feet and made short work of the soft doeskin slippers. The delectable scent of her wafted across him, lifted him up, and coaxed him to continue. A sweet floral mixed with the promise of a woman ready to be pleasured. With his fingers resting on her ankles, he smiled up at her. "Sit, and I'll help ye with yer stockings, aye?"

"That would be lovely," she said in a breathless way that told him more than any words.

She seated herself among the cushions with her arms spread across the top of the bench. Open. Waiting. Ready.

He knelt at her feet and slid his hands to the ties above her knees. Once loosened, it took little effort to slip the stockings down and toss them aside. "So smooth," he murmured, running his hands higher. Warm and silky. Nay, better than silk or any velvet he had ever touched. He kissed the soft inner skin of her knee, then pressed his face against her thigh, forcing himself to slow down and take his time. *Savor her*, he silently repeated over and over.

She hitched her chemise higher as if coaxing him onward. But when he had kissed his way up her leg, she stopped him by planting a hand on top of his head. "Why don't we both finish ridding ourselves of these clothes before we continue?"

"As ye wish." He rose and shucked off his surcoat, belt, and boots. When she stood and skimmed her shift off over her head, he nearly dropped back to his knees. Her long, lean, naked glory glowed golden and magnificent in the candlelight.

"Well?" She arched a brow at his tunic and trews, then turned and reached for her wine, giving him a different mouth-watering view.

He stripped off his remaining clothes and pulled her into his arms, sloshing her wine down her front.

"Shame on you! You have spilled my wine." Delicious teasing dripped from every word of her scolding.

"Forgive me, m'lady." He scooped her up into his arms, then laid her across the bench. "Allow me to clean ye up." He hovered over her, hands planted on either side of her head.

She smiled and framed his face with her hands.

He took that as permission to lick away all traces of his clumsiness. The wine's fruity tartness mixed with the sweet saltiness of her skin made him hungrier. Never would he drink wine again without thinking of this delectable flavor.

"You do that quite well, sir."

"Sir?" He paused at her naval and lifted his gaze to hers. "I am yer husband, dear one. Never anything less."

She tickled a toe up the outside of his leg and gave a seductive rubbing of her knee against his flank. "Forgive me, *my husband*."

"Nay, m'love. I shall give ye a penance to make ye remember." He moved lower still, settling between her thighs to ensure he licked away every possible drop of the spilled wine.

"Penance," she repeated, arching to meet him. Her fingers tangled in his hair. She guided him with a wanton abandon that made him wonder if the penance punished him more than it did her. He ached with the need to take her.

After crying out and clutching him tighter, she gasped, "The floor."

The floor? Aye. The floor. More room. He gathered her up and lowered her to the floor in front of the bench, thankful that he'd given the housekeeper free rein to lavish the room with every comfort. The heavy weave beneath his knees was much kinder than hardwood. Although, at this point, he would readily kneel in hot coals if it meant he could sheath himself in Evie's wondrous heat. "I can wait no longer, m'love."

"Then don't," she said, pulling him down on top of her. She arched and shuddered. Welcomed him in with the same hunger burning through him.

"Wife," he groaned with a hard thrust.

"Husband," she gasped, matching his every move with her own.

"Ye are mine, Evie," he rasped, pounding harder. "Mine alone."

"That goes both ways." She bucked higher, matching his urgency. "Don't you ever take me for granted."

He grabbed her wrists, held them above her head, then ground in deep and halted. "I will never take ye for granted, m'love. I swear it."

"Convince me," she dared. "Make me believe it."

"As ye wish, m'lady." He obeyed the command until they screamed each other's names.

SUNLIGHT CREPT ACROSS the floor, making it seem as though she watched the minutes of her life slipping away. Sprawled on her side. Feather pillow plumped under her head. She was too exhausted to sleep. Or move. Her arms and legs felt heavy as lead. They had most definitely consummated their vows. So many times, in fact, she had lost count. Never had she experienced such a night. Such...well...words couldn't describe it. A thoughtful and generous lover, Quinn had given his all and then some.

The weight of his hand resting on her hip triggered a sad smile. She had married the man for protection. Not for love or money. But protection. What would those who knew her in the twenty-first century think of her now?

As he shifted in his sleep and pulled her back against him, a mixture of guilt and something she couldn't quite put her finger on burned in the center of her chest like a bad case of indigestion. Was she taking advantage of him? Was it bad to use him for protection when he was the one who offered it? She had always taken care of herself before. Never depended on anyone. But now. Here in this time. She had no choice. But was it deceitful?

He hugged her tighter, as if sensing her uncertainty. The gesture increased the guilt settling like a rock in her gut. She liked him. A great deal, in fact. Come to think of it, she liked him better than she had ever liked a man before. Past relationships paled in comparison to this. She'd never met a man quite like Quinn. He said what he thought, whether she wanted to hear it or not. Honest to a fault, the man didn't con or charm to get his way. He simply charged forward like a bull in a china shop.

"Sleep, m'wee hen," he said quietly in that deep intoxicating rumble that made her melt.

"How did you know I was awake?"

"Yer breathing." He kissed her shoulder, gave her a squeezing hug, then palmed one of her breasts. "When ye dozed for a wee spell last night, yer breathing slowed. Ye were at peace. All soft and warm. Ye're troubled now. Tense as a bowstring. What worries ye, Evie? I wish ye to find contentment in our life together. Are ye already regretting yer choice?"

She hugged his arm tighter around her. "No. I do not regret my choice." Brutal honesty nagged at her to be as blunt and forward as Quinn. "But my conscience says I'm taking advantage of you. Using you for protection instead of—love." There. She said it. The knot in her chest burned less and loosened a notch.

"I offered my protection." He rolled her to face him and tucked a finger under her chin. "And who is to say that as time passes, we willna grow to love one another?"

"Have you ever loved anyone?" She didn't know what made her ask. The words came out all on their own.

His dark brows drew together as he tickled the side of his thumb back and forth across her bottom lip. "I have known a fondness once or twice, but I wouldna say I have ever truly loved anyone." His thumb stilled, and the intensity of his gaze held her prisoner. "But I believe I could love ye, m'wee hen. Quite easily, in fact." His fingers slid along her jaw and combed their way into her hair. "Do ye think ye might one day be able to love me?"

"Possibly," she whispered, thrumming with the building energy between them. The same ravenous force that had consumed them last night. "I do care about you already."

"Well then." He grazed her mouth with his. "Caring is a promising start, aye?"

"I agree." She slid a leg up his side, her exhaustion chased away by the need to return to the mindless oblivion of blissful sensation. Everyone always told her to get out of her own head. Quinn provided that escape in quite a delightful manner.

He rolled her to her back. With an arm around her shoulders and a hand cupping her bottom, he returned to the slow rhythmic thrusting they had perfected last night. Their own seductive dance.

"I will love ye someday," he rasped as the tempo increased and the thrusts became a delicious pounding. "I will love ye with all my being."

"Someday," she gasped, raking her nails down his back. "Someday, I will love you, too." She arched to accept all that he gave. A keening groan escaped her as she peaked, and waves of pure luscious sensation washed across her.

He plunged to the hilt and halted, body taut and hard as stone. A fierce growling rumbled from deep within him. He threw back his head and roared, shuddering uncontrollably. Then he collapsed atop her, gasping.

When he went to roll to the side, she held him in place. "No. I like you on top of me."

"I dinna wish to crush ye, m'love." He propped on his elbows and pressed his forehead to hers. "I weigh a mite more than ye, ye ken?"

"I don't care." She slid her hands down his back, reveling in the sensations of a simple touch. Ripple of hard muscle beneath warm, smooth skin. Ridges of scars. The *feel* that made up all that was Quinn. "I'll let you know when I can't breathe." She held him tighter.

An insistent rapping on the door interrupted their serenity.

Quinn lifted his head and glared back over his shoulder. "Do you wish to die?" he shouted.

"Forgive me. We have received word that King John is imprisoned in the Tower of London." Kendric sounded ready to charge off into the fray. "Additional castles have also fallen to Edward."

"How close are they?" Quinn gave her a quick kiss and an apologetic smile as he leapt from the bed, yanked a pair of trews from his wardrobe, and stepped into them.

King Edward I. The summer of 1296. Evie struggled to figure out the exact date. She remembered this part of that long-ago history class because they had delighted in ripping apart that motion picture that had so inaccurately portrayed William Wallace and the beginning of Scotland's first battle for independence. "The date. What is today's date?"

Quinn halted halfway toward the door and gave her a puzzled look. "The date?"

"Yes. Today's date."

"Fourth of August, I believe. Why?"

Kendric knocked on the door again. "'Tis urgent we discuss this, Quinn. Their troops have nay gotten this far north yet, but we must be prepared."

"He's headed to Scone," she blurted without thinking. "He means to take the Stone of Destiny along with the Scottish crown, the archives, and the Black Rood of St. Margaret. August 8th. Edward will seize all those things in four days."

Quinn's eyes flared wide. Shock and defensive leeriness registered in his stance. In his expression. In everything about him.

She covered her mouth with one hand and held on tight. Oh, bloody hell. What had she just done?

"Go to the library, Kendric," Quinn ordered, without taking his gaze from her. "I will meet ye there."

"As ye wish." The war chief's hurried steps faded into the distance.

"How close to King Edward are ye, Evie?" Quinn eased toward her as if stalking big game, and she was the dangerous beast in question.

"Not close at all." She wouldn't lie, but she needed to figure out a cover story. Fast. "Never met the man, actually."

"Then why would ye say such a thing about the loss of Scotland's treasures? Even go so far as to give a specific date of when they would be abducted?"

She pulled in a deep breath and chewed on her bottom lip. Bloody, bloody hell. She wished she was better at making up believable lies.

"The truth, Evie."

"If I tell you the truth, you won't accept it." That was true enough. She still grappled with her current reality herself.

"Try." He stared at her with a look that isolated her, made her cold.

"I have to explain it in my bedchamber. There's something I need to show you." If she expected him to even come close to accepting her fantastical tale, she needed additional proof than what he had already seen. She had explained most of those things away, and he'd seemed to accept it. Her one hope was the one thing she had never shared with him. Never openly shown him. Hadn't even pulled it from its zippered pouch on her backpack since leaving the waterfalls.

He didn't comment. Just watched her.

She nodded toward the door. "Could you get my shift? It's still in there."

Without a word, he yanked open the door and disappeared into the sitting room. A few moments later, he returned with the linen chemise in hand and tossed it to the foot of the bed.

She slipped it on, shook it down in place, and hurried past him. "Come with me." A sense of doom filled her. Doom and an aching loss that hit her harder than she expected. Instinct told her that no matter what she told him, what proof she showed, he would never believe her. Any chance at winning his trust would be lost forever. She hated that. Hated it more than she had thought she would. Any caring, any possible love they might have shared would never happen now. An aching lump in her throat threatened to choke her. She didn't want to be alone again. She wanted Quinn.

"Over here." After fetching the key from her dressing table, she led him to the trunk where Lorna had locked away her things for safekeeping. She unlocked the chest and lifted the heavy lid. Before reaching for her backpack, she turned and looked up at him. "Promise me you won't interrupt and that you'll do your best to keep an open mind."

"I will do my best." He folded his arms across his chest, looking just as miserable as she felt. Why in Heaven's name hadn't she just kept her mouth shut?

"Too late now, Eves," she muttered as she pulled the backpack out of the chest and tossed it onto the bed. Before she revealed her proof, she would do her best to explain. "You remember when I tried to go behind the falls? When the ledge collapsed, and you dove in after me?"

"Aye."

"And you asked me why I had done it, and I told you I did it to get back where I belonged? Or something like that." The exact words didn't matter. She just needed to lay the groundwork.

"I remember, Evie. What has this to do with what ye said a few moments ago?" He resettled his stance as though bracing himself.

Bracing was good. He would need that.

"You thought I was talking about getting to the other side of the pool. Up on the embankment." She opened the backpack and noticed the tag sewn into its inside seam. Another bit of proof.

"Kendric is waiting in the library, lass. 'Tis urgent I speak with him."

"I assume that's your way of telling me to get to the point?" She really didn't blame him. People who rambled irritated her as well.

He didn't answer. Just arched a brow.

Fair enough. "I wasn't trying to get to the other side of the pool," she said. "I was trying to get back to my time."

"Yer time?" His eyes tightened into narrow, disbelieving slits.

"July 2019." She braced herself, not feeling nearly as safe and protected as she had just an hour ago.

"2019?" he repeated, then took a step closer. "Ye're a canny woman, Evie. I wouldha thought ye could come up with a better lie than that."

"Now is the part where I need you to not interrupt," she reminded, determined to make him understand. "I ended up here, in the thirteenth century, when I foolishly attempted to save a cat. The silly thing darted behind the falls. Screeching and crying like it was lost. I couldn't go off and leave it, so I followed."

He started to speak, but she held up a finger. "No interrupting, remember?"

She motioned for him to come closer. "As I slid my way behind the water, I felt kind of woozy, but then I was fine. I figured it was just because of all the noise. When I came out on the other side, I saw you." She shook her head. "But I didn't realize I had traveled back in time over seven hundred years until the next day." A hard swallow didn't ease the tightening of her throat. "When I found the second set of falls and everything was different, I knew something was wrong. That's why I asked you the date then and acted so strangely."

He flinched as though she had struck him, then scrubbed both hands down his face. "I want the truth, Evie. Are ye an English spy? One of Edward's mistresses? What? Tell me the truth."

"I am telling you the truth. Come here. Look at this tag and tell me what it says." He had to believe her. She couldn't bear the pain and accusation in his eyes.

With a disgusted sigh, he took hold of the tag and scowled at it. The scowl slowly dissolved to dark pensiveness. "Manufactured by Crance and Nolan. Established 2009."

"2009 was the year Crance and Nolan became a company. I bought this bag the year after they opened. In 2010. At that time, it was the best on the market. I needed it for a trip to Africa."

He didn't speak, just slowly lifted his head and locked eyes with her. She sensed his leeriness growing stronger, morphing into complete fear and disbelief. All the emotions played across his face.

"I volunteered abroad for a while. Did medical work to help others. That's what took me to Africa." Babbling didn't help, but she couldn't stop it. Exhaustion and desperation had shifted her mouth into high gear. She unzipped a pocket, pulled out her phone, and held down the button, praying it would power up. If it didn't, she could get a full charge one last time with the emergency battery charger stored in another pocket. Bitter satisfaction filled her when the screen lit up. She had a ninety-eight percent charge. Plenty to show Quinn the date and time stamps on the pictures she had taken to send to Maggie and Human Resources. "Here. Below this picture of the tourist sign for the waterfalls. See the date and time?"

He stared at the thing as if it would attack him.

She held her finger down on the photo, and the image came alive. Leaves fluttered in the breeze, and the people moved because she had taken the photograph with the live image option on the camera app.

All color drained from his face. He backed up a step. "So, ye are a witch, then?"

"No." She swiped through her photos to one taken in front of Finchcrest and held it for him to see. "I am a surgeon at this hospital. Finchcrest. In London. I am lost in time. Trapped in the year 1296, where if I tell the truth, everyone will want to burn me at the stake because what really happened to me is too impossible to understand." She shoved the phone into his hands and showed him how to move through the photos. "Here. Look. This is the life I left behind. Places. People. Medical notes. All of them time stamped. Dated, so you can see I'm not lying."

His gaze slowly lifted from the phone and settled on her. He stared at her. His expression blank. Unreadable. The only hint at his thoughts was the muscle ticking in his clenched jaw. After what seemed like forever, he threw the phone back on the bed, stormed out the door, and slammed it shut behind him.

Locks clicked with a heart-stopping clank of doom. Evie sank to the floor. It was all over. She had no doubt that Quinn's offer of protection had just been rescinded. She was on her own. Again.

CHAPTER THIRTEEN

H OW COULD IT be true? How could anything she had said be true? Quinn charged down the steps, trying to outrun the nightmare his new wife had laid at his feet. He halted partway down. *His wife.* The woman he had offered his protection. He sagged back against the cold hard wall and drew a shaking hand across his eyes. Evie. Not just any *woman*. But Evie, the one who already held his heart.

Last night came back to him in a flood of wondrous sensations and fierce emotions. He raked both hands through his hair, fighting against the memories. She had loved him. And he had loved her. Maybe not in words, but with each caress, every intimacy shared, they had melded their bond. Given it strength. God help him, he did love her. Even now. After everything she had said, he still loved her.

He pulled in deep breaths and blew them out as he lowered himself to sit on the steps. He could neither move forward nor go back. Not until he calmed and figured out this impossibility. With arms propped on his knees, he held his head in his hands. The grey stone stairs stared up at him, silent and unhelpful.

The future. The year 2019, no less. Scratching at the stubble of his beard, he concentrated on the facts, remembering every detail. All the way back to the day they met. The tiny torch she controlled with the flick of a finger. The white pebbles that lessened the pain in his head. Her tasty bars of power. Her knowledge. A guilty uneasiness squeezed his chest. She had saved Fern and the wee bairns. Never had she done any harm.

Her inability to tell a convincing lie pushed to the forefront of his turmoil as if pleading her case. He saw through her as easily as looking through water from a Highland spring. Evie couldn't lie to save her soul. The lass was from the future. Not a witch. Nor one of the Fae. But a woman who had somehow tumbled back through time. The eerie certainty weighed heavy in his gut like a poorly digested meal.

He pushed himself up from the steps and continued downward, at a loss for what to do now. If anyone else ever found out, it would not bode well. They would accuse her of witchery and hunt her down no matter how hard he tried to protect her. As he passed the archway to the second floor, he paused, then backed up a step. Fern. His sister would know what he should do. She had always possessed a quickness for decisions that he envied. He hurried down the corridor and knocked on the door to her suite, hoping that arse, Gilbert, wasn't about.

Her maid Janet answered, bobbing a quick curtsy and throwing the door open wide when she saw it was him. "My chieftain. Her ladyship will be verra pleased to see ye."

"She is strong enough for a visit?" He prayed she would be. If not, he would have to sort out this mess himself, and he preferred to do it with the help of Fernie's level-headed opinion.

"Aye, m'chieftain. I shall let her know ye're here." Janet lumbered across the sitting room and slipped inside the bedchamber.

When the door opened again, it was Fern, taking one slow step at a time. "And why are ye not still in bed with yer wife getting her with yer first child?" Even with the dark circles under her eyes, they still sparkled with mischief.

"I need to speak with ye. Badly."

All mischief left her, replaced with concern. She held out a hand. "Help me to my chair, aye? I'm still fearsome sore."

"I imagine ye would be," he said. "She cut ye open like field dressing a deer."

"Thank ye for the observation, brother." She shot him a stern look as she settled into her cushions. "Now, what is wrong? I see it in yer face. Have the English gotten to our people?"

He glanced around, noting that Gilbert's chamber door was closed. "Where is yer husband?"

"Gone to the village. The tanner wished for help with his books." Fern folded her hands across her middle. "Isla is getting Evalie and Alexander settled for their morning nap."

"Evalie and Alexander. Proper names." Although he wasn't certain she would agree when he told her what he had to say. It was obvious she had named her daughter after Evie.

"Out with it, Quinn. Ye know I canna stand a dawdler." Her hands twitched atop the much smaller swell of her stomach, her thumbs tapping impatiently.

"Evie finally told me where she is from." He stared down at the floor, unsure how to continue.

"And why is that so dire?"

He leaned forward, lowering his voice. "She said she is from the year 2019. From London. In the future."

Fern blinked as though waking from a daze. "2019, ye said?"

"Aye."

Her head tilted first to one side and then the other. She studied him as if trying to see into his mind. "Do ye believe her?"

"I dinna ken what to believe." He scrubbed a hand across his mouth, wishing he could pour all he knew into his sister's head so she would know all the unbelievable facts, too. He had never done well with explaining. "I think...aye, perhaps, I do."

With a thoughtful look, she pursed her lips. "Has she ever caused ye harm? Or caused anyone harm?"

"Nay." Evie didn't have it in her to harm anyone. He for certain believed that about her.

"She saved my life and the life of my bairns." Fern gave him an impressed nod. "Perhaps, she is from the future to know the things she knows."

"Aye, but what should I do?" He sagged forward, propping his forearms on his legs and wringing his hands. "What should I do, Fernie?"

"I am going to ask ye again. Do ye believe her? Do ye believe she is being truthful with ye?"

"Aye, Fernie. I do." He slowly shook his head. "I dinna ken how what she says could possibly be so, but there is so much proof to what she claims." A heavy sigh escaped him. "And the poor lass couldna tell a lie if her life depended on it."

"Her life does depend on it." With a slight wince, Fern eased herself up from the chair and turned toward the bedroom. "I am weary, brother. I must get my sleep when the babes do." After another few steps, she paused and smiled back at him. "Tell no one of this, and protect Lady Evaline as long as she does no harm. I trusted her with my life and the lives of my children. I owe her. For my sake, grant her yer protection and trust her until she proves ye shouldna do so, aye?"

"Ye wouldna think me foolish to trust her then? To keep her as my wife?"

Her smile widened. "Nay, brother. I have thought ye foolish for many things. But not for this." With her hand on the door latch, she paused. "And I see more than worry for the clan in yer eyes. I believe ye already love her." Before he could reply, she went into her room and closed the door behind her.

Aye, he loved her. May God have mercy on his soul. But that didn't mean he knew what to do with her. And then there was Kendric and the English to deal with. He pushed up from the chair and headed for the library, knowing exactly what he would tell his friend. He knew the man's thirst for battle. The war chief would want to send warriors to find the nearest English troops and oust them. But if what Evie said was true, the English would stay far south of them. At least for a while. That would give them time to plan for when their troops made it this far north. Time they could use to strengthen their fortifications and better protect those who trusted them.

He strode into the library, determined to concentrate on the matter at hand and give no hint about what Evie had told him. They couldn't prevent it, anyway. The abbey near Scone, where the Stone of Destiny was kept, was too far south to reach in time to protect it from Edward. They might make it there by August 8th, but it would be a hard ride, leaving them weary and ill-prepared for a defensive confrontation.

"Forgive me for interrupting yer time with yer new bride," Kendric said as he paced back and forth in front of the wall of books. "But we must make haste and ride out to push the English back."

"Have ye seen them anywhere inside our borders?" Quinn went to the sideboard and poured himself a drink. The difficulty of the morning demanded it. When Kendric didn't answer, he turned and held up another glass. "Yerself?"

"Nay, Quinn."

"To the drink or the fact that the English havena yet showed, and ye're overreacting to the information from the messenger?" He waited, knowing Kendric would not appreciate the wording of the question.

His friend's face hardened into a familiar scowl. "Both," he spit as though the word tasted bad. "What would ye have me do? Take no action, so they perceive us as defenseless?"

"If ye take all our forces south," Quinn said. "We will be defenseless, as well as foolhardy." He waved his glass to encompass the entire room. "We have a fine, large keep here, my friend. Double...nay...triple the guards and increase our stores. Make our stronghold even fiercer." He shook his head as he strolled closer. "Dinna leave our people unprotected with few to walk the walls and keep them safe. Spend yer energies on warning those who dinna live within these walls. Bring those unable to defend themselves back to the keep for protection. They can return to their homes once things settle."

Kendric pounded his fist on the map spread across Quinn's large desk. The candelabra wobbled, and melted wax splattered everywhere. "We must take a stance! Not herd our people into a pen and wait for the slaughter."

"We will take a stance." Quinn downed his whisky and upended the empty glass on the sideboard. "Our stance will be within the protection of these walls." He could tell by Kendric's expression that the man strongly disagreed. Longtime friend or not, he would not be countermanded. "Do you understand me?"

Kendric's scowl twisted tighter, but he gave a curt nod. "By yer leave then, my chieftain."

Quinn dismissed him with a nod, regretting that he had angered his friend but knowing he had done the right thing. Their first duty was their people. Many a castle fell into enemy hands while its men fought elsewhere. He would not allow that to happen here.

He walked over to the window and leaned against the frame. As he rubbed his chin against his shoulder, he drew in a deep breath, then closed his eyes. Her warm, alluring scent clung to him, reminding him of things he'd rather not think of right now. What to do about Evie? What had he ever done, what sin had he committed for Fate to place such a dilemma in his lap? This was worse than trying to discover who wanted him dead. Because this risked his heart as never before.

A hesitant pecking at the door made him turn. Lorna and Agnes stood side by side, worry wrinkling their brows and their hands clasped in supplication.

"Aye?" They wouldn't speak until he granted permission. "What is it?"

"Yer lady wife," Lorna started, then stopped and gave a hard swallow.

"Go on," he encouraged.

"Her bedchamber is locked from the outside, my chieftain," she finished, taking care to keep her gaze lowered. "We dinna have the key."

"We called out to her to see if she had need of anything," Agnes said, almost whispering, as she kept her head bowed. "She didna answer even when we rapped hard on the door and called out to her a second time." She stole a glance up at him and gave a quick dip of her chin. "Mrs. Dingwall said for us to tell ye so we might know what ye wished us to do."

What should they do? Aye, that was the question of the day, and dawdling about did nothing to answer it. Time to speak to Evie and sort this impossible mess out. But to do so, he needed privacy with his unusual wife. With a flip of his hand, he shooed the maids away. "Get with Cook and order yer mistress a fine tray to break her fast." As they turned, another thought came to him. "And hot water," he called out to them. "For her morning broth." Her precious tea. Now, he understood her dread about using up the last of it.

"Aye, m'chieftain." Both girls dipped another curtsy and scurried off.

He stared after them, battling with himself. With a determined rolling of his shoulders, he charged forward. Time to face her. Talk to her. Perhaps he shouldn't have locked her in her room, but instinct had taken over. The need to protect himself and his people. When he explained, surely, she would understand. At least, he prayed she would.

When he reached her door, he paused, focusing on the latch as if the bit of brass would grant him wisdom. Instead of unlocking it and pushing in, he knocked.

Silence answered.

"Evie?" he called out softly, the bitterness of remorse flooding through him. He unlocked the bolt and eased the door open a crack. The snuffed candle left the room dim and filled with shadows. The window covering remained closed, refusing to flood the chamber with sunlight. He crept deeper into the room, squinting at the mounds of pillows on the bed. Maybe she slept? Sometimes women wept until exhaustion overcame them. Didn't they? She had looked ready to weep when he left her. The memory of her fear, her lonely urging for him to believe her, haunted him. She had seemed so…lost. His chest ached. A burning hole had taken the place of his heart. Evie had told him the truth, and he had deserted her.

"Evie?" He tapped on the privacy screen that partitioned off the chamber pot and washstand from the rest of the room. Continued silence. The type of empty quiet that raised the hairs on the back of his neck. He stepped around the screen, and his gut clenched, almost bending him double. No hit to his middle had ever left him as winded as he was right now.

Every corner of the room was empty. Evie was gone. She had found a way to leave him.

⟫⟫⟩⟨⟨⟨

STILL ON THE floor, leaning on the bedpost for support, Evie stared at the locked door for what seemed like forever. It was as if time stood still. Held her suspended. Made her achingly numb. At least most of her was numb. Her heart hurt like it had been ripped in two.

He hadn't believed her. Even after all she showed him. He still hadn't believed. Of course, she didn't much blame him. After all, it was a large pill to swallow. She covered her face with shaking hands and bowed her head. What would become of her now? What could she do? How would she survive in this godforsaken century without Quinn? Not because he protected her, but because, damn and blast it all, the bloody fool had made her love him. That hard-headed Highlander who thought himself invincible had weaseled his way into her heart.

"Pull it together, Eves," she whispered as she lifted her head. "You're on your own now. Done it before. Just need to do it again." She grabbed hold of the bedpost and pulled herself to her feet. "Time to get moving. I'll be damned straight to hell if I sit here and wait for them to come for me." If he didn't believe and accept her for the oddity she was, then by jings, she would find a way out and make it on her own. Somehow.

She repacked her backpack with everything from the twenty-first century and then some. As much as she longed to wear her jeans, she refrained. No. If she was to fit in and survive this medieval hell, she had to dress the part. She relented a bit and wore her boots. The long skirts should hide them well enough. She donned the plainest kirtle in the wardrobe, braided her hair, and covered it with the fresh white kertch that Agnes had explained all married women wore.

As she fastened a braided leather belt low around her waist, her wedding ring caught her attention. She stared at it, twisting it to make the emerald sparkle. His mother's ring. He had touched her heart when he placed it on her finger. The beauty of the stone meant nothing to her. What it represented meant it all. With hard, fast blinks against the threat of tears, she slipped it off and set it on the table. The ring needed to stay with Quinn.

Backpack on her shoulders, she lifted the candle and examined the walls closer. If Fern's room had an entrance to tunnels, surely hers did, too. At least, she hoped so, because if it didn't, she would have to rappel out the window with whatever she could fashion into a line. No matter what, she was leaving.

Fern's opening to the tunnels had been hidden behind a tapestry. Evie turned and eyed the one with the demonic-looking bunnies. "What better place to hide a door?" She flipped a corner back and peered behind it. Disappointment made her huff. Nothing but a solid wall of stone. So much for that idea.

She returned to the center of the room and turned in a slow circle, determined not to give up. There weren't any other tapestries large enough to conceal a way out. What else would hide the door to the tunnels? Her focus locked on the two monstrous wardrobes and the bed. It had to be behind one of those three. She fished out her penlight and flashed it behind the bed curtains hanging at the head of the bed. Another solid wall of stone blocks.

There had to be a tunnel entrance. Wouldn't they wish for the lady of the keep to run and hide if they ever came under attack? She shined the light behind the wardrobe to the right of the door. Nothing but solid wall. And what looked like a dried-up mouse. Lovely.

"You are my only hope," she informed the matching wardrobe on the left. With her cheek pressed to the wall, she tried to see behind it, but something blocked her view. She stepped back and frowned at the thing. Why couldn't she see behind it? She tried again from the other side but had no luck. Apparently, she would have to move it.

"This should be interesting." She slid her backpack off and leaned it against the door. With her back pressed against the side of the large, solid mahogany monstrosity, she shoved with all her might. It didn't budge. Not the slightest centimeter.

"I have moved big furniture before," she told the thing as she set her shoulder against it and pushed again. It didn't even shudder. "Stupid thing!" She thumped the side of the cupboard and immediately regretted it. "Blast it!"

After shaking off the sting of the hit, she returned her backpack to her shoulders, then paced back and forth in front of the closet while twiddling her penlight between her fingers. "I can't see behind you or move you, so you have to be hiding what I'm looking for."

A book about a wardrobe leading to a magical place came to mind. She pulled open the double doors. Penlight on, she pushed aside the clothes hung on the pegs along the back wall. "There you are, my precious exit." At least she hoped that hinged panel was her way out. She popped it open and swept the tiny beam of light into the black void. "How about if we use our full-grown flashlight, shall we?"

She clicked off the penlight and returned it to the safety of its slot in the backpack. After crawling all the way inside the wardrobe, she crouched and rummaged through her possessions. There was the awesome tactical flashlight the infomercial had convinced her she couldn't live without. In a moment of weakness, she had ordered the thing. Thank goodness it had turned out to be legit. The small black flashlight had a beam brighter than a searchlight. She clicked it on and closed the wardrobe's outer doors. At least if someone walked in, they wouldn't discover her right away.

The light revealed a narrow set of stone steps leading downward. She leaned into the hole and cast the light upward. Nothing but cobwebs fluttering down from a massive beam of wood.

She sat on the edge, her boots planted firmly on the top step. "I have to leave," she argued to any entity wishing to listen. A gutted emptiness threatened to reduce her to a curled-up mess of tears. She sniffed and cleared her throat. No. Not the time for tears. She would weep for all she had lost later. If she survived. She clenched her teeth and shoved the doubt away. No. *When* she survived and started a new life, she would cry for what might have been.

She cared about Quinn, but that didn't matter because he obviously didn't care about her. If he had, he would've believed her. She admitted to a maybe when it came to that, but surely, in the end, he would've come around. Instead, he had locked her in her room and stormed off. Probably headed to fetch guards or something. She made an angry swipe at a determined tear and lifted her chin. "Stop it, Eves.

No wallowing, remember?"

With a hard yank of her pack through the narrow opening, she started down the steps, pausing only long enough to close the hatch behind her. She needed it to look as if she had never found the escape tunnel. At least, she hoped it was an escape tunnel.

One hand on the cool damp wall, the other clutching the flashlight, she eased her way down the narrow steps. Something scratched and scurried somewhere, making her skin crawl. She hated rodents. They spread so many diseases. Water dripped and echoed. She halted. Water? What if she came out somewhere and had to swim for it? The fortress was built overlooking the ocean. "Well then, you will just have to swim for it." There was no turning back. Not after all she had seen in Quinn's eyes.

"Onward, Eves." It made her feel better to talk out loud. Helped her feel not so alone. The psychologist reporting to Human Resources would have had a field day with that one.

After she descended for an endless span of time, she halted again, reconsidering the situation. She wished she had packed some food. At least some bread or something. As it was, she might still have a power bar or two. She couldn't remember. With a shake of her head, she continued on. It didn't matter. She would figure it out. One obstacle at a time. The current priority was to escape whatever judgment Quinn had reached.

The rhythmic shushing of moving water echoed through the darkness. She tipped an ear toward it and concentrated. Strong waves. Definitely not some sort of underground moat or cesspool. The steps led to the sea. She hoped they also led to some dry ground and not a submerged chamber. "Press on, Eves. Press on." No sense wasting worries on what might be.

As silly as it seemed, the darkness didn't look as dark. With a hand firmly planted on the wall, she clicked off the flashlight and waited for her eyes to adjust. Off in the distance, as the steps became less and less steep, a light glimmered, and the sound of waves crashed louder. She hoped that meant there was somewhere to walk as well.

She clicked the flashlight back on and hurried down the last of the steps. As the passage opened up, relief made her breathe easier. Blessed daylight shone right up ahead. The tunnel opened out into a hidden cave with plenty of room to walk and a small opening that would take her outside to the shore. Even when the tide came in, the high, broad shelf of stone wouldn't be submerged. She scurried around the perimeter and stepped out into the sunshine, blinking against the brightness.

On the cliff above loomed MacTaggart Keep. That meant if she went left, she would find herself along the shores of Cromarty Firth. To the right lay the mouth of the Moray Firth and open ocean. Fishing settlements might line the banks of Cromarty. Maybe even a village. If she expected to survive, she needed to find someone who would pay her to work. At what? She didn't have a clue. But surely, she could do something. First, she needed to put some distance between herself and Quinn. She wished she had some idea where his clan started and stopped. He had told her where the borders of his land lay, but now she couldn't recall what he had said.

The rocky strand made for difficult walking, especially since she did her best to hug the cliffside. If anyone above happened to look down, she would be spotted right off with her white kertch and blue dress. She snatched the cloth off her head and tucked it into her belt. It could be worn later. Around people. When the effectiveness mattered.

Terns keened overhead. Waves crashed. A brininess filled the air, leaving behind the saltiness she tasted every time she licked her lips. If someone followed her, she would never hear them. Constant glances behind slowed her. It looked as if the cliffside sloped lower up ahead. She climbed to the grassy hillside, pausing to tie the kertch back over her hair, hoping it would disguise her. Quinn's people had only seen her for a short time at the wedding feast with an uncovered head.

Hopefully, none would remember her well enough to recognize her.

She peeped over the low embankment, scanning the horizon for people or dwellings. Nothing but tall grass, clusters of gorse, and a few trees here and there. "Brilliant." She scurried onward, yanking at her skirts as they snagged on thistles and bushes. Now and then, she paused and glanced back at the sprawling keep. Somehow, she got the impression the fortress disapproved of her escape. The arrow slits and windows scowled at her with a formidable glare, silently swearing she would fail. No. She would not fail. They didn't know who they dealt with.

After adjusting the straps of her pack on her shoulders, she hitched up her skirts and ran, heading for the closest clump of trees. She shouldn't stay out in the open. Once they discovered her gone, they would initiate a search.

When she reached the safety of the small wood, she halted to catch her breath. A minute or two of rest was most definitely in order. The first energizing spike of adrenaline had waned, leaving her to battle weariness alone. She sat with her knees bent and arms propped atop them, surrounded by the knobby roots of the largest tree. As soon as she fully caught her breath, she'd run to the next copse. It would be a hearty jaunt to that one, deeper inland and farther down the glen. But that woods was larger. She would rest longer there.

The distinct sound of thundering hoofbeats made her roll to her belly and keep her head low. From the sound of it, the horses were headed toward the keep. Not away from it. Whoever that was, they weren't searching for her. She grabbed hold of her pack and eased to the edge of the temporary hideaway.

A long stretch of open ground lay between her and the next forest. Long enough that it made her wonder if she should wait until nightfall. Another look back at the entirely-too-close skirting wall convinced her not to wait. Guards walked the wall. If she could see them, they could see her. At least the height of the grass was well above her waist. If any more riders passed by, she could duck. That would work. As long as she spotted them before they spotted her.

After a deep breath, she charged forward, once again wishing she had worn her close-fitting jeans instead of the impossible yardage of linen and wool skirts. When she had almost reached the next line of trees, the distant sound of horns came to her on the wind. Loud horns. Blaring a long time and accompanied by drums. An alarm. Either the English had made it this far north and her history professor had forgotten to teach that part, or the alarm sounded because of her. At the moment, she wasn't certain which option would be worse.

She ran hard the last of the way, not stopping until she made it deep inside the protection of the trees. When she felt sheltered enough, she dropped to her knees. Doubled over, she hugged herself, fighting to catch her breath. Heaven help her. If anyone happened to be close, they would find her from all her wheezing and coughing.

As her labored breathing slowed, she pulled her water bottle from the pack and allowed herself a small sip. She wanted to guzzle it but refrained. Who knew where the next spring might be? Every resource needed to be conserved and rationed. Everything. Another sip, and she'd make her way to the far edge of the trees and see what lay ahead. She wished she had noticed additional details on the ride in, but no sense lamenting that now. All she could do was keep moving until...

She clenched her teeth to keep from sobbing. Until what? They found her and killed her? Tortured her? They'd covered that in history class as well. What would she do if people didn't believe she belonged here? Especially with her bloody English accent.

"Stop it!" she ordered in a ragged whisper. Panicking helped nothing. One task at a time. She needed to focus on one task at a time. Find the basics first. Food. Water. Shelter. She wouldn't stop moving until she checked those three goals off her list. At least, for today. She had the distinct feeling that every day would bring a new set of priorities, whether she wished it or not.

CHAPTER FOURTEEN

"S HE LEFT?" DUGAN backed up a step and swept a quick glance around the stable. As a lad led a horse down the aisle, he craned his neck and watched the boy until he'd gone well past the stall. "Why did she leave?" he asked while still keeping watch.

Rosstan thumped Dugan's shoulder. "It doesna matter *why*, ye arse." He threw out his chest and gave Quinn a curt nod. "Ye know ye can always depend on me." With a backward glance at Dugan, he added, "No questions asked."

"I thought it might help us to know where the lady might ha' gone." Dugan shuffled in place and drew up like a sullen child.

Quinn tightened the straps of his saddle, paying no attention to their banter. "She canna be far. Nary a horse is missing." He stopped himself, clutching the worn leather of his gear as yet another memory about Evie came to mind. "She doesna ken how to ride." With a stern shake to free himself of the thought, he gathered up the reins and led his horse out of the stable. "I would welcome yer company in finding her."

"Shall I fetch Kendric as well?" Rosstan followed close behind with his own horse in tow. Dugan and his mount exited the stable last.

"Kendric is busy ensuring our clan is secure from the English. I willna take him from that task." Quinn hoisted himself up into the saddle. With a nod at Dugan and Rosstan, he led the way out the gate.

Once they cleared the skirting wall, Dugan brought his mount even with Quinn's, riding to his left. "Have ye any hint of where she might she go?" He leaned forward, looking past Quinn to shoot Rosstan a hard look. "And that's a valid question to help find her, ye ken?"

Rosstan laughed.

"I have no idea," Quinn said. That was the problem at hand. Evie didn't know the people or the land. Where would she try to hide? "The tunnel from her room ends in the cave on the shoreline beneath the keep. We keep a boat there."

"Ye feel she would try to manage the sea when she canna even ride a horse?" Rosstan shaded his eyes with one hand as he scanned the landscape.

Quinn didn't know what the lass might try. She was afraid and probably angry, as well. He just prayed she had worn the garb of this time instead of her strange clothes. At least that way, if anyone came upon her before he did, she might be some safer. If anyone harmed her, he'd hunt them down and kill them. "The guards on the wall reported nothing on the seaside."

"Did they check the cave for the boat?" Rosstan asked.

"I sent them there but couldna bear to wait for them to report back. They'll send a runner if the boat's missing." Quinn slowed his mount to a stop and studied the land he had loved since birth, wishing it would share the secret of Evie's whereabouts. "I feel in my heart she would keep to the land. 'Twould be easier going for her."

"If she nay wishes to be seen, she'll keep to the trees," Dugan said with a thoughtful scowl at the scattering of trees dotting the glen. "There's but a few copses to choose from. Shall we separate to cover more ground?"

Dugan's suggestion held promise. If she took to the meadow and not the shoreline, she couldn't be far.

"If she followed the water's edge, she's had time to reach Muiry. I know it's mainly docks and fishermen's shanties, but this time of day, their women will be out mending nets and baskets. They could tell us if they've seen her." Rosstan resettled his grip on the reins. His horse side-stepped as if eager to be on the move. "Shall I go there and see?"

"Aye." Quinn nodded. "Check Muiry. Dugan and I will scour the trees."

With a curt tip of his head, Rosstan wheeled about and rode off at a hard gallop.

"West or south, my chieftain?" Dugan sat ready to ride, alert as a dog waiting for a stick to be thrown.

"Search west 'til ye reach the village. If ye ask about her there, mind yer words. I'd as soon keep this as quiet as possible. I've already had to share this with too many." His wife running off the day after their wedding night shamed him, and he had no one to blame but himself. If he had not locked that feckin' door or left her feeling that he'd turned on her, he'd not be searching for her now. Of course, at that time, he hadn't known what to think about all she had shared. "Dinna leave a blade of grass untouched, Dugan. I want her back, ye ken?"

"Aye, my friend." Dugan gave him a sympathetic look. He spoke with uncharacteristic quietness. "We will find her, cousin. Dinna fash yerself."

Quinn watched him ride away, then spurred his mount toward the cluster of trees closest to shore. It was naught but a smattering of scraggly birches and one or two decent-sized oaks, but she could've hidden there for a short time while she gathered her bearings. The leaf mold beneath the trees appeared disturbed. He studied the ground closer. Not the work of a wild boar foraging for food. The layers of leaves weren't laid aside as though plowed by a snout. 'Twas a delicate roughing up of the woodland floor. Maybe deer. Hopefully, Evie. He rode in and out among the trees, eyeing the tracks until he reached the other side.

Across the way waited a much larger woods that would serve as a fair enough shelter for the evening. He headed toward it at a hard gallop. All the while scanning the sea of tall grasses rippling in the wind. The sedge was tall enough to hide her. If she kept her wits about her, she could lay flat and go undiscovered. He hoped she hadn't realized that.

The next stand of trees flourished in the dip between twin hillocks rolling across the glen. Oaks outnumbered the birch and rowan populating this forest. Grand trees big enough to provide ample cover this time of year with their thick, leafy canopies. He paused just as he entered the tree line and listened. Water. The trickling teased like quiet laughter. Aye, this place would be a grand bit of cover for a night or two.

The ground sloped downward on both sides, hinting that the copse hid a shallow ravine at its base. Gnarled roots of the ancient trees clutched the ground like knobby fingers coated in velvety green moss. Odd to find such a forest this far north and so close to the sea, but the lay of the land sheltered the woodland enough to allow it to thrive and mimic the forests farther south.

A gentle breeze shushed through the leaves as if telling them to keep their secrets from him. Birdsong serenaded his search. A red squirrel fussed and chittered, sounding the alarm that an intruder had entered their shady sanctuary. Evie had to be here. Fresh water. Wild cherries. Blackberries. Sloes everywhere. If she knew of such things, she could hide here and do well. At least for a little while.

He started to call out to her but stopped. Nay, she wouldn't answer. If anything, she would hide as best she could. He would have to hunt her with the stealth of stalking skittish game. Slipping out of the saddle without a sound, he quietly patted his mount. "Wait here, Fenn. I dinna wish our lady to hear us."

The horse would stay in place 'til sundown, then return to the keep, with or without him. As it had done on the day of the attack at the waterfall.

As silent as a spirit of the woods, Quinn slipped through the trees, heading toward the gurgling burn. Evie was canny enough to go to water. At least she would if she came this way. The farther he went with no sign of her, the more doubt became a fearsome demon gnawing at his gut. If she hadn't come this way, he wasted precious time on this hunt.

He reached the water. The shallow stream danced across a bed of multicolored stones, rounding them with its endless caress. A double handful of the cold sweet stuff refreshed him. He drank his fill and wet his face. As he crouched beside the trickling burn, he trailed his fingers in the water and silently prayed, *help me find her.*

When he lifted his head, the tiniest flash of white at the base of a tree on the embankment across the way caught his attention. He went still, locked on the bit of pure whiteness that didn't belong among the shadowy greens and browns of the copse. Quiet and slow, he rose to his full height. Enough of the white showed to make it recognizable as cloth.

The urge to charge toward it raged through him, but he held fast. Nay, even though he could easily outrun her, he didn't wish to frighten the lass. Heel to toe, he eased toward her without the slightest sound. She must be sleeping behind the rise of that root. Completely spent from her escape. His hands twitched with every step, making him cringe when his knuckles popped. She didn't move. Poor lass. He had mistreated her into exhaustion.

Hopefulness filled him as he rounded the base of the tree. But then he dropped to his knees, as all hope left him. The white cloth, a woman's kertch, had snagged on a broken branch and remained in place while its mistress had continued on her way. Its brightness revealed its newness to the area. That soothed him somewhat. Surely, it belonged to Evie. She had to have come this way. He snatched it up and buried his face in it, breathing it in like a hound on the hunt. Heaven help him. It was hers. Even if struck blind, he could find her by her scent. As he clutched it to his chest, he bowed his head. "Forgive me," he whispered. "I am so verra sorry."

A loud splash made him jerk around and search the stream. Nothing out of the ordinary appeared. Harried rustling through the forest floor's dried leaves yanked his attention back to the hillside beyond the tree where he knelt. "Evie!" He sprang up and bolted after her, not caring that he had shouted like a lovesick lad. It didn't matter. She was so close.

She stumbled and landed on her knees but scrambled back to her feet and took off again. Not as fast this time. In fact, she limped.

"Evie, wait! I willna hurt ye. I swear it." He was almost to her. A bit closer, and he'd snag hold of a loop on her pack and halt her.

She swerved under a low-hanging branch and tripped again. The weight of her bag threw her off balance, sending her tumbling down the hillside into the stream. Skirts soaked, she clambered out of the water, then collapsed, pounding on the ground with her fist. "Bloody hell! Bloody, bloody hell!"

As he drew closer, she clawed a rock free and threw it at him. "Leave me alone! Just let me go! Haven't you done enough?"

He halted within three strides of her. She reminded him of a snared rabbit—terrified, fighting for its last bit of life. The vision tormented him, pushed him down to his knees. "Evie—"

"Leave me be. I'll just go away and won't bother anyone." She shoved her wet skirts out of the way and leaned to one side, massaging the lower part of her right leg. Desperation filled her eyes and lent a tremor to her voice. "You should know I would never hurt anyone. So, just let me go. All right?"

"I canna let ye go," he said quietly. "I..."

"What? I suppose you're going to say you have sworn some sort of oath to the Church to burn all witches? Is that it? Well, I'm not a witch. I told you that." Her face crumpled as a high-pitched sob escaped her. She angrily swiped at the tears and gasped for breath. "I bloody wish there was such a thing as magic. I'd spell myself back home and be done with this godforsaken time."

He stared at the ground, letting her rant as long she wished. It was fear making her beg for her life. It ripped through him because he alone had sent her into such a state. When at last she quieted, he lifted his head and pressed a hand to his chest. "I canna let ye go," he repeated softly. "Because I love ye, Evie."

She stared at him, tears streaking through the grime on her cheeks. "Are you really that cruel? You would toy with me like that just to con me into going with you so you could throw me into some sort of dungeon? So, you can torture me? Well, stop it!" Another hiccupping sob escaped her. "Haven't you tortured me enough?"

"I mean it when I say I love ye, my own. Never have I told anyone that I love them. Not ever." Not even his mother. Yet another regret he would carry to the grave. "And I believe everything ye told me, Evie. I promise, I believe."

"Well, I don't believe you."

Leeriness. Fear. Doubt. It all held her prisoner, poisoning her against him. And it was his fault. He deserved no better. "I should not have left ye locked in yer chambers." He shifted atop the stones biting into his knees, oblivious to the pain. "Forgive me, Evie, but ye scared me with all ye told me."

"I'm sure I did." She scooted back, increasing the distance between them. "I'm still not too keen on it myself." Still rubbing her leg, she clenched a rock in her other hand, ready to throw it at a moment's notice. "What caused your sudden change of heart? Convinced you that I told the truth?" She edged back again and winced as she bumped into a tree. "Last I saw of you was a disdainful look and a locked door."

He lowered himself the rest of the way to the ground. Maybe if he sat, she would be easier. At least she seemed to be calming. "I remembered everything I knew about ye." He kept his gaze locked with hers, watching for any flicker of renewed trust. "How ye never harmed a soul, but saved many, whether or not ye knew them. Me. Fern. The wee ones. Ye didna hesitate to fight for all our lives." He leaned forward, willing her to feel his sincerity. "I remembered yer odd words and even stranger tools." A sad smile tickled his mouth, and he didn't attempt to stop it. "And last of all, I remembered ye to be the worst liar I believe I have ever met." He couldn't bear it any longer. Shifting to all fours, he eased toward her. "But most of all, I realized I didna wish to lose ye. I love ye, Evie. I swear I do."

"You love me," she repeated as if to convince herself she heard correctly.

"Aye, m'precious wee hen." He couldn't resist a quiet laugh. "Fernie saw it in me, too. As my twin, she sometimes knows me better than I know myself."

"I want to believe you," she whispered, still as cautious as a cornered animal.

"Then do." He held out his hand and waited, not daring to move any closer. Now it was her turn to choose. He prayed she would choose him.

Ever so slow and timid, she reached out with her left hand. The bareness of her fingers sent his heart to the pit of his stomach. "Yer wedding ring."

She drew back and curled her fist to her chest. "I left it. On the table in my room." With a shudder that matched the quaking in her voice, she bowed her head. "I didn't think it right to take it. Thought you probably regretted putting it on my finger."

He closed the distance between them, pulled her into his arms, and tipped her face up to his. "The one thing I regret is hurting ye. Can ye ever forgive me?"

"You really think you love me?" The fragile need to trust him echoed in her voice, pained him to no end. Fear lingered in her eyes.

"I dinna *think* I love ye," he said quietly. "I *know* I love ye." He kissed the soft damp curve of first one cheek, then the other. "I need ye, my own. I canna imagine a life without ye at my side." He kissed her eyelids, her forehead, then the tip of her nose. Before covering her mouth with his, he stared into the gold-rimmed green of her eyes. "Please come back with me, Evie. Please come back and be my wife."

She didn't answer. Just clung to him, looking ready to weep.

"I will do better by ye. I swear it," he added, not too proud to beg.

"I will come back." She pulled him down for a kiss and held tight with a fierceness unmatched.

Nay. That was a lie. He clutched her just as fiercely. "I love ye," he whispered against her mouth.

"You better," she whispered back, her tears flowing over again. "Because I love you, too."

⇒⇒⇒⟩⟨⟨⟨⟨

HEAVEN HELP HER. She had actually said it. With his face framed between her hands, she stared up at him, frustrated that her blasted tears refused to stop. "I thought I loved someone once before," she said as he dried her cheek with a tender swipe of his thumb. "But compared to how I feel about you, I don't believe I loved him after all."

"Perhaps the Fates sent ye back in time because we are such a well-matched pair." His smile, that powerful dimple that had won her heart the first time he flashed it, made her wish they could stay right here in this woods forever.

"Perhaps so." Trust and love shone in his dark eyes. She prayed both would always remain. Life and love seemed hard enough back in the future, with every known convenience. How could a relationship survive here? "Can we stay here a while?" She wasn't ready to go back to the keep and face all the questions. All the looks that would pick her apart. She needed to stoke her determination to face them eventually, but not yet.

"We can stay here as long as ye wish, m'lady." He settled them back against the tree root that curled around them. "However," he murmured as he bent his head and nibbled at the tender flesh behind her earlobe. "If we tarry here past sundown, we shall have to fetch Fenn and bring him here. Either that or walk back to the keep whenever we're ready. He willna stay into the night unless he's within sight of us. That's how Dugan found us at the waterfall. Fenn returned to the keep, then led Dugan back to me." The stubble of his beard tickled more than it scratched, sending shivers through her.

"Fenn," she repeated, finding it difficult to concentrate and sort out everything he had said. His mouth on her throat shifted to her collarbone, making it impossible to think. She must have failed at lacing the front of her kirtle properly since he had already slipped both the dress and her shift partway off her shoulder. "What was that you said about Fenn?"

His rumbling laughter vibrated against her. "It nay matters. All that matters is the two of us. Here. Now."

She agreed wholeheartedly, closing her eyes and arching into his touch as the gentle breeze kissed the part of her revealed by skirts shoved up to her waist. This era's disbelief in undergarments simplified things. She agreed with that, too.

Passion overpowered any semblance of patience as she tugged on the front flap of his trews that insisted on remaining securely buttoned. Kilts would be so much easier. When the devil did kilts come to the Highlands? Apparently, not in 1296. "You have me at a disadvantage," she informed him with another frustrated yank.

He laughed again as he took her hand and guided her. "Like so." The barrier of the flap fell away, revealing the treasure she sought. With an impatient push, she rolled him to his back and mounted in a single satisfying move.

"Yes. This." Flashes of all they had shared last night returned, then dimmed, outshone by the moment at hand. When it came to this, the century didn't matter, nor who might be from which year. She rode hard and fast, neither able nor inclined to pace herself in returning to the blissful release found with Quinn.

He bucked beneath her, lifting her up as he roared her name and shuddered.

She raked her nails down his chest, clutching, crying out as wave after wave of the most delicious sensations washed across her. Once the delightfulness ebbed, she collapsed atop his chest, content to melt into him 'til the end of time itself. Yes. She loved this man. Heaven help them both.

He tightened his arms around her. "A perfect way to start anew."

"I agree." She nestled in closer and kissed his throat, licking her lips to revel in the salty sweetness of his skin. Without realizing it, she pulled in a deep breath and released a heavy sigh.

Quinn tensed beneath her, every fiber of his muscular body hardened. "What is it, m'love? Pray tell me yer fears. I would have no other misunderstandings between us."

"I dread going back to the keep," she confessed, voicing her worries. "I've never survived rumor mills well. I always come out on the bottom."

"A keep always swarms with rumors." He slowly rubbed her back, his rhythmic caress lulling her into a warm, fuzzy daze. "When ye shelter so many inside the walls, 'tis impossible to stop it." He kissed the top of her head. "But remember, ye are the lady of the castle. Ye answer to no one."

"Not even you?" she teased.

"Most especially not even me."

"You impress me."

"How so, m'love?" He paired the rubbing of her back with an

occasional squeezing of her rump.

"I would have thought your clan a strong patriarchal society."

His palming of her rear paused. "A what?"

"A patriarchal society. Male-dominated. Men, especially yourself as chieftain, make all the decisions. A woman's opinion counts for naught." She countered his gentle cupping of her buttocks with an idle twisting of his chest hairs. "A poor society, but the norm in this time just the same."

He shifted beneath her with a sigh as heavy as hers, then caught hold of her hand and stilled her twirling of his chest hairs. "Aye, ye described Clan MacTaggart aptly. Not the poorly part, but the part regarding a man's place versus a woman's." He kissed her fingers then nudged a kiss to her forehead. "But that was before."

"Before?"

"Before I loved ye." With his cheek resting against her forehead, he slid his hand to her waist and pulled her closer as if to place proper emphasis on his explanation. "I was a pompous arse before I met ye. Considered myself the only man fit to lead my clan. Fit to decide the fate of my people. I listened to no one—even when I should have."

"Considered yourself a legend, did you?"

He chuckled. "Perhaps—but that was before yer wisdom, yer kindness, all that makes ye such a rare woman came into my life and opened my eyes. I would be a damned fool not to consider yer counsel as important as my own."

Humbled and amazed, she propped herself up on an elbow and stared down at him. "Truly?"

"Truly." Not a hint of guile came from him.

"I'm not too sure if I don't find that frightening." She climbed off him and shook down her skirts, needing to think, needing to pee, and needing a drink of water. None of which could she do while lolling about in his arms. "I know little about this century."

"You know enough." He rose to his feet, sorted himself out, then frowned and shot a quick look all around.

The need to freshen up left her, replaced by a prickly uneasiness. "What is it?"

With a slow shake of his head, he scrubbed at the back of his neck. "A feeling. As if we are not alone."

She tightened her laces with a hurried tug, all the while stealing glances at their surroundings. "Was anyone helping you look for me?"

"Dugan and Rosstan." His eyes narrowed with a continuous scanning of the landscape as he stepped toward her. "But Rosstan went to Muiry, and Dugan rode westward."

"What about…" The name evaded her, but she could see Quinn's war chief as if he stood right in front of her. "Your war chief. I can't think of his name. What about him?"

"Nay." Quinn shifted the slightest bit, then turned, increasing her uneasiness tenfold. "Kendric is ensuring we are ready for the English if they make it this far north." Pressing finger and thumb to his lips, he split the air with a whistle so sharp, she jumped.

A low rumbling, like distant thunder, answered. The thudding grew louder. Closer. The forest joined in, adding snapping branches, crunching leaves, and splashing water to the song. As Fenn galloped into view, he greeted his master with a snort and a toss of his head.

Evie knew nothing about horse behavior. Was such a feat normal? "I thought you said we would have to fetch him?"

As Quinn greeted the horse and untangled the reins, he tossed a glance back at her. "A whistle is fetching with Fenn." He patted the saddle and motioned for her to join him. "Come. This place no longer feels safe."

As much as she hated leaving their sanctuary, she agreed. She grabbed her backpack and held it out to Quinn to lash behind the saddle. A distinct hissing whooshed so close to her right ear, she instinctively dodged to the left and flung the pack up into the air. The arrow meant for Quinn hit the bag with a solid thunk.

She whirled around, searching for the bowman. A flicker of movement caught her eye. Enough to spot the man and make out his garb. She had seen that style of cloak before. His face hidden within the shadows of his hood, the sniper nocked another arrow and pulled back.

"Evie! Now!" Quinn hoisted her into the saddle, tossed her backpack into her hands, and launched himself up behind her. He bellowed some sort of battle cry she couldn't make out. But Fenn understood. The horse charged forward, weaving through the trees like a demon of the woods.

Hunched over her bag, she held tight to the saddle, praying the assassin couldn't get off another shot. Quinn's exposed back would be a tempting target. Her single hope was their mount's amazing ability to swerve through the trees.

They cleared the forest and flew across the glen. Heart pounding. Stomach churning. Throat closing off in fear. Evie tucked her face to her pack and concentrated on not throwing up. Everything would be all right. They would make it to the skirting wall, get inside, and be safe. Eyes closed, she relived the terrifying moment, bringing the archer back to the forefront of her mind. The hood of his cloak had shielded his face. But that green cloak. And leather armor. Black leather armor. Then startling realization rushed across her. The men from Clan Munro, the warriors given as part of Annag's dowry. They wore the same clothing as the shooter.

She opened her eyes and discovered them almost to the keep. "Slow down. We must talk before we go inside."

"We can speak once I have ye safe within those walls. I willna risk ye further."

Still unsure how to drive a horse but determined to slow them down, she yanked back on the reins. "Halt, Fenn!"

The beast slowed but didn't stop. Just seemed somewhat uncertain.

She jerked the arrow free of her bag and twisted in the saddle to show it to Quinn. "We are not safe inside the keep because two of his friends are in there. It was one of the Clan Munro men who shot at you. I saw him."

The horse halted as if Evie had discovered the magic word to make him listen.

"Are ye certain?" Quinn took the arrow from her and examined it.

"Absolutely." She knew about being fired upon from her work abroad in field hospitals. Not with arrows, but the concept played out the same. They trained her to commit everything about such adverse events to memory. Her life and the lives of her team had depended on it whenever the troops providing them protection needed answers. "I saw him. Clearly. Not his face, but the armor and his cloak."

"Then we must see which of the three is not within the walls." His eyes flexed to thoughtful slits, then relaxed. "The cowardly attacks on me always happened someplace other than the keep or nearby protected grounds." He gave a slow nod, and the horse moved forward with a purposeful trot instead of the wild gallop of before. "We shall narrow it down and have our foe by sunset."

As selfish as it sounded, Evie hoped the incident would take the spotlight off her escape from the locked bedchamber. Of course, she would still have to face Lorna, Agnes, and Mrs. Dingwall. They would have to be told something. But those three weren't nearly as intimidating as the entire keep.

As they entered the courtyard and came to a halt in front of the steps, she patted his hand. "Shall I just say we had a fight, and now we're all sorted?" She kept her voice low, certain that the gossips had her in their sights.

Quinn dismounted, then held up his hands to help her down. "Aye, m'love, and now we are once again a happily married husband and wife." He tucked a finger under her chin and lifted her face for a kiss. "I told no one but Fern the details," he whispered across her mouth.

Thank goodness for that. So far, she got on well with Fern and her maids. Mrs. Dingwall? She still wasn't sure.

"Lady Evaline and I were attacked in the woods," Quinn announced to the pair of guards emerging from the gatehouse. "I want a runner sent for Dugan, Rosstan, and Kendric. Dugan rode to the west. Rosstan should be in Muiry, and I dinna have a feckin' clue where Kendric's got to, but I want him found. 'Tis urgent they return immediately, ye ken?"

"Aye, my chieftain," said the man on the right.

"And I want the Munros brought to the hall," Quinn added as he escorted Evie up the steps. When they reached the landing, he took hold of her left hand and kissed it. The intensity of his gaze made her heart beat faster. "I want that ring back on yer hand, m'lady. Never take it off again, understand?"

"Yes, my chieftain," she promised quietly. "I understand." Out of the corner of her eye, she spotted her maids and Mrs. Dingwall headed her way. Instead of facing them head-on, she tiptoed for a lingering kiss to ensure no doubt of her intentions remained. "After I've freshened up, I shall join you in the hall. Yes?"

"Aye, m'love. Dinna tarry, ye ken?"

She nodded, then charged forward, ready to face her welcoming committee of two friendly maids and a formidable housekeeper.

CHAPTER FIFTEEN

"**M**'LADY?" LORNA'S NERVOUS call echoed through the passage as she and Agnes scurried along behind her, trying to keep up with her hurried stride. Mrs. Dingwall had quickly abandoned the chase, snorting out a disgruntled huff as she veered off toward the kitchens.

"I'd like to freshen up, please." Evie gave the request, as if nothing unusual had taken place, and every bride ran away from her groom the day after their wedding. "I fear I have managed to get myself quite grubby."

"Aye, m'lady. As ye wish." Agnes raced around her and made it to the chamber door first. Face red and puffing for air, she pushed it open with a polite curtsy. "Would her ladyship like some water prepared for her special broth?"

Tempted as she was, this was no time to sit and enjoy the last of her tea. She needed to clean up and be quick about it, so she could have a word with Fern before she joined Quinn downstairs. Fern might have answers she needed. "No, thank you. Perhaps, later." She unlaced the front of her kirtle as she rushed across the sitting room. It was then she noticed a tear at the base of the seam. "Oh dear, I tore it when I fell."

"When ye fell?" Lorna squeaked. "Be ye injured, m'lady?"

"Scraped my leg a bit. Nothing serious." As she wrestled the gown off, she hurried to her dressing table. There it was. Right where she had left it. She slid the precious wedding ring back on her finger. The weight of it, the band's comfortable fit, was like a proper welcome home that made her smile.

"Is everything all right, m'lady?" Lorna asked, easing around her with the unmistakable hopefulness that she would soon hear some juicy secret.

"No, it is not." What better way to find out information than to feed some news to those who might overhear everything in the keep?

"M'lady?" Agnes crept closer with a fresh shift clutched to her chest.

Evie leaned in as if sharing the deepest, darkest secret with them. "Someone tried to kill Qui... Himself again. In the woods to the south."

Both maids drew in a sharp intake of breath and backed up a step.

"That makes three times, m'lady," Lorna whispered. She stole a glance around the room as if they weren't alone. "During a hunt a sennight afore he met ye was the first. Then at the waterfall. Now, today."

"Nay, Lorna. Ye have it wrong." With a prim scowl, Agnes held up four fingers. "The first was before the hunt. Remember Himself's trip to Edinburgh back in the spring?"

Recollection arched both her dark brows to her hairline as Lorna bobbed her head with dizzying speed. "Aye! I had forgotten the trip to Edinburgh."

"Four times?" Evie wanted to ensure she had the details straight. She counted off on her fingers. "Edinburgh, a hunt, the waterfall, and now today?"

"Those are all we know of," Agnes assured.

"Thank Heavens the man has the nine lives of a cat." Evie waved them forward. "Hurry, help me wash and dress. I must speak with Fern before I go downstairs. I'm sure she has thoughts on the matter. This bloody fool has to be stopped before he gets lucky and robs us of our chieftain."

As if leading a charge into battle, the pair of maids descended upon her.

After a quick scrub, fresh clothes, and a passable straightening of her hair, Evie hurried down the steps to Fern's suite of rooms. While she hated to bother Quinn's sister when the woman needed rest, it had to be done, and she felt sure Fern would agree. She tapped on the door.

Janet answered, gracing her with a welcoming smile and opening the door wide. "The bairns are doing so well, m'lady, and Lady Fern gets stronger by the day."

"That is truly wonderful news, Janet." Evie tipped her head toward the partially ajar door to Fern's room. "Is she awake? I'd like to look in on her if I may."

"Aye, yer ladyship." The grandmotherly maid trundled across the room and eased the door open wider. "M'lady? Lady Evaline is here to visit with ye."

Propped among a barrage of pillows, Fern smiled and waved her forward. "Praise God Almighty, ye came back to him." With a kindly smile and a nod at the door, she dismissed Reah and Janet. "Poor things. I've worn them 'til their edges are frayed. Janet there used to help watch over Quinn and myself when we were bairns in the nursery. And Reah's so inexperienced with babes, she's afeared she'll do something wrong. She's constantly fretting about Alexander being so much smaller than Evalie."

"I promise I shan't keep you long." Evie made her way to the wide wooden cradle in the corner beside the bed. She bent to admire the babies, pleased with their healthy coloring and plump little cheeks. "All of you should sleep when the babies do," she softly advised. The precious newborns lay tucked in close together, swaddled and peaceful, their tiny pink lips working as though they were still at the breast. Alexander had some catching up to do with his sister when it came to size. She made a mental note to keep a close eye on his progress. "Still latching on and eating well? Both of them?"

"Aye, both are fierce eaters. Thank goodness, I've a wet nurse to help. Isla's a blessing for sure." After a glance at the door, Fern patted the bed. "Come, sister. Sit. We need to speak of things other than bairns."

Something in Fern's tone gave Evie pause. "He said he told you?"

"Aye, he told me." With a thoughtful smile, Fern pushed herself higher among the pillows. "But dinna be afraid. I would never bring harm to the woman who taught my brother how to love." She patted the bed again. "Please, sit. I swear I would never risk yer life by sharing anything that Quinn said."

"You trust me then?"

Fern gave a soft laugh. "Ye saved my life and the lives of my bairns. I'd say that's fair payment for my trust." Then her mirth left her just as quickly, and confusion puckered her brow. "But I canna imagine how such a thing could come to pass."

"I wish I knew how it happened." Evie rose and strolled over to the window, unable to sit still. A gentle breeze fluttered across her hair with a refreshing caress. She smiled. Fresh air and sunshine. Arguably, the best medicine for healing minds as well as bodies.

"Would ye go back if ye could?"

A few days ago, she would've answered that question without hesitation. But now? Without taking her gaze from the waves sparkling beneath the sun, she barely shrugged, then shook her head. "Only if Quinn agreed to come with me."

"A fair enough answer." Fern blew out a heavy sigh. "I canna imagine how strange everything here must seem to ye."

"It is strange." Evie wandered back to the cradle and touched tiny

Evalie's soft cheek. "But it's getting better thanks to Quinn." Thanks to Quinn. But what would happen to her heart if the killer succeeded? She looked up and locked eyes with Fern. "Someone tried to kill him again. A man dressed like the Munro warriors."

Fern clutched a fist to her chest. "When? Where?"

"Today. In the woods to the south. An archer."

"I knew they werena pleased to be here, but I didna think them so filled with hatred." Fern's attention shifted to her children as a pained expression pulled her face tight. "They asked to stay here. All three of them did. Almost begged to stay because Annag's father is such a cruel bastard."

"Then why would they want Quinn dead?"

"It makes no sense." Fern twisted the hem of the bedsheet in her hands. "Unless one of them was Annag's lover, but why now? The woman is dead. Why would he wish to kill Quinn now?"

"Who else might want him dead?" Evie needed as much information as possible before she went downstairs. She always thought things were simpler in the past, but so far, that theory had disproved itself.

Fern's expression hardened as her scowl locked on Evie. "Gilbert hates him because Quinn doesna attempt to hide the fact that he thinks my husband a useless fool."

"Does he hate him enough to kill him?"

"I fell in love with Gilbert because he is a decent and gentle man. Gentler than any of these warriors who think the best way to settle a disagreement is with a blade." Worry dripped from her words. "I dinna think—nay, I pray Gilbert is not the one responsible for these acts against my brother." She plucked at the coverlet as if doing so helped her think. "But ye said ye recognized the man as one of the Munros."

"I didn't see his face. His cloak and armor, but nothing else." She knew what she needed to ask but dreaded it. "Where is Gilbert? Is he here?"

Fern's hands trembled as she pressed them to her cheeks. "Nay," she whispered. "He said the tanner in the village needed help with his books. So, he left early this morning." With her head bowed, she covered her eyes. "Gilbert would never have done such a thing. I know in my heart he wouldna."

"I have to get downstairs now. Quinn has ordered the Munros brought before him." Stricken with guilt at having stirred such trauma in Fern's mind, she backed toward the door, wishing she hadn't troubled the poor woman in her weakened state. "If just the two are brought forward, we'll know the third to be the assassin. I'm sorry I bothered you, Fern. I'm sure Gilbert told you the truth."

"I pray ye are right." Fern stared down at her lap, lost in her thoughts. "I truly pray ye are right."

"I'll let you know what happens," Evie promised. Although, she felt sure the servants would keep their mistress apprised of everything much quicker than she could. "Again, I'm so sorry to have upset you."

Fern managed a half-hearted smile. "Find the person trying to kill my brother. No matter who it might be, ye ken?"

"I will do my best." She hurried from the room and headed down the main stairs that would take her straight to the library behind the hall. Rumblings from the large gathering room filled the passage as she exited the stairwell. At least it didn't sound as though anyone shouted in anger—just the conversations of several men.

When she stepped through the arch, she spotted Quinn, Dugan, and Rosstan. They stood close to an ornate chair placed in the center of the dais where the head table had sat during the feast the night before. The long, heavy oak table and its chairs now waited beside the far wall. The chair on the dais resembled a throne. Massive. Legs carved with intertwining knots and arms the shape of enormous paws of a mighty beast.

Quinn turned as if sensing her presence. He smiled and held out a hand. "Come, m'lady. Join me."

Dugan and Rosstan both gave her a respectful bow and backed away. Each took a stance beside the exit to the left of the chieftain's chair. Evie noted they both kept their hands on the hilt of their swords.

She glanced around the room but didn't see the warriors of Munro anywhere. Several men, their weapons in plain sight, meandered among the benches and loitered in the center aisle, but not the Highlanders in question. Servants flitted here and there. Cleaning tables. Polishing candelabras. Readying the room for the evening meal.

"Any sign of them yet?" she asked as she edged closer and kept her voice low.

"They have not reported." Quinn glared at those gathered in the hall, his jaw tightening as though he ground his teeth together.

"For Lady Evaline," a servant explained as he placed a chair next to the chieftain's.

"Thank you." She smiled at the shy young man, then wondered if she shouldn't have because of the furious red blush bedeviling the poor lad's cheeks. "Am I not supposed to thank them?" she whispered to Quinn.

His mouth quirked to the side as he took her hand and led her to her seat. "Dinna fash yerself, m'love. It is yer way." His gaze settled on the ring, and his smile grew. "Good. Back where it belongs." He placed a lingering kiss across her knuckles, then waited for her to seat herself before he did the same.

A ruckus at the front of the hall grabbed her attention. The Munro men. All three of them. But one wore an ill-fitting tunic and a pair of trews made for someone half his height. He looked like a beggar instead of the stoic warrior from last night.

Quinn's knuckles whitened on the arms of his chair. "This is how ye dress when ye are summoned to yer chieftain?"

All three from Clan Munro stared at Quinn as though they thought him addled. One of the two, still wearing the green and black uniform of their clan, stepped forward. "Summoned? We know of no summons."

"Then why do ye stand before me, Fraser?" Quinn's hold on his chair relaxed.

"To report yet another affront to us," the man growled. He jabbed a thumb at the man dressed in the garb that didn't fit. "Alec was robbed of his clothes." He shifted and pointed at the man on his other side. "And Dorne's bow and arrows are gone." Standing taller, he threw out his chest. "We swore our fealty to Clan MacTaggart, and yet we are treated worse than lepers. What say ye, Chieftain? This is not the first time we have discussed this."

Evie reached across and rested a hand on Quinn's forearm. His muscles flexed and rippled beneath her touch. She leaned close and spoke behind the cover of her hand. "I'm sure you realize the assassin stole those things to make you think the Munros are the ones trying to kill you." She paused, straining to keep her voice low. "If they really are innocent, you need these men as allies. Have they been slighted, as they say? Do you think they can be trusted?"

He cut his eyes over at her but didn't answer. Instead, his focus slid back to Fraser. "Ye speak the truth. This isna the first time we have spoken about prejudices against ye. But this will be the last."

All three of the men resettled their defensive stances as if preparing to fight their way out of the room. "Go on," Fraser prompted.

Quinn swept a hard look around the hall, pausing on several men Evie assumed were members of his guard since they seemed to be doing just that. "From this day forward, the three of ye shall be the highest-ranking of my personal guard, reporting directly to myself. Should I be unavailable, Rosstan Corbett and War Chief Macwaters will be yer superiors." He rose from his chair, and the hall went silent. "Fraser, Alec, and Dorne Munro will be honored with the respect their positions command. They are a valued part of this clan, and anyone who has an issue with that will be brought before me. Is that understood?"

Even though most in the room nodded and either clapped or thumped their fists to their chests, Evie noticed a few who did not. Those would be the ones to watch. She committed their faces to memory and added them to the list of suspects in her head.

"I would ask yer forgiveness for not doing this sooner," he said to the Munro trio. "I turned a blind eye to the issues ye wished me to address. That makes me just as guilty as the ones mistreating ye." He tipped his head to each of them. "Forgive me. It willna happen again."

Fraser took the lead and dropped to one knee. Alec and Dorne followed. With his dagger held as though it were a cross, Fraser kept his focus locked on Quinn. "There is nothing to forgive, my chieftain. We pledge to serve ye well."

"Aye!" echoed Alec and Dorne as they held their daggers the same.

Quinn touched each of the daggers and motioned for the men to rise. "Find yerself some better clothes, Alec. Ye look like a beggar."

Alec grinned. "Aye, my chieftain."

"And as soon as we discover who took yer things, ye can punish them as ye see fit," Quinn added.

Alec's grin became a broad smile as he thumped a fist to his chest, then strode from the room.

Fraser and Dorne moved to stand on either side of the dais. Their stern looks dared anyone to make the wrong move.

Quinn seated himself and turned to her. "How was that, m'love?"

"A promising start." She kept her sights on the men who hadn't seemed to agree. "Now all we have to do is narrow down who wasn't in the keep today since it had to be an inside job... I mean someone within the clan who's trying to kill you."

"Aye," Quinn agreed in a dry tone. "In other words, I'm right back where I started."

"Not really." She needed a pen and paper. Or more aptly, a quill and parchment. "Do you write?"

"I am an educated man," he said in an insulted tone.

"Then let's go to your library." She headed toward the door without waiting to see if he followed. They would write everything down. Everything. It was the best way to hone in on the assassin.

⟫⟫⟫⟨⟨⟨

"A LIGHT TOUCH. Light, m'love. That is why they keep breaking." Quinn cringed as Evie soused a third quill into the ink after splitting the nib of a second. "And not so deep into the well. Just touch the surface of the ink, ye ken?"

"You will die of old age before I learn to write with this bloody feather!" With every fingertip black and a smudge on the end of her nose, she tossed the quill aside and glared at him. "Find me another sheet of parchment. I'm sure I packed my favorite pen. I can't imagine leaving London without it." She popped up from behind the desk and stormed out the door.

He didn't see what a pin would do unless she intended to attach the page to the wall and throw daggers at it. But he daren't comment nor deny her. Not with that look in her eyes. He hadn't lived this long by being foolish. She seemed intent on writing all they knew about the attempts on his life. He didn't understand her need to write it. Why couldn't they just discuss it?

After long enough for her to make it to their chambers and return downstairs, she burst back into the room, with a small metal stick held high as if leading a charge into battle. "Now, I can write!"

With a tip of his head toward the blank parchment centered on the desk, he pulled out the chair. "Yer seat, m'lady."

"You know—if you had agreed to list the names as I suggested, it wouldn't have come to this." She flounced into the chair, clicked one end of the silvery tube, and waited, poised to write. "But you refused to do the writing."

"Aye, I did. And I'm not sorry for it. I dinna enjoy sitting at a desk and scratching marks on paper. I am a man of action—not a man of words on a page."

"Even when your life depends on it?" She gave him a judgmental hike of a brow that made him laugh.

"I have a canny wife to handle such things now." After a kiss to her cheek, he tapped on the parchment. "Get on wi' it, m'fine wee hen."

"You and I are going to have a long talk about your cheekiness one of these days." She wrote a column of numbers on the paper. "First three suspects are the Munro gentleman."

"I thought ye told me to trust them?"

"I asked you if you *could* trust them. Just because their alibi for today seemed convincing, that doesn't mean they're entirely in the clear." Eyes narrowing, she stared off into space and tapped the tip of her amazing writing stick on her chin.

"How does it make the marks without dipping it in the ink?" He leaned closer and hazarded a touch of the letters. Amazing. The ink had already dried.

"The ink is on the inside," she said, speaking as if in a dream. With an apologetic tilt of her head, she tapped on the page again. "Do you feel Gilbert should be listed? Fern said he wasn't inside the walls today."

"Ye can list him if ye wish, but I dinna think that fool intelligent enough to pull it off." He strolled over to the window and stared out at the garden, itching to take action rather than make lists.

"Don't be overly cocky. Remember how a mere shepherd slew a mighty giant with a stone?"

"I doubt verra much that Gilbert is a David to my Goliath," he said with a backward glance. Her expression halted him, made him focus on her. "What is it?"

"Could you please step back from the window?" She nervously patted on the desktop and motioned for him to come back to her side. "What if the assassin is in the garden waiting to get off another shot?"

While her concern warmed his heart, what she suggested enraged him. "I willna cower within my home, m'love."

"I don't want you to cower," she argued quietly. "I merely want you to be careful. Aware of risks. Please?"

With an indulgent nod, he moved away from the window, poured them both a drink, and returned to her side. He brushed a soft kiss to her temple, then hugged his cheek to hers. "I will heed yer wishes, dear one, because ye have my heart."

"Good." She tapped the nib of her writing stick on the next space she had numbered. "I saw a few in the hall who didn't seem to agree with your promotion of the Munros. Did you notice them, too?"

"Aye, they never agree, and trust me when I tell ye they're harmless."

"You feel certain of this?" The doubt in her eyes was unmistakable.

He leaned down until the tip of his nose nearly touched hers. "There is nay a person in this clan who hasna felt anger toward me or disagreed with a decision I've made at one time or another. We canna list everyone, or we'll surely overlook the one we wish to catch."

"I suppose that's true."

"We must focus." He kissed the tip of her nose, then frowned down at the list. Four names, and none of the prospects he felt were likely. "I spoke with Rosstan and Dugan. Both are doing what they do best. If neither discovers the man we seek, we'll set Kendric on the hunt as soon as he returns. He'll find them."

She blew a very unladylike snort. "If Kendric is the man you say he is, then he should've already found them by now. Four attempts on your life? What's he waiting for? Would he prefer to solve your murder instead of protect you?"

"Now, now...dinna be too hard on the man. I know he's a bit arrogant and set in his ways, but he's busy ensuring we're ready for any attacks from the English. The bastards have overrun many a castle in the Highlands." With an apologetic grin, he interjected, "No offense intended, of course." He meandered back to the center of the room, almost went to the window, but remembered his promise and swerved away again. "And according to Dugan, Kendric's woman died a little over a year ago. I must admit, the man changed around that time. He's nay been the same since."

"According to Dugan?" she repeated. "I thought you and Kendric were close friends? Why didn't he tell you himself?"

"We are—but when it happened, I was so embroiled with Annag's dealings and her backstabbing father that I had no time for anything else." He paused, clenching his teeth against the bitter gall of guilt and regret. "I failed my friend when he needed me most. I was a selfish bastard. Concerned with nothing but my own affairs. Poor Kendric suffered his loss alone." He slowly shook his head as he faced her. "The man saved my life once. Nearly lost all the fingers on his right hand in the doing of it. Stopped a blade meant for my throat. If not for old Merdrid binding them tight for months on end, he'd have nothing but a thumb on that hand. He never complained once, and yet I still failed him."

"We all do things we wish we hadn't. You seem on good enough footing now."

"I apologized and did my best to make things right by naming him war chief. At the time, he said he forgave me, but I'm nay so sure."

"I'm sure he did. That's what friends do." With her thumb on the end of her strange quill, she made it click, then pinned it to the neckline of her gown by the sliver of metal attached to its side. She noticed his quizzical stare and gave a sad smile. "Habit. In my time, I kept it clipped to me for signing off on orders." She twitched a slight shrug and looked aside as if lost in her memories. "My parents sent it to me when I graduated since they didn't wish to interrupt their holiday in Sardinia to attend the ceremony."

"Sardinia?" He wasn't familiar with that place, and she graduated from what?

"On the Mediterranean." She shooed away the subject with a wave of her hand. "Not important."

He returned and knelt beside her. "Everything about ye is important. Never forget that."

Blinking rapidly, she pressed her knuckles to her mouth, then reached out and held her hand to his cheek. "I shall be very cross with you if you continue to make me cry."

"I dinna wish to make ye cry," he said softly as he turned and kissed her palm. "I love ye, m'wee hen. More with each passing day."

"Same," she murmured. With her arms wrapped around his neck, she kissed him with an urgency that roared and set him on fire.

He yanked her tighter to his chest.

The kiss broke with her surprised squeak as the armless chair scooted out from under her, sending them both toppling to the floor.

"Oh, bollocks! Are you all right? You didn't hit your head, did you?" Sprawled across him, elbows on either side of his head and her lovely bosoms almost touching his nose, she combed her fingers through his hair and gently felt his scalp. "I am so sorry. The chair just tipped out from under me."

A deep, rumbling laugh escaped him. He couldn't help it. Nuzzling his way inside the neckline of her chemise, he nibbled a kiss behind every word. "Dinna apologize, lass. More room on the floor. Ye taught me that on our wedding night. Remember?"

"You are incorrigible," she murmured but cradled his head and encouraged his progress. "I don't suppose you happened to lock the door, did you?"

He hadn't and didn't really wish to stop long enough to see to it now. "No one will bother us," he promised between samplings of her sweetness.

She repositioned herself farther down his torso, took hold of his face, and pressed her forehead to his. "Are you certain your library…"

He interrupted her with a kiss and a not-so-subtle hiking up of her skirts. A sound of encouragement came from her, like the purring of Cook's cat when given a saucer of cream.

"Well, perhaps just a quick one," she said as she broke the kiss, slid her hand down between them, and undid the flap of his trews with ease. She gave him a wicked smile as she reached inside and stroked him. "I'm a quick study."

"Ye are at that, m'love." Hands on either side of her waist, he lifted her up, then set her back down, impaling her nicely. "Ye are at that," he groaned as she settled into a rocking rhythm that took hold of him, body and soul.

"If you had locked the door, you could have bent me over the desk," she said, riding harder and faster.

"A future endeavor," he growled, then rolled her beneath him and pounded. This rare woman unleashed a fury within him he couldn't nor wished to delay.

When she keened out her bliss, it finished him, making him shudder as he emptied into her. He held fast, an ecstatic prisoner of their mutual trembling and clenching. Completely spent, he collapsed atop her, the force of their joining leaving him barely conscious enough to brace so as not to crush her.

"Quinn!" Dugan shouted as he burst into the room. "Quinn! Where are ye? Are ye hurt?"

"Halt!" Quinn roared, doing his best to ensure Evie was properly covered. At least they were partially concealed behind the desk but wouldn't be if Dugan came much closer. "Do not take another step."

"I told you to lock the door," she hissed, looking ready to kill him.

"Oh." Dugan's tone spoke volumes. The man understood completely what he had interrupted. "Forgive me," he mumbled as he backed toward the door. "Heard noises of distress. Or so I thought." As soon as he cleared the threshold, he slammed the door shut but called out from the other side, "I'll stand guard here to ensure yer…well…I'll stand guard."

Evie rolled her eyes. "God help that poor man."

"He needs a proper woman." Quinn grinned down at her. "Like mine."

"Next time, lock the door." She shoved him. "Shall we make ourselves presentable? I'm sure he wasn't coming to the library for a book."

"I suppose we should," he agreed with a sigh, making a mental note to speak with Mrs. Dingwall about thicker weavings to cover the floor. He stood and helped Evie to her feet, then arched a brow at her chest. "Uhm...ye're a bit exposed, m'love."

"I am well aware of that." She tucked her breasts back behind the modest covering of her shift and the laced bodice of her kirtle. After smoothing her skirts and patting her hair in place, she gave him a nod to summon Dugan back inside.

"Dugan!"

The door eased open the barest crack. "Aye?"

"Ye may come in now."

The wooly man's plump cheeks shone red as fire. He kept his gaze locked on the floor and halted just inside the doorway. "—forgive me again for barging in."

"You are forgiven, Dugan," Evie said. She shot a stern look in Quinn's direction. "I told him he should've locked the door." With a quick kiss to Quinn's cheek, she headed toward the exit. "I shall leave you two to discuss whatever it is you need to discuss." She tossed a glance back and smiled at them both. "It is time for my tea," she said, then closed the door behind her.

"What is tea?" Dugan asked, his bewildered look still locked on the door.

"A drink she makes with hot water and dried leaves." That was another thing he needed to do. Find some sort of acceptable replacement for Evie's tea until he could convince her to tell him exactly where he might find her the genuine brew. "Have ye discovered anything?"

The man shook his head. "Several in the barracks and many in the courtyard attest to the Munros being within the walls the entire day. A few even heard Alec's raging when he couldna find his cloak and armor."

Quinn went to the desk, inked the last quill that had escaped Evie, and drew a line through each man's name. "That leaves Gilbert as the likeliest."

Dugan made a face and scrubbed the stubble on his chin. "Gilbert still hasna returned from the village. He left the keep early."

"If he left before I discovered Evie gone, he would have no idea that I would be out and about."

"Aye, but if he was still here and heard of her leaving, he would know ye'd go out searching for her." Crossing his arms over his barrel chest, he scratched his chin again. "Does the man even know how to use a bow?"

"I dinna ken." Quinn thought back over every encounter he'd ever had with Gilbert. While he sorted through the memories, he idly rubbed the tender wound on the back of his head. There was no way a man as slight as Gilbert could've dealt him such a blow. He had the height but not the brawn. Aye, they hated each other, but he'd be surprised if Gilbert was the one responsible for all four tries on his life. Maybe he'd hired someone to kill him. Now *that*, Quinn would believe. "What about Rosstan? Have ye spoken to him since earlier in the hall?"

"I told him what so many said about the Munros. He was headed to the village to verify yer brother-in-law's whereabouts." Dugan sidled his way to the window and scowled at the garden beyond. "Keep away from the windows, aye? There's too many unanswered questions."

Remembering Evie's same advice, Quinn smiled. "Aye. We've many unanswered questions for sure. As soon as Kendric returns, we'll step up the pace and start finding those answers, aye?"

Dugan nodded and boomed a hearty, "Aye."

CHAPTER SIXTEEN

E LBOWS PROPPED ON the windowsill behind the bench, Evie stared out at the sea. The green-blue waves undulated in an endless dance, some cresting with lacy white froth, some glistening as if tilting mirrors toward the sun. The distant horizon gave her the sensation of perching on the edge of the world. And heaven help her, what a strange world it had become.

Weary from everything, she had planned to indulge in a quick nap after enjoying the last of her tea, but her mind decided otherwise. It wouldn't shut off until she found answers. Even the rhythmic shushing of the sea against the shore failed to relax her.

The memory of the archer kept flashing through her head. She wished the bloody fool had been arrogant enough to show his face. But no matter how hard she tried to sharpen every detail, not once could she recall a silhouette or shadowy profile. Whoever it was knew enough to keep themselves concealed. Even though she had met Gilbert only a single time, intuition told her he wasn't the one. The assassin was meatier, a muscular frame that didn't resemble the lanky Gilbert. So, if not Fern's husband or the Munros, then who?

She drummed her fingers on the cool stone of the sill. Instead of playing the role of indulgent wife and giving the men their privacy, she should've stayed down there and helped them work this out. What a ridiculous attempt at molding herself into something she wasn't. Modifying her behavior hadn't worked in her time. Why would it work now? "I won't make that mistake again." Well…she would work harder at concealing her backstory. For safety's sake. But other than that, she would be herself.

"Time to engage." She rose and marched across the room, energized with determination. Four attempts on Quinn's life were enough. Time for it to stop.

When she reached the library's closed door, she started to knock but stopped herself. Perhaps a bit of eavesdropping was in order. After a glance up and down the hallway, she leaned in close and strained to hear every word. "Blasted oak." She scowled at the door. Thick and solid, it muffled the deep murmurings on the other side.

"In for a penny, in for a pound," she said as she entered without knocking. She was the lady of the keep. Time to act like it.

All conversation stopped as the four men turned and looked at her. Rosstan and Kendric now stood with Quinn and Dugan. She strode across the room like she owned the place. The key to winning any battle was acting like she knew what she was doing. "Gentleman. Have we discovered the identity of our assailant yet?"

Quinn met her halfway, tucked her arm in his, then kissed her cheek. "I thought ye were going to enjoy yer tea?" he asked in a low tone meant just for her.

"I did, thank you." She fixed each of them with the unflinching stare she always reserved for first-year students during their introduction to the arts of surgery. "Well? Any progress?"

Quinn chuckled as he tipped his head in her direction and winked at his men. "I told ye she was fierce and canny."

Rosstan offered a polite bow, then grinned. "Not yet, m'lady, but allow me to say it is good to see ye safely returned to us."

"Aye, m'lady," Dugan chimed in, his ruddy cheeks flaring to an even deeper shade of red.

"Thank you, Rosstan." She couldn't resist shooting a teasing smile Dugan's way. "And thank you, too. By the way, you are quite forgiven. I know you were trying to watch out for my husband."

He ducked his head and gave a sheepish twitch of a shoulder. "Aye, m'lady. 'Tis verra true."

"What did ye do now?" Rosstan asked him.

"Never ye mind." Dugan cleared his throat and flipped a hand in Kendric's direction. "Kendric here thinks the English might ha' shot at Himself."

"The English?" she repeated, turning to the war chief who still hadn't properly greeted her. "How would the English get the Munro garb?"

Kendric's light blue eyes flared wider, then narrowed. Apparently, the man didn't appreciate her question. She didn't care. It was valid. "Well?"

"I received word that they have infiltrated Munro lands." After a snubbing dip of his chin in her direction, he returned his attention to Quinn. "That is why I feel it proper we march south since their lands abut ours."

"That makes no sense," she said, determined to keep Quinn's attempted assassination at the core of the conversation. "Alec Munro reported his clothes stolen. How do you explain that?"

The man's nostrils flared, and a muscle in his cheek ticked with his tightening jaw. "Who's ta say?" With a dismissive shrug in her direction, he added, "Coincidence, I am sure."

Evie slid her arm free of Quinn's and stood her ground. Kendric didn't like her. Thought he could passively bully her. Poor man. He didn't have a clue who he was dealing with. "There have been four attempts on my husband's life, Mister Macwaters. I daresay, we shouldn't discount anything as coincidence and concentrate on finding the assassin instead of fretting about the English who are still quite far south of us. Are they not?"

"Munro lands are nay that far south."

She almost laughed out loud when the man had the audacity to bare his teeth like a dog guarding a bone. "My husband met with you in this very library this morning and yet, had to send several of your own guards to find you this afternoon. If we couldn't find you without sending so many to look for you, how could you receive word so quickly from some mysterious informant about the lands south of us? How were they able to find you so easily?"

He took a threatening step toward her, then stopped himself. "Are ye calling me a liar, m'lady?

"Of course not," she said as sarcastically as possible. Actually, she had called him a liar and obviously struck a nerve. "You are war chief. Why would you need to lie?"

"Evie," Quinn rumbled softly, sounding like an amused parent scolding a bratty child.

Kendric squared his broad shoulders and stood taller, scowling down his nose at her as he directed his words to Quinn. "I am done here. If anything new develops, I shall be at the training field. I have yet to inspect the guards today and test the swordsmanship of the new ones." He pulled a single black glove out of his belt and yanked it on, his glare filled with loathing. "Good day to ye, Lady Evaline."

Evie found herself unable to breathe. "That glove," she whispered.

Kendric flexed his right hand, making the metal eyelets and brads decorating the long, broad cuff of the heavy leather gauntlet rattle. "Aye, m'lady. I must wear this glove when I grip my sword because my fingers sting with a vengeance. They have done so since I nearly lost them while saving yer husband's life."

"Nerve damage," she said under her breath. A sickening weight settled firmly in the pit of her stomach and threatened to send her tea spewing back out.

"What did ye say?" he snapped.

"Kendric." Quinn's tone held an unmistakable warning. "Mind yerself, man."

"As I said, I am done here." Kendric gave a curt nod to the men and turned to go.

Evie darted back to the library door, pressed her back against it, and spread her arms across its width. "I have seen that glove before. It is very distinctive." Unsure as to how the man would react, she braced herself. This could all go very badly.

Kendric's eyes narrowed again. He eased toward her as if stalking game.

She glanced around for something to use as a weapon.

"What are ye saying, love?" Quinn asked, looking first at Evie, then at Kendric.

"It was you." She kept her gaze locked on Kendric, recalling it clearly now. The sunlight had filtered down through the leaves and bounced off the metal bits on that glove as he nocked the arrow and pulled back the bowstring. None of the Munros wore gloves, and Kendric's was unmistakable. "It's been you all along. Every time. Hasn't it?"

"Yer bride has gone mad," he growled, then shot a scowl at Quinn. "Who do ye trust? Me or this English woman ye've known but a few days?"

Quinn's focus slid to her, and he barely arched a brow.

"I promise it was him. I saw the cloak, the black leather armor, and that glove as he tried to get off a second shot after the first missed you." Her heart warmed as she caught the slightest quirk of a smile deepen Quinn's dimple. Yes. He not only trusted her, but he also believed every word she said.

Kendric snorted. "Lies. That is all the English know, how to lie."

Closing the distance between them, Quinn grabbed hold of Kendric's shoulder and yanked him around to face him. "Ye will mind yer tone and yer words when ye speak to my wife."

"All I will mind is seeing ye dead at last." He spun and threw a hard blow at Quinn's jaw.

Quinn dodged and countered, knocking Kendric back several steps. "Why?" he shouted. "Why do you want me dead?"

Rosstan and Dugan started toward them, but Quinn held up a hand to stay them. "No! This is my fight." He advanced on Kendric. "Answer me. Why do ye want me dead?"

"Because ye took her from me," Kendric spewed, hatred rolling off him. "Ye killed her and my child."

Quinn's furious scowl melted into one of confusion. "What the devil are ye saying? I took no woman from ye."

"Aye, ye did." Kendric sidled closer to Evie and the door, moving slow and deadly as the rising tide.

Evie searched again for a weapon in case he made it to her. Finding nothing, she widened her stance and prayed.

"She loved me." Kendric thumped his chest, then flung a hand at Quinn as though dismissing him. "But her father wouldna let her marry a simple guard." His sneer hardened even more. "Nay, he wanted a chieftain for his daughter. An alliance to protect his clan."

"Ye were Annag's lover?" Quinn backed up a step, his fisted hands relaxing as they dropped to his sides.

"Aye." Kendric shook with the simmering rage he had kept contained for so long. "I loved her from the first time I laid eyes on her. Our verra first visit to Clan Munro's keep. Remember it? Ye said ye wanted to see the woman they had offered ye?" His knuckles popped as he flexed his uninjured hand. "She fell in love with me, too. Said she couldna stomach the sight of ye but had no choice but to marry ye. Her bastard of a father threatened to slit her mother's throat if she didna go through with whatever he wished."

Evie noticed the veins pounding in Kendrick's temple. His red face. The sweaty sheen to his skin. At this rate, the man risked a heart attack or stroke at any moment. If they didn't stop him, his body would.

"I had no idea," Quinn admitted quietly. "Why did ye not tell me? We couldha remedied the situation. Somehow."

"How?" Kendrick spat at him and took another step. "With her mother's life at risk, Annag would do nothing to force her father's hand." Again, he thumped a fist to his chest. "That child was mine," he said with a sobbing growl. "She told me the day before she wed ye."

"I didna kill her, Kendrick," Quinn reasoned quietly. "'Twas God's will. Ye know the dangers of bringing new life into this world."

"I know the dangers of drinking a witch's brew to keep the bairn inside ye long enough to make it look like it belongs to the man ye married." He shook his head. "She did it all to save her mother. My poor lass wouldna believe the woman was already dead. Her father killed her mother the day she left, but she wouldna believe the hard truth of it because of the letters he forged and sent to her."

Poor Annag had died because of her father, not Quinn. She had taken some sort of medieval concoction to stop or delay labor. Evie pondered the herb and the level of its dangerous toxicity. Apparently, quite high if it had caused Annag's death. "Who gave her that poison?" That person needed to be dealt with as well.

"Merdrid," Kendric said, his eyes filled with hatred. "I killed that witch when she finally confessed to helping Annag die." A heart-wrenching sob tore free of him as he pounded his chest yet again, then jabbed a shaking finger at Quinn. "My child. My love. Killed because of that bastard who didna care if my sweet Annag lived or died."

"Annag's father killed her. Not Quinn." She couldn't keep quiet any longer. While she sympathized with Kendric, the man's hatred was misplaced.

"Oh, I took care of him," Kendric said, then gave a chilling laugh. "Sent him to hell to pay for his sins." He pointed at Quinn again. "And now it's time for ye to pay. But first a taste of the pain ye gifted to me."

Before Evie realized what he intended, Kendric dove, grabbed hold of her, and yanked her back against his chest. With an arm locked around her waist, he clamped his gloved hand around her throat and squeezed. "But I will do ye the honor of letting ye watch the terror in her eyes as she dies."

"If ye harm her—"

"Ye'll what?" Kendric taunted, bumping his back against the door and squeezing harder. "There's not a damn thing ye can do but watch her die, just like I watched Annag."

All the self-defense talks she had ever heard raced through her mind as she struggled for air. She mustn't panic. Arms and legs were free. She could do something. Lights flashing through her blurring vision warned her to get on with it.

Ink pen. She snatched it off her neckline and thrust backward, driving it deep into Kendric's eye, as deep as its steel barrel would go.

He roared in pain, freeing her to clutch his face. Blood streamed through his fingers.

Quinn charged forward with his dagger drawn. He buried the blade in Kendric's gut and shoved it up beneath his ribcage. "I am sorry, old friend," he rasped as he drove the man back against the wall and held fast. "May God help ye find the peace ye never found here." As Kendric sagged in his hold, he slowly lowered him to the floor.

For the first time in her life, the bloodletting sickened her. Still coughing and wheezing for air, she struggled not to heave. She needed to breathe, not vomit—such a tortured mess of pain and misunderstanding all because of greed. So much blood covered her hand. To think a mere ink pen had saved her life.

"Evie." Quinn's quiet voice made it through her inner storm.

She fell into his arms and clutched him. "Hold me," she whispered, burying her face in his neck. "Don't let go."

"Never, m'love. I swear it." His arms tightened around her. "It will be fine now, Evie. Thanks to ye."

"No," she rasped with a shake of her head. "I don't want to be known as his killer." All her adult life, she had worked to save lives, not take them. She didn't want the memory of this day to stain that. "Think of a lie to explain it," she whispered. "Save his honor and mine."

"I will, m'love." He tenderly kissed the tip of her nose, then smiled. "I'll think of a lie because I know that's not one of yer gifts."

"I'm glad you know that." She was more than glad. She was bloody thankful that he knew her for the lousy liar she was. "I think I'll go see if I can coax a smidge more tea out of those leaves and have a nap now."

He helped her to her feet, swept her up into his arms, then shot a look back at Dugan. "The door?"

Dugan hurried to open it just enough to let them pass. "Rosstan and I will see to this, cousin."

"Bury him beside Annag," Quinn said quietly. "It's the least I can do for him."

"Thank you, Dugan," she added in a croaking whisper. "I appreciate you."

Dugan shook his head. "Nay, m'lady. 'Tis we who appreciate yerself."

»»»«««

"TEA LEAVES." HE sniffed the bag after she turned it inside out, hoping to get every last bit that might have clung to the seams.

"It will become the favorite drink of the English," she said with a sad smile, then nudged a slight shrug. "Scots and Irish, too. Even many Americans will love it." She wrinkled her nose as she added cream to her steaming cup. "But many of them will drink it iced down."

"Americans?"

"Continent to the west." Her smile seemed thoughtful. "Many will emigrate there." The smile faded to a troubled frown. "Some will end up there against their will." After a heavy sigh, she shook her head.

239

"But you'll be happy to know, those colonists, who will include a great many Scots among their ranks, will win their freedom from British rule. Permanently."

"When will this be?"

"1776." She sipped her tea, closing her eyes and flinching as she swallowed.

The purplish bruising of her throat stirred both anger and guilt within him. His reflection in the glass of whisky between his hands stared back up at him, both accusing and forgiving for the unknown part he had played in fostering Kendric's madness. "1776," he idly repeated, not really caring.

Her soft touch on his hand made him look up.

"It wasn't your fault, Quinn." She held his gaze, willing him to believe. "You didn't know about Kendric and Annag."

"He was my friend." How such an unreasonable evil could take hold of Kendric befuddled him to no end. But as he lost himself in Evie's golden-green gaze, he understood a small part of it. He would kill for Evie. Already had, in fact. He kissed her hand, then pressed it to his cheek. "I love ye, dear one. Love ye more each day."

"Same," she said with a tender smile. "More than you will ever know."

EPILOGUE

Two years later...
MacTaggart Keep

"LADY EVALINE WAS right," Rosstan reported with a thankful tip of his head in her direction. "She saved us for certain."

"They say a third of Wallace's men died at Falkirk. The rest fled for their lives." Dugan puffed out his chest and sent a smile over at Evie as well. "Mairi's prouder than proud to help Lady Evaline with wee Tavish there." He leaned toward Quinn and held a hand to his mouth to hide his words. "And praise God for Lady Evaline. Thanks to her, Mairi's nay so wild and is even learning to read."

Quinn smiled at his amazing wife and their equally amazing son of six months. He was indeed blessed more than he deserved. Evie, Tavish, and Dugan's ten-year-old Mairi sat on a blanket spread in the shade of the old oak that ruled the corner of the garden. Tavish gurgled and laughed out a constant stream of babbling that no one but his mother understood. "God smiled upon us when he brought us Lady Evaline."

"Aye, and for certain," Dugan agreed, then turned and called out, "Mairi—we must go now. Come, lass."

"But Da," the little girl argued in the most pitiful whine imaginable. "I havena seen Tavi since yesterday."

Evie leaned close and whispered something that made the child smile and nod. After kissing the baby on his chubby cheek, she hopped up and scampered to Dugan. "Lady Evaline says if I behave and do my chores, I can help her prepare wee Tavi's supper. Smashed beetroot and pork today, and then I get to see if he fancies it."

"I'm sure he will if ye're feeding it to him," Dugan said as he turned her toward the garden gate. "Because he already fancies yerself."

"I'll be going, too," Rosstan said. He glanced at Evie again. "I dinna ken how she knew, but thank her for protecting us from joining in at Falkirk."

"I will, my friend." Quinn was glad to see them leave, greedy to have his family all to himself. He'd never get enough of the contentment that consumed him when it was just them and no one else. "Dugan and Rosstan are quite grateful that ye saved us from Falkirk," he announced as he joined Evie on the blanket.

Wee Tavish waved both pudgy hands in the air and unleashed a loud stream of serious baby gibberish.

"Do ye now?" Quinn picked up his son and held him in the air until he crowed with joy. "Ye see?" He tossed a wink at his lovely wife. "Ye're nay the only one who speaks fluent *Tavish.*"

"Well done, you." Evie scooted closer and leaned against him, smiling at their son. "He just nursed, so I wouldn't jiggle him too much. You know what will happen."

Quinn immediately seated his son back on the blanket. "Trying to trick me, are ye? Ye wee scamp."

The baby patted both legs and kicked, wiggling with happy chortles.

Chest so tight with love and contentment, he risked bursting, Quinn pulled Evie into his arms and leaned her back against him. "I never imagined a happiness so complete," he whispered.

"Nor did I." She hugged his arms tighter around her. "I truly don't believe I would have ever found such contentment in my time."

"*This* is your time now, m'love. Here. With me and our son."

She turned and rewarded him with a tender kiss and a smile that meant the world to him. "Yes. Our time. Forever."

About the Author

"No one has the power to shatter your dreams unless you give it to them." That's Maeve Greyson's mantra. She and her husband of almost forty years traveled around the world while in the U.S. Air Force. Now, they're settled in rural Kentucky where Maeve writes about her beloved Highlanders and the fearless women who tame them. When she's not plotting her next romantic Scottish tale, she can be found herding cats, grandchildren, and her husband—not necessarily in that order.

SOCIAL MEDIA LINKS:
Website: maevegreyson.com
Facebook Page: AuthorMaeveGreyson
Facebook Group: Maeve's Corner
facebook.com/groups/MaevesCorner
Twitter: @maevegreyson
Instagram: @maevegreyson
Amazon Author Page: amazon.com/Maeve-Greyson/e/B004PE9T9U
BookBub: bookbub.com/authors/maeve-greyson

Made in United States
Orlando, FL
17 December 2021